THE L1

SERIES TITLES

The Continental Divide
Bob Johnson

Keeping What's Best Left Kept Secret
David Ricchiute

Soaked
Toby LeBlanc

The Path of Totality
Marie Zhuikov

Shocker in Gloomtown
Dan Libman

The Three Devils and Other Stories
William Luvaas

The Correct Response
Manfred Gabriel

Welcome Back to the World: A Novella & Stories
Rob Davidson

Greyhound Cowboy and Other Stories
Ken Post

Close Call
Kim Suhr

The Waterman
Gary Schanbacher

Signs of the Imminent Apocalypse and Other Stories
Heidi Bell

What We Might Become
Sara Reish Desmond

The Silver State Stories
Michael Darcher

An Instinct for Movement
Michael Mattes

The Machine We Trust
Tim Conrad

Gridlock
Brett Biebel

Salt Folk
Ryan Habermeyer

The Commission of Inquiry
Patrick Nevins

Maximum Speed
Kevin Clouther

Reach Her in This Light
Jane Curtis

The Spirit in My Shoes
John Michael Cummings

The Effects of Urban Renewal on Mid-Century America and Other Crime Stories
Jeff Esterholm

What Makes You Think You're Supposed to Feel Better
Jody Hobbs Hesler

Fugitive Daydreams
Leah McCormack

Hoist House: A Novella & Stories
Jenny Robertson

Finding the Bones: Stories & A Novella
Nikki Kallio

Self-Defense
Corey Mertes

Where Are Your People From?
James B. De Monte

Sometimes Creek
Steve Fox

The Plagues
Joe Baumann

The Clayfields
Elise Gregory

Kind of Blue
Christopher Chambers

Evangelina Everyday
Dawn Burns

Township
Jamie Lyn Smith

Responsible Adults
Patricia Ann McNair

Great Escapes from Detroit
Joseph O'Malley

Nothing to Lose
Kim Suhr

The Appointed Hour
Susanne Davis

PRAISE FOR

THE CONTINENTAL DIVIDE

"Bob Johnson understands angry men and the damage they do, especially in fits of jealousy or revenge-seeking. These hard-wrought stories chart a course through a richly textured world of bullies, ex-cons, wise guys, psychotics, crooked cops, abusive churchmen, exhausted women, and confused kids. Johnson's clear-eyed sensibility and honest prose show us where the trouble starts and why it's so hard to find a happy ending that doesn't include violence."

—BONNIE JO CAMPBELL
author of *The Waters* and *American Salvage*
National Book Award Finalist

"To borrow a phrase from William Carlos Williams' poetry, the pure products of America go crazy in these stories, whose narrative acceleration is the literary equivalent of a souped-up car. The characters here are often desperate and on-the-run from something, and that 'something' usually catches up to them and overtakes them. Forget anything you thought you knew about the Midwest—these stories will set you straight."

—CHARLES BAXTER
author of *The Feast of Love*
National Book Award Finalist

"*The Continental Divide* is a riveting, powerful literary debut, and Bob Johnson is my new favorite writer. From the first story to the last, he has his foot on the gas and never lets up."

— DONALD RAY POLLOCK
author of *Knockemstiff*
PEN/Bingham Prize Winner

"What Eudora Welty does for Mississippi, *The Continental Divide* does for Indiana, revealing inner desires and conflicts its citizens have tried so hard to bury beneath the facade of respectability. Again and again, Johnson shows us the crucial moment when the facade cracks and reveals all, to startling effect. These stories ripple with life."

—MATTHEW NEILL NULL
author of *Allegheny Front*
Mary McCarthy Prize Winner

"Recalling Flannery O'Connor in its merciless judgment and surprising grace, *The Continental Divide* maps the American Midwest in new and unsettling ways. With quiet lyricism and great precision, Bob Johnson reveals to us the brutal beauties of the human heart. Riveting, chilling, the stories in this masterful collection will startle, unsettle, and amaze you. Johnson is an astonishingly gifted writer."

—E.J. LEVY
author of *The Cape Doctor*

"In *The Continental Divide*, Bob Johnson brings storytelling back to its roots, with precisely drawn characters mucking around in the deep chasms between freedom and safety, tradition and progress, and individualism and community. You might need a breather between stories, but you'll keep returning to these Alice Munro-esque depictions of heartbreaking humanity in a broken but beautiful world."

—SUSANNA DANIEL
author of *Stiltsville*
PEN/Bingham Prize Winner

"A dynamite collection. Johnson's Mount Moriah is at once mythical in scope and powerfully earthy and granular in its rendering—a threshing ground where no space is safe, and everything is the opposite of copacetic, and the soft, lonely spaces of the soul struggle to wriggle free of their violent, often nihilistic entrapments. The dramatic tension on the page is so visceral and intense it makes your hands tremble."

—ROBERT COHEN
author of *The Varieties of Romantic Experience*

"Bob Johnson's stories are so complex, so powerful, that from the first line you know you're going to finish shaken to your core. This is the Midwest no one talks about. This is the Midwest I know well. There's not a collection out there like this."

—ERIKA WURTH
author of *White Horse*

THE CONTINENTAL DIVIDE

STORIES

BOB JOHNSON

CORNERSTONE PRESS
UNIVERSITY OF WISCONSIN-STEVENS POINT

Cornerstone Press, Stevens Point, Wisconsin 54481
Copyright © 2025 Bob Johnson
www.uwsp.edu/cornerstone

Printed in the United States of America by
Point Print and Design Studio, Stevens Point, Wisconsin

Library of Congress Control Number: 2024947476
ISBN: 978-1-960329-64-6

All rights reserved.

This is a work of fiction. Names, characters, businesses, places, events, and incidents are either the products of the author's imagination or used in a fictitious manner. Any resemblance to actual persons, living or dead, or actual events is purely coincidental.

Cornerstone Press titles are produced in courses and internships offered by the Department of English at the University of Wisconsin–Stevens Point.

DIRECTOR & PUBLISHER
Dr. Ross K. Tangedal

EXECUTIVE EDITORS
Jeff Snowbarger, Freesia McKee

EDITORIAL DIRECTOR
Ellie Atkinson

SENIOR EDITORS
Brett Hill, Grace Dahl

PRESS STAFF
Cora Bender, Paige Biever, Madalyn Carpenter, Zoie Dinehart, Allison Lange, Sophie McPherson, Hannah Rouer, Ava Willett

To Cindy, Nick, and David

STORIES

The Continental Divide	1
Bird Fever	17
Plucked From the Lame and Afflicted	29
Please, Mister, Please	46
Blue Moon	60
Man on the Tracks	74
Little Dude	87
Lady Liberty	100
Her Precious Things	117
A Vigorous, Mostly Happy Couple	135
Wicked Heart	147
Tell Me About Bobby Kennedy	159
The Half Hour	174
The Devil's Age	192
Acknowledgments	209

The heart is deceitful above all things, and desperately wicked; who can know it?
—*Jeremiah* 17:9

The Continental Divide

Edith's son LT was driving her to town when he took a turn past the community college where the young girls walked. She knew what he was up to and had a notion to object, but he was a grown man who'd paid his debt, so she bit her tongue at first.

"This ain't the way, LT," she said finally.

"I like the view," he said, like he'd never seen short pants before.

That's how their two minds worked. Of all the people in her eighty years—her mama and daddy when they were alive, her sister Rose in Elkhart, the Mister—Edith was the one to see the most sensible road to getting somewhere.

LT chose the path beset by peril on all sides.

"Keep your peepers in your head," she said. He was forty-five years old and a month out of the penitentiary downstate in Plainfield, while the girls were mostly in their teens. The way he slowed the Buick to watch them gave her the creepy crawlies, and she changed the subject. "When we seeing my grandson, or has his mama turned his head for good?"

LT didn't answer. Since Plainfield he dosed his words by the spoonful.

"She's a haughty one," Edith said. "Like she never did wrong herself."

"A cunt, is what she is."

LT's ex-wife lived with their son Wallace in Mount Moriah, where she ran a tattoo parlor. "I don't like that word, LT," Edith said, though she might as well have scolded the thunderheads gathering in the west.

They turned onto Highway 23, where the IGA butted up to the Rite-Aid on one side and Waffle City on the other.

"As sure as there's a sunrise," LT said, and Edith followed his gaze to where the Law, a county boy, was sitting at the Conoco station, radar gun aimed at the road.

"He ain't after you," she said, but then the Law pulled out and followed them into the IGA parking lot.

"Bastard," LT said. His papers allowed him to drive when Edith was along or back and forth to a job, though of course nobody hired a two-time loser. The meth might be forgiven, but indecent liberties shut every door for good.

"For all he knows you became chaplain while you was inside." Edith twisted to watch the brown and white slink back onto the highway. "Run afoul of the Law, and there ain't no coming back. I always said so."

She went into the store while LT waited in the car. He drove her to town because her eyes weren't what they used to be. The doctor said he could cut the cataracts out and her vision would improve manifestly, but Edith saw what she needed to see, and now that a man was in the house again to take her on errands, she was satisfied. The Mister had died while LT was away, giving her a suspicious glance one morning and crashing to the kitchen floor. Even before she got to her knees to look at him, she knew her husband was dead. No living body hits the floorboards with that kind of determination.

"At least he's at peace now," Edith's sister Rose had said at the vigil, though Edith doubted it. If there was a spade awry in the devil's toolshed, the Mister would notice and jaw the subject to death.

At the cash register she looked out and saw LT in a phone booth, though by the time she wheeled her groceries to the car he stood ready to unload.

"Who you talking to?" Edith asked. His papers told him to stay clear of prior associates, though she'd overheard enough whispered conversations to doubt he obeyed.

"Your grandbaby," LT said. He grunted as he lifted a bag of dog food into the back seat, and his T-shirt rode up to show a white belly hanging over his belt. He'd always been full-sized, though he'd come out of Plainfield big as a house.

"You mean Wallace?"

"Ain't he the only grandbaby you got?"

The clouds chased them home, and soon the sky was black, and rain was falling in sheets. LT stopped beneath the carport, and Edith hurried what she could inside while he got the rest. The dog Zeke met her at the door, tail between his legs and whining with each breath.

"It's just rain," she said. "It won't hurt you none."

She was pleased beyond words at LT's news. Her grandson Wallace was coming for supper that night and bringing his fiancée Aubrey. Edith hadn't seen the boy in five years, and of course she'd never met his girl. It seemed impossible that the teenager she'd last seen at LT's hearing was now twenty years old— a mechanic, she'd heard—and getting married in the fall.

"What you think about that?" she said to Zeke. "Your brother's coming to visit."

She put the groceries away, then swept the place from top to bottom. Zeke shed like a house afire, the bulk of his hair collecting in the parlor, a room he rarely visited. Why that was Edith didn't know, though she enjoyed fussing on such questions, same as why did the moon seem larger at the horizon, or did a flock of starlings change direction by mutual agreement or leave the decision to an outlier among them?

Later she peeled a handful of potatoes, leaving them to boil while she got dressed. She planned to fry porkchops and open some lima beans because she remembered Wallace the boy saying that lima beans looked like the kind of ears a frog would have if a frog had ears.

"I can't deny it," she'd said. "They do at that."

A familiar darkness came over her when she remembered the Mister telling Wallace to hush up and eat, but she brightened again to think the boy would have his first meal at her table without the old man there to pick at him.

She washed her face, then changed into her good dress, the lavender one with pink flowers. It had been hung to dry in the sun so many times the cotton was soft as a butterfly wing. She looked at herself in the mirror and patted her hair. It was a frizzy horror, though she'd seen it worse. Finally, she fetched her choppers from a glass and put them in her mouth. She'd taken to not wearing them for every day, but she didn't want Wallace to be embarrassed introducing his grandma to his girlfriend. What was her name again?

When the young people arrived, Edith hurried to greet them. Wallace had changed little from the boy she'd last seen at the courthouse, but for a near-invisible mustache and a teardrop tattoo beneath his left eye that signaled his own time in juvenile lockup.

"Oh, Wallace, my sweet child," Edith said. She pulled him to her and wept.

"Hello, Gamma."

"And this must be Audra," Edith said, stepping back to eye the young woman beside him. She wore black basketball shoes and jeans cut so short the pockets flopped against her milky thighs. Her hair was jet black and she wore purple lipstick, and Edith decided she'd fit right in at a haunted house.

But then the girl smiled with surprising sweetness and said, "It's Aubrey, ma'am." Her gaze shifted, and Edith felt a tingling one feels standing too near an electric fence.

She turned to see LT at her elbow. He was stuffed into a cream-colored bowling shirt with vertical stripes, his thin hair tied in a ponytail.

"This here's Pap," Wallace said, and when Aubrey reached to shake his hand, LT bowed wordlessly and pressed her fingers to his lips.

The girl turned pink. "Well, lah-dee-dah," she said.

At the table Aubrey told them she'd met Wallace at a meeting, and both would be a year sober in November. She was a cashier and Wallace was getting his mechanic's license, and they would soon move into the apartment above his mother's tattoo parlor.

At the mention of his ex-wife, LT spoke for the first time. "All I can say, boy, is check the small print on the lease. Your ma wouldn't piss on a body was it on fire."

Edith looked to see if Wallace might bite back, but he put on the same droopy face he'd always shown when his father said something mean. She felt a shiver of loathing toward her son as she remembered stories of the Law kicking in a door in Mount Moriah, only to find LT and a teenage Wallace so dazed on fumes they didn't look up from their cooking.

The storm raged on, and Edith lifted her voice above the thunder. "Did Wallace tell you about his *National Geographics*?" she asked, and when Aubrey shook her head, she continued. "When he was a boy, he'd come over to the house and look at my *Geographic* magazines instead of play." She closed her eyes and swayed gently. "The Mister would be at work, and I'd be doing laundry or whatnot, and this little boy would come in and say, 'Hey, Gamma, did you know there's a firefly in China that lights up the exact same time other fireflies do, and nobody can figure out how?' Or, 'Hey, Gamma, did you know only girl mosquitoes bite?'"

She opened her eyes. "That's when I knew he was my grandson. We're both the curious sort." She laid a veiny hand on Wallace's arm. "When you went away I packed them magazines in Tupperware. I'll get them out if you like."

"That's okay, Gamma."

"He ain't a little boy no longer, is he?" LT said to Aubrey. He hadn't stopped staring. Wallace looked more hangdog than ever, and Aubrey went pink again and stared at her lap.

The pork she was chewing turned bad in Edith's mouth, and she spit it into her napkin. "Whenever it rains like this," she said, "I remember Wallace reading about the continental divide." She looked at Aubrey. "Do you know what that is?"

"No, ma'am."

"Most folks know it as mountains that go from Alaska to Mexico, and how a drop of rain that falls on the west side flows to the Pacific Ocean, and one on the east goes to the Atlantic." She peeked at her grandson. "But what is it folks don't know?"

"There's more than one," Wallace said.

Aubrey smiled at them back and forth.

"There's more than one continental divide, he means," Edith said. She rapped the tabletop. "Tell the rest, boy. Don't make me beg."

Wallace sighed, then recited as from a printed page. "This house, Gamma's house, sits square on what's called the Saint Lawrence divide, only here the water goes north and south. Any rain that falls in Gam's backyard ends up in the Gulf of Mexico, and any in front goes north to Lake Michigan."

Edith clapped her hands. "How about that? He spends all day reading about Hottentots and crocodiles, when there's a real, natural wonder right under his nose. He got so excited he fetched a glass of water and dumped it onto the backyard to see what might happen."

"So, what happened?" Aubrey said.

LT snorted. "It soaked in and disappeared. I could of told him it would."

After supper the two men went to the carport to smoke, and Aubrey followed Edith into the kitchen. Before Edith knew it, the girl had filled the sink with soap suds and begun to wash the dishes.

"Where'd you get your manners?" Edith said, picking up a towel.

"My mama," Aubrey said. "If I don't help clean up, she says, 'Who made you Queen for a Day?'"

"I like her right now."

They worked side-by-side in the tiny kitchen, shoulders bumping lightly, and by the time they'd finished, the storm had grumbled to the east. Edith hung up her towel and turned to face the girl. "I hate to say this, but don't get caught up alone with LT. I wish it warn't so, but there it is."

Aubrey's eyes widened. "I don't expect I'll be here without Wallace." She stuck out her chin. "Besides, I can take care of myself."

"I believe you can," Edith said, "but I got two more things to say. First, I love my grandson, but he ain't never stood up to his daddy, and I doubt he'll start now." She patted Aubrey's cheek. "And second, sometimes a smart young lady says, 'Yes, ma'am, I'll take your advice and thank you for it.'"

"Yes, ma'am," Aubrey said and, to Edith's surprise, gave her a hug. Edith hugged her back and smelled her freshness and wondered why life would give an old woman three generations of foolish men to look after, with nary a girl in the mix.

When she and Aubrey returned to the sitting room they heard LT shouting from the carport, "I'm still your pap, ain't I?"

In another moment Wallace stalked in and grabbed Aubrey's wrist, and the two left the house without a word. Edith watched from the door as they hurried to Wallace's pickup, the girl still in her grandson's grasp as she ran-walked to keep up. The yard—a mess after any rain, tonight an unholy bog—sucked her black basketball shoes so deep she might have been walking on stumps.

Edith turned to look for LT, but he'd disappeared. She let the dog out a last time, then climbed the stairs, changed into her nightgown, and got into bed. Zeke turned round and round before settling, his bones thumping the floor like a bag of dry sticks. She stared a while at the ceiling, then rose and went into the hall. LT's door was ajar, and a wan blue glow came from within, and she knew he was watching the old RCA he'd dug from the attic when he got out of the penitentiary.

She stepped to the door and hollered. "Whatever you're planning for that girl"—she heard him curse and the mattress squeak violently—"put it out of your mind. This family don't need no more trouble."

When no answer came, she padded back to her room. "I won't allow it," she told Zeke when he lifted his head.

EDITH ROSE AT DAWN AND PUT on her everyday dress and the Mister's boots. She ate a bowl of peaches, then started a load of laundry and went outdoors. The sun was shining, though the ground was still muddy, and her boots squelched as she descended the northern slope of the property, where wild raspberries grew in abundance. The Mister had used the berries for wine, but Edith had seen enough of intoxicants, and she used them for jam and raspberry pies, both Wallace's favorites.

She hummed as she worked, slowly forgetting the unhappy close to the evening before. When she'd picked enough, she climbed to the house and washed the berries in the sink, then stood on the porch and looked at the day. A spent, tattered quality to the trees told her cold weather was nigh, and the darkness came over her again as she pondered a winter shut up indoors with her son. She might stand it better if the young folks visited now and again, but, like Mister before him, LT behaved himself only when temptation was beyond his reach, and the way he'd looked at Aubrey…

"I'll spend the winter without then," she said aloud.

"Without what?" a voice said, and she turned to see LT at the screen door. He was in his underwear and wiping sleep from his eyes. She went inside to start his breakfast.

At the table LT told her that Wallace had found him part-time work at the garage in Mount Moriah. He'd be fixing tires, changing oil, checking fluid levels—duties below a mechanic's pay grade.

"He called while you was picking berries just now," LT said.

Edith paused over her dishes. "That's a start, ain't it?"

"I'll need the Buick, of course."

"I expect so." He rarely changed his shirt, let alone a tire, but she wasn't about to argue with a paycheck. The Mister's pension had been cut by half when he died, and LT ate like a lumberjack. She looked to where he sat, kneading a bit of toast between his fingers and watching her. "You don't need an old lady's permission to do what your papers allow," she said finally. "Just remember the Law got his eye on you."

"Bastard."

Over the next week LT left the house after breakfast and returned by evening, as clean as when he'd driven away. When she asked how that was, he mumbled about coveralls and Lava soap and handed her a five-dollar bill, which she put aside for heating oil.

Before two weeks passed, the money dried up and LT began staying out until all hours and smelled of pot when he came home, and Edith knew the job was no more, if there'd been one in the first place.

"Tell Wallace Gamma says Hey," she said one day before he drove off.

LT glowered. "He's proud, that one. He forgets who his daddy is."

Edith studied on those words as the Buick disappeared, remembering suddenly Wallace the boy at the supper table, waving a *Geographic* and telling her and the Mister about a tribe in Africa who dyed themselves blue for so many generations their babies came out blue naturally.

The Mister had looked up from his beans. "I'd dye myself too, was I African."

Edith covered her grandson's hand with her own. "Those people is less advanced than us," she said. "We think every baby starts new, no matter who his folks are."

EDITH WENT TO SLEEP IN AN empty house and woke before dawn to Zeke growling at the window. She rose and looked for what had got his attention and saw lights off in the woods where the Mister had put up a deer stand. The lights flickered as figures passed back and forth, and when she cracked the window she heard men's voices. She went downstairs and saw the Buick in its place beneath the carport, then climbed to her room and dug from the bureau the Mister's Colt revolver she fired sometimes at chicken hawks.

She sat in bed with the pistol in her lap, and later a vehicle roared from the woods and stopped below, and then voices exchanged hard words. She rose to see Wallace's pickup speed away and then heard LT stomp up to his room, where he would stay until suppertime.

It was bad business. She held the pistol a while longer, comforted by its heft and coolness. The sun was halfway above the horizon when she returned the gun to the bureau, dressed herself and went downstairs to begin her work.

LT DIDN'T LEAVE THE HOUSE for the next three days, and on the morning of the third he was on the porch and Edith was trimming sugar peas in the kitchen, when the Law drove up the lane. An Indiana trooper in a Smokey-the-Bear hat, and the young marshal from Mount Moriah.

Edith left her peas in the sink and stood watching through the screen door, as the men climbed the slope to stand below the porch. The trooper wore sunglasses and had a paunch that rivaled LT's. The marshal doffed his hat and smiled at Edith.

"Good morning, ma'am," he said. "Beautiful day, isn't it?"

Edith had a notion not to answer, though her rearing forbade such rudeness. She crossed her arms. "I wouldn't say it was, and I wouldn't say it wasn't."

The young marshal laughed. "Fair enough. It's early yet."

LT said something from his chair, and the state trooper turned sharply. "What's that, LT? I didn't make out what you said."

"I didn't say nothing," LT said. "Nothing anyhow for your consumption."

The exchange caught Zeke's attention, and he growled where he stood beside Edith. She made a *whist* sound with her lips, and he slunk to his place beside the stove.

"We're here on a missing person matter," the marshal said to Edith. "Do you know a girl named Aubrey Sykes?"

Her heart skipped. "I don't know that I do."

"Well, that's curious, because she's living with your grandson, and we have reason to believe the two were recently here to the house."

"I don't keep track of Wallace. He's growed now."

"So, Aubrey Sykes hasn't been on this property? Her ma's worried something awful."

Edith steadied herself against the door jamb. "I'm sorry for that woman, but I don't know of no Aubrey Sykes."

"How about you, LT?" the state trooper said. His eyes were hidden behind his sunglasses, though his beak thrust forward like a hawk's. "You like the young ones. You know anything about the girl's whereabouts?"

LT yawned. "What Mama said."

The men looked at each other. "Mind if we poke around a bit?" the marshal said to Edith. He smiled again. "Just so we can say we did."

She peered at them back and forth. "I don't see no paper in your hands."

LT chuckled. "If they had cause, Ma, they'd of got one from a judge and brought it with them." He nodded at the troopers. "That's how it works, ain't it?"

The men stood another moment, Hawk Nose speaking before they turned to the cruiser: "There's talk you're cooking again, LT, you and that string bean boy, but my gut tells me you'll soon have bigger worries."

The Law drove away, and Edith returned to her peas, though twice she paused to study the back of LT's head where he rocked in the sun.

EDITH ROSE THE NEXT MORNING at first light. She put on her everyday dress and the Mister's boots, and she and Zeke followed the tracks of Wallace's pickup into the woods, four days old but still plainly visible. They led to a clearing where pieces of the Mister's deer stand still clung to an oak tree, and pines loomed silently like judges robed in green.

She paused to let her eyes adjust to the dimness. A pileated woodpecker screeched nearby, and a far-off answer came so immediate it sounded like an echo.

She found where the truck had stopped and walked in ever-expanding circles away from the place, stepping around fallen logs and mucky places that never dried, and likewise Zeke ranged with her among ferns and puffballs and mayapples, and after a time he came to her with a black basketball shoe in his jaws. She took it with a tiny cry, and then followed him to a spot where branches of young wood were swept atop one another, their torn places fresh and their leaves wilting where they ought yet to have been stiff and green.

She called Zeke off his sniffing, then sat on a stump and cradled the shoe in her hands, her tears raining onto it. After a time, she tossed the shoe onto the soft earth, remarking to herself how foolish her two men had been, to think that the Law wouldn't find a grave when an old lady and her dog had done so in less than an hour.

She wiped her face on her sleeve and studied a while longer. The woods were ghostly quiet, yet she sensed the living and dying everywhere around her: the movement of earthworms in the muck, the shrews that hunted them, trees shedding their leaves.

Whatever LT had done to the girl—it was he and not Wallace, of that she was certain—her grandbaby would be stained with it and sent downstate to Plainfield.

"Where a hundred LTs are waiting," she said aloud. She stood and walked back to the house.

There she went upstairs and laid her good lavender dress across her bed and rummaged in the closet until she found the pumps she saved for weddings and funerals. She put these on the bed also and fetched the Colt pistol from the bureau and laid it beside them.

A chair scraped below, and she went downstairs to find LT at the kitchen table. She got to work, mixing batter and bacon in the skillet, then frying potatoes in butter and garlic salt the way he liked. She hovered at his side, heaping pancakes and bacon onto his plate and refilling his coffee, until finally he groaned and waved her away. He stood and belched, then pulled a cigarette from his breast pocket and went outside, where the stone footing of a tumbledown barn was his bench, and where he sat looking over the southern hills as he smoked.

Edith put the dishes in the sink and went upstairs. There she changed into her good clothes and put her dentures in her mouth, then went outdoors to where LT sat. Despite her intentions, she couldn't help but see how plush and extravagant the clouds were on the horizon, and how closer by the trees gleamed in the morning sun.

LT heard her steps and turned, though if he noticed her finery he didn't have time to say so, because she pressed the Colt to his temple and pulled the trigger.

A pink mist bloomed from the opposite side of his skull. His shoulders convulsed, and he fell to the ground. There he sprawled at the edge of the slope, face down in the crook of an elbow, like a man examining the earth's surface one grain of sand at a time.

Edith looked to where he lay, then walked to the shed and returned with a spade. She wedged it beneath the dead man's hip and pushed until the body tilted over and tumbled down the hillside. It rolled and bounced in the grasses and milkweed until it was out of sight, though she followed its path a bit longer by the wake it made in the green.

She stood until something invisible chucked her beneath the chin and she began to move again. She leaned the spade against the stone footing and walked to the house. For the second time that morning she found that she was weeping, and she rubbed her fists against her eyes, telling herself she had more work to do.

In the kitchen she dug through the phone book until she found the number for Wallace's garage, then asked the man who answered if she could speak to her grandson.

"He's busy right now, or he better be," the man shouted over the sound of impact wrenches and revving engines.

"I'm afraid it's an emergency," Edith said, and, though she despised old ladies who did so, she made her voice small and helpless.

When Wallace came on, she told him there'd been an accident at the house.

"What is it, Gams?" the boy said. "Is it Pap?"

"Just come. Come right away." She dropped the handset so it bounced against the counter, then went to the porch and sat in LT's rocking chair. A tiny voice shouting *Gams! Gamma!* came from the kitchen. When it went silent, she knew the boy was on his way.

She closed her eyes in the sunlight, forgetting for a moment what her business was. Why was she sitting so idly? Where was LT? The Buick sat beneath the carport, so he hadn't left for the day. Might he be wanting lunch soon? Also, she hadn't liked the man at the garage. He clearly thought poorly of her grandson—a sweet, curious boy who, given the proper chance might yet—

She bit her lip, the pain clearing her head.

When Wallace's truck appeared, she would walk to meet it, then shoot him so his body fell down the north slope into the raspberries. Anyhow, that was her plan. She had learned that morning that a dead body goes where it wants to go, yet she was determined there'd be no taking a spade to her grandson like he was one of Zeke's droppings.

She tilted her ear for sounds of a pickup, determined to stay alert. Soon, though, her thoughts drifted, and she remembered herself and Wallace the boy walking in the woods and coming upon a calf that had wandered from a farm and died. Maggots filled the animal's nostrils and eye sockets, and its body was so bloated its legs stuck out stiffly like the legs on a hobby horse.

"Why is he so fat, Gamma?" the boy had asked, and she'd told him that a dead body gets that way, and then bursts to release all the liquids inside, and those soak into the ground to help whatever comes next to grow.

She winced, knowing that LT and Wallace would soon bloat in a like manner, but then she remembered the night she'd met the girl Aubrey and how hard the rain had fallen, and she was comforted to know that LT's vitals would wash to the south, where moss and copperheads hung from the trees and old women danced to voodoo music, while her grandson's best parts would flow north to a great blue lake, where eagles plucked salmon from the glassy surface, and moose dipped their muzzles in the froth and came up blowing clouds of steam.

After she'd finished with Wallace, Edith intended to climb to her room, where she would invite Zeke onto the bed with her. There she'd take care of him as he would wish her to. He was an old dog and wouldn't be happy anywhere else.

The final job would be easiest of all. The Law would find her in time, and there'd be the question of what to do with her remains, but Edith and her people would be ended by then.

What came next wasn't her concern.

Bird Fever

When the baby's fever reached 105, they decided they could stand it no longer. A call to the pediatrician had reached an answering machine, and they'd waited an hour, but the child was hot as a charcoal briquette and had recently begun vomiting a white, mealy substance—a cross between grade-school paste and cottage cheese—that was unlike any spit-up they'd seen. Finally, they loaded the baby into the Volvo and drove to the emergency room. Thomas kept the accelerator to the floor, and Allison sat in back with their son. The boy cried hoarsely with each breath, and Allison asked if Thomas finally agreed the turkeys were to blame.

"Let's not go off the deep end," he said. "We're not the doctor."

"When this is over, you're speaking to Johnny Baker," she said. "And don't talk to me like I'm crazy."

The emergency room doctor took the baby's temperature, now 106, and declared the first order of business was to cool the child down. Febrile seizures were a possibility if the fever remained so high. Thomas spent the next half hour lowering his screaming son again and again into cool water while a nurse tracked his temperature. The boy held tightly to him with arms and legs between soakings, and to get him free Thomas had to break the child's grip each time. He found himself panting and crying with his son, as Allison leaned against the wall in the mercilessly bright exam room, her face in her hands.

When the fever dropped to 102, the nurse wrapped the child in a towel and laid him in his mother's arms, where he fell into a croaking sleep. The doctor sat with them and asked how long the boy had been ill.

"We think it's bird flu," Allison said instantly.

Thomas laid a hand on her arm. "Of course, we don't know what it is, Doctor. He's been listless for two days, no appetite, his diapers soft and yellow. The fever came on late this morning and has been building all day."

Allison swung toward him, the child against her breast like a shield. "I was on the patio with Declan four days ago," she said, "where we allow turkeys, wild turkeys, to come out of the woods and up to the house. He was on a blanket, and I was reading, and I thought I'd swept all the droppings into the grass, when I looked and saw him playing with one of them—one of the bowel movements, I mean." She glared at Thomas. "It was at his mouth."

The doctor's eyes darted between them. This was good information, he said, though bird flu was doubtful. He nodded at Allison. "Despite what you hear on the news, the transmission of avian influenza from bird to human is rare, and there are no reported cases in the US. It's more likely your boy has a case of the everyday flu, though we'll need further—"

"Can we at least acknowledge," she cried out, "that a five-month-old child handling bird shit is a bad idea? Can we at least acknowledge that?" She said "bird shit" so loudly conversations beyond the exam room curtain went quiet.

The doctor lifted his palms. Yes, he said, handling bird feces was never a good thing. Several illnesses might result from such contact, and knowing the child had done so would inform their testing. Allison's face crumpled, and she began to weep so convulsively that Thomas took the baby from her, and the nurse helped her to the examination table where she could lie down.

In the hallway the doctor put a hand on Thomas's shoulder. "This is hard on both of you. That's perfectly understandable."

Thomas sensed the man was prompting him to talk about Allison. He pressed his cheek against his son's hot forehead and whispered, "It's bad enough having Declan so miserable, but she always jumps to the worst—"

"She's right to be concerned," the doctor said. "The boy is very sick."

Allison had always been fearful, though there'd been a time when Thomas found her timidity appealing. She was blonde, honey-skinned, and an inch taller than he, and she walked with the loping, pigeon-toed stride of a model on the runway. Her father owned three restaurants in Chicago and had played outfield one season for the White Sox, and he'd made it clear in word and deed that his daughter deserved better than a high school math teacher.

When Allison turned girlish and needy, it salved a raw spot in Thomas's pride.

Once, soon after they were engaged, she'd made a roast beef dinner at her apartment, and when they sat down she asked if he would light the candles. When he looked at her curiously, she told him she'd never struck a match in her life.

"Father always did it when we were little," she said. "And then later on it became like a family custom, and before you know it, I'm in high school and college and"—she shrugged and laughed—"I've still never done it."

Thomas lit the candles and savored knowing he'd taken the old lion's place. He bent to kiss Allison's cheek in the firelight and said if she needed someone to strike matches for the rest of her life, he would be that man.

And he meant it. But in the years since, her qualms had begun to eat at him. If he stood at an open refrigerator door more than ten seconds, she worried about the milk going bad. If they were sitting on the patio in the evening and a bat flew overhead, she bolted for the house for fear the creature would tangle in her hair.

But whenever Thomas had explained the flaws in her thinking, the few times he'd tried to help her face her fears logically, there'd been hell to pay.

Shortly after he'd begun his first teaching job, they spent a weekend in Chicago with another couple and visited the Sears Tower, where the observation deck promised a view of four states from its thirteen-hundred-foot perch. Better yet, you reached it by one of the world's fastest elevators.

Allison stood at the ticket booth, reading the description and biting her lip, but when their friends suggested going for it, she shook her head. Thomas had drunk a second beer at lunch, and he laughed more loudly than he meant to and said, "Of course not. We could *all die*."

Allison scowled and walked away in the Wacker Drive lobby, arms folded across her chest. He followed, and their argument in front of a Baskin Robbins had clerks staring and mothers gathering their toddlers close.

"You didn't have to embarrass me," she said when he caught up and took her elbow.

"Do just one thing," he said. "Admit this is ludicrous. On an intellectual level at least, admit there's nothing to be afraid of."

"You treat me like a child."

Thomas's voice took on a tone he used with his most obstinate students. "A child gives in to irrational fears, but an adult knows better. An adult knows there's near zero chance the elevator will malfunction. An adult knows—"

Her chin snapped up. "Leave me alone or I'll claw your eyes out. That's what I know."

He sighed. "Have you ever once considered telling your demons to fuck off?"

She startled him by smiling. "Fuck off," she said.

In the end she waited in a tea shop while Thomas and the other couple rode in silence to the top of the world.

THE BOY'S TEMPERATURE HAD BEGUN to climb again, and the doctor suggested admitting him for a day or two. A regimen of anti-viral meds, fever reducers and a cool-mist vaporizer should do the trick. Allison insisted on staying, and Thomas volunteered to drive home and pack an overnight bag for both of them. She shook her head. "I want you to sleep at the house and talk to Johnny Baker first thing," she said. "I don't want to see you again until you've talked to him."

"I don't think there's any reason to—"Thomas began, but she'd turned away.

THEIR NEIGHBOR JOHNNY BAKER was the town marshal. When he and his twelve-year-old son Mitch weren't hunting or fishing, they were stacking bales of straw at the wooded end of their back yard and shooting steel-tipped arrows into them. They cleaned bluegills and bass on their deck and threw the guts into the weeds, where raccoons feasted in plain sight. Lately Allison had seen Mitch spreading ears of field corn in the grass, so wild turkeys and quail would come out of the pines to feed.

And though the quail scurried for cover the moment Thomas or Allison opened the door to the patio, the turkeys had grown bolder by the day. One June evening Thomas and Johnny Baker had stood at the hydrangea bed connecting their backyards, and the man told him that springtime was the birds' mating season, and the young males—jakes, he'd called them—were loaded with spunk.

"We're either wives or rivals to them," Baker said. "They want to fuck us or fight us." As if on cue, a male turkey stepped from the trees and strutted toward them, its head high and thrusting, its eyes fixed on their faces.

"Whoa, uncle," Baker said. He broke off a woody hydrangea shoot and met the bird halfway. The turkey stretched its naked skull toward him, and the man stood tall and whipped the stick through the air so it made a whistling sound. "Shoo now, chief."

The bird bobbed and flounced and retreated into the woods, its legs like ostrich legs, muscular and springy.

"They have to know who's top dog, is all," Baker explained.

IN THE MORNING ALLISON CALLED to say that Declan's fever had spiked again overnight, and they'd repeated the cooling baths. He had a rash and made no tears when he cried, so the doctor had ordered intravenous fluids.

"They couldn't find a vein," Allison said. "They poked him and poked him, and finally had to go into his neck." Her voice was exhausted, but their conversation was less than a minute old when she asked him if he'd spoken to Johnny Baker.

"Not yet," Thomas said. He put down his coffee and rubbed sleep from his eyes. "His pickup's still in the driveway." The line buzzed with a reproving silence, and Thomas looked out the window to see the marshal and his son hoisting a portable generator onto the truck bed. "Oops, there he is now," he said, hanging up before she could respond.

PREGNANCY HAD LIFTED ALLISON to the top of a green hill, but the birth itself had pushed her into a helpless, tumbling roll down the other side. Labor was a bruising, thirty-six-hour grind, and when Declan's head got stuck in the birth canal, the doctor gripped it with forceps and yanked the boy so violently into the world his cheek was bloodied. Thomas woke to find himself on the tile floor, a nurse swabbing his face with a towel and his son's squalls in his ears. And though friends had told him how wonderful the moment would be when the boy was at last laid on his mother's chest, Allison began to hemorrhage, and the room filled with shouting medical staff. The baby was hustled away, and Thomas was sent, still in gown and mask, to a couch in the waiting area.

When mother and child finally came home, Allison slept in Declan's room every night for months. Even after nighttime feedings tapered off and she'd joined Thomas again in their bed, she continued to check the boy four and five times a night.

Once when they lay sleepless in the early dawn, she told Thomas about being a child and learning about glaciers. "I thought they were like rainstorms," she said. "I thought you'd wake up one morning and there'd be a glacier on the horizon where yesterday there was just sky." She'd dreamed about her father picking her up and running, while a wall of ice loomed behind them, tearing houses asunder, gouging sidewalks from the earth, shredding trees.

"I've started having that dream again," she said, pressing her damp face into his shoulder. "I'd forgotten about it, and now it's back."

Thomas smoothed her hair and listened to Declan's clotty breathing on the baby monitor, turned to full volume on the nightstand.

NOW HE STEPPED FROM HIS YARD into Johnny Baker's driveway and watched the man and his son wrestle the generator to the back of the truck bed and strap a gasoline can against it with a bungee cord. Only after they'd finished and jumped to the ground did the marshal acknowledge Thomas's presence.

"How do, neighbor," he said, wiping his forehead with the back of his fist. He wore a sleeveless khaki shirt half-open to his chest, and his biceps were round as softballs. "What can I do you for?"

Thomas told him Declan was in the hospital, the doctors were trying to pin down what was making him feverish, Allison had spent the night with him there.

"That's no good," Baker said. "I'll let Helen know." Mitch stood beside him and stared at Thomas. His hair was cut short to the same length all over his head and was so blond it was nearly white.

"Anyway," Thomas said. "The doctors think it might have something to do with the turkeys, with their droppings on our patio."

"Is that right? That's what the doctor said?"

"They think it's a possibility. That's correct," Thomas said.

The man rubbed his chin. "We're sorry to hear the boy's sick. Declan, is it?" He glanced at Mitch, whose gaze hadn't strayed from Thomas's face. "I don't think it's the turkeys though, do you?"

"Probably not," Thomas said, "but I have my orders." He smiled, but when the marshal looked at him blankly he hurried on. "We're going to try to keep them out of the yard, just to be on the safe side."

"Shoot, that's easy," the marshal said. "Get a tennis racket and run them off."

"No, that's not what I mean." Thomas felt hot blood in his cheeks. "I'm teaching Drivers Ed this summer, and I can't expect my wife to be chasing wild animals from the yard. Not with a new baby."

"Wild animals," Baker repeated, and then his face brightened. "I tell you what. Get a dog. Turkeys can't stand a yapping dog."

Thomas sighed and gripped the truck bed rail with both hands. "Allison doesn't like"—he felt the silence, then heard a breeze rustle high in the pines—"we're not dog people."

Baker glanced at the treetops. "What is it you need from us, Tom?"

Thomas stepped around the wheel well so his back was to Mitch. He stared into Baker's eyes and spoke rapidly. "Look, it's probably nothing, but my wife...*we* think it would be better if you didn't spread corn in your yard. The birds are losing their fear of us, and if there's the slightest possibility they carry disease—"

"Done," the marshal said. "If that's all you need, we're glad to help. More than glad." He bent to retrieve a spade and pickaxe and threw both into the truck bed so they clattered heavily. "Is there anything else your wife needs? Anything Helen can do?"

"No, nothing else," Thomas said. "Thanks for understanding."

"It's nothing at all. You tell your wife she needn't worry about turkey turds any longer," Baker said. He laughed, and Mitch smiled and unsmiled quickly.

When Thomas returned to the house, he found a push broom and swept the patio clean of a fresh collection of gray-green droppings. He saw Mitch watching from the deck and nodded, but the boy stepped onto the lawn and began scouring the grass with a rake, sending naked corn cobs flying into the trees.

AT THE HOSPITAL DECLAN SLEPT open-mouthed, each inhalation a squeaking whimper. A tube snaked from an IV bag to a bruised place at his jugular. The doctor sat with Thomas and Allison and told them their son had a virus, likely the flu, and would probably be better in a few days.

"What about the turkey droppings?" Allison said.

"That's our conundrum," the doctor said. "We've ruled out bird flu, of course, and the symptoms aren't consistent with *E. coli* or salmonella. It's possible he has a case of West Nile, and that's no laughing matter." The rash, the high fever, and the dehydration all suggested the mosquito-borne virus.

Thomas stroked Declan's head. "So, it doesn't come from the turkeys after all?"

"On the contrary, it might," the doctor said. "A mosquito bites an infected bird, and then it bites us." West Nile usually disappeared on its own, he continued, but in rare cases it turned to encephalitis, especially in infants. He asked if they had any standing water in the backyard—a goldfish pond or a tire swing—that might be a breeding place for mosquitoes.

A cool feather brushed Thomas's heart, but Allison said Declan was too young for a swing, and a pond wasn't safe for a child. She looked at Thomas. "Is there anything else you can—"

"No," Thomas said. "There's nothing else." He felt the doctor eyeing him. "I'll check though. Just to be sure."

Allison rocked back and forth as the doctor recommended their son stay in the hospital until they knew he was out of the woods. When he left the room, she continued to rock, hands twisting the waistband of her sweatshirt. "He'll never be out of the woods," she said.

"Don't be silly. Of course, he will," Thomas said. He stood and paced the room, squeezing fistfuls of hair until his scalp stung. He told her Johnny Baker had agreed to stop spreading corn in the yard. He'd seen Mitch raking the grass clean. Soon the turkeys would learn their place. "I'll call off from Drivers Ed for a week. I'll show them who's top dog."

"We can't keep our baby safe," she said.

"Yes, we *can*." Thomas knelt and grabbed her shoulders. She stared past him, and her bleakness moved him to panic. He took her face in his hands. "I'll fix this. I promise."

He left the hospital and drove to the hardware store, where he bought one hundred feet of chicken wire, two dozen rebar stakes, a mini sledgehammer, five citronella candles, and a propane mosquito fogger.

At the house he went immediately to work. Since Declan's birth, he had stopped gardening, and his watering can and the birdbath were full to the brim with rainwater. An amber film coated both surfaces, and he emptied the can and flushed the birdbath clean with a hose. He climbed a ladder to inspect the eavestroughs and found them choked with pine needles. He circled the house with the ladder, scooping crud from the gutters with his hands, then snaking the hose into each downspout until the clogs gave way and water flowed freely into gravel beds. He fetched a rake from the garage and swept the back yard clean of droppings, flinging them into the pines.

Finally, he used the mini sledge to drive the rebar at intervals along the property line and stretched the chicken wire from stake to stake, anchoring it with ground staples.

Once he looked up to see Johnny Baker watching from the deck. The man called to him, but Thomas bent again to his task.

When he was finished, the fence stood four feet high and wove tautly from one corner of the backyard to the other. It spanned the width of the pine woods and sliced through the hydrangea bed.

Thomas's clothes were fouled with pine sludge, his hands bloodied from the wire, but he unpacked the citronella candles and placed one on the outdoor bistro table and the other four at each corner of the patio. The sun was low in the trees when he unboxed the fogger and filled the reservoir with insecticide. He lit the pilot light and walked from one edge of the yard to the other, sending clouds of poisonous smoke into the grass, the bushes, the trees. The fogger made a wet, throaty sound, and the breeze wafted the smoke skyward, where it disappeared into the gloom.

When he was finished Thomas turned off the machine and stood in the gathering dusk. The pines loomed above him like a wall, the oldest more than eighty feet high. The woods extended a mile behind the house to wetlands, and as the noise from the fogger died, he heard in the trees the drone of a billion crickets and katydids, peepers, and toads. Crows heckled him from the uppermost branches. Sandhill cranes called from the marsh.

He put the tools in the garage, then sat in the kitchen to call Allison. Declan was better, she said. His temperature was normal. They'd removed the IV. Whether West Nile or the flu, the illness had passed.

"Oh, god. Oh, sweetheart." Thomas sagged into his chair. He sucked in a huge lungful of air, and as he released it he began to weep like a child. He described the fence, the candles, the fogger, and when she didn't respond he gripped the phone and sobbed. "Did you hear me? Did you hear what I did?" His heart was full to bursting. "I won't let anything bad happen to either of you. Don't you know that?"

"I know," she said quietly. "Take it easy."

They hung up and Thomas sat for a few moments in the dark kitchen. Then he rose, poured a scotch, and walked back to the patio, where he lit the citronella candles and fell into a deck chair. His eyes burned, and his bloody hands throbbed. The sun had set, and a soft glow suffused everything.

A half dozen turkeys emerged from the pines onto Johnny Baker's lawn. They pecked and bobbed, snatching at the ground in reptilian syncopation. One of the jakes neared the fence, examined it briefly, then flared its wings and sprang lightly into Thomas's yard.

Soon another followed, and then another.

Plucked from the Lame and Afflicted

There was only one vacancy, a room with a double bed, when Nelson and Pastor Snow checked into the motel. No bother, Snow told the desk clerk. He and his young friend would sleep side by side, like boys on a campout, and be on their way at first light.

When the clerk glanced curiously at Nelson, he beamed and nodded, and ten minutes later he was slumped on that double bed, listening to the old pastor urinate in the bathroom. His thin shoulders were lost in his dead father's sportscoat. A clip-on tie poked his budding Adam's apple. He held a stenographer's pad limply in one hand.

He had made a show of taking notes during the day's tour of the university—Snow's excited description of this or that ivied hall, meetings with seminary students, sit-downs with aging professors—but his scribbles, like the trip itself, were a sham. Nelson Froelich had no intention of studying for the ministry, despite what Pastor Snow thought of his keen mind and searching heart, despite his mother insisting he give up "one silly weekend" to make an old man happy.

"It's the least you could do," she'd said, swirling ice in her glass, "after the comfort he was when your father died."

Nelson had objected a bit longer, though anyone who knew him could have predicted the outcome: a smile followed quickly on its heels by surrender. He had just finished high school, life yawned before him like a valley of shadows, and the one thing he was good at was pleasing people. Adults, most of all.

Pastor Snow appeared from the bathroom, vivid as a road sign in green pajamas. "I think you'll agree, my lad. Today has been a banner day."

"It was terrific, sir." Nelson lifted the notepad. "I have everything here."

"But all good things must come to an end, hey?"

Nelson made a rueful sound, then went to the bathroom himself, where he changed into jeans and a T-shirt. The boy in the mirror was slender and downy-cheeked and might have been mistaken for fourteen instead of seventeen. Large glasses gave him a startled, owlish gaze.

When he opened the door, the pastor was beneath the covers. He frowned at Nelson's change of clothes. "Not ready for bed, I gather?"

"I believe I'll take a walk, if that's okay."

Snow yawned. "I'll leave the door unlocked, then." He propped up on an elbow. "Mind, though...I have important matters to discuss on the drive home. I'll need you awake and alert."

Nelson promised a speedy return and stepped outside. A cold spring wind made the treetops swirl. A paper bag skittered across the parking lot like a headless cat. He walked toward a diner where he and Snow had eaten an hour earlier, and a young waitress in blue eye shadow had smiled at him.

He had never been alone in a city where no one knew his name.

No one, that is, but the old man in bed behind him.

PASTOR SNOW'S ATTENTIONS HAD BEGUN shortly after Nelson's father died, six months before. Nelson Sr. and his son had been visiting the elder's birthplace in Cairo, Illinois, when the man's heart sputtered and failed, leaving Nelson stranded with cousins he barely knew. His mother collapsed into a three-day jag when she heard, so Snow volunteered to fetch the boy home. He took the Greyhound instead of his old Valiant, arranging for the father's body to return in the luggage hold, while he and the son rode above.

Nelson remembered only pieces of the journey: sleeping fitfully, crying at times, describing to the pastor how he and his father had made a game of counting red-tailed hawks during their trip south.

Once he'd awakened to Snow nudging him and pointing out the window at a red-tail, riding updrafts in the clouds. "That's your dad," the pastor said, "seeing you home."

The boy knew better. Nelson Sr. had been a newspaperman and naturalist and unabashed non-believer, an unheard-of combination in Mount Moriah, Indiana, 1983. He was partial to hawks, he'd often said, because they were fierce and lonesome and relied on their wits to survive, and Nelson knew that all that remained of his father lay in an aluminum shipping casket beneath him, steeped in mortician's brine.

Nevertheless, the boy's bearing on the journey persuaded Snow he might be a fit for the ministry. "He has his father's doubting heart, but he's smart and inquisitive," the pastor told Nelson's mother on graduation night. "A lad either has those qualities or he doesn't."

A clergyman's charge, he said, was to find young men for the pulpit, and a weekend pilgrimage to Ohio's Wittenberg University, the Lutheran church's best-known divinity school, might be just the ticket.

Nelson's mother had fixed the pastor with a radiant smile, then turned its heat on her son. "He would be thrilled to go," she said.

THE DINER WAS NEARLY EMPTY, save for a boy at the counter in an orange shirt and black tie and straw-colored hair, and the young waitress, swapping a cigarette through the serving hatch with the cook.

Nelson found a booth, and, after glancing reluctantly at him several times, the waitress came over. Her uniform was blue like her eye shadow and hugged her thin chest.

Nelson ordered coffee and watched her hips as she walked away, and then the booth shifted and the boy with straw-colored hair sat across from him.

"If your eye causes you to stumble, pluck it out," the boy said. He grinned at the girl as she returned with a coffee pot. "It is better to enter into the kingdom of God with one eye," he said through the steam, "than have two eyes and be cast into hellfire."

Nelson wasn't surprised. Something about him attracted panhandlers and conmen. His father would have dismissed the boy in a cold instant, but Nelson freed himself in such moments with clever words and a smile.

"Forgive me," he said. "I'm not sure we've—"

"It ain't for me to forgive. Lust is of the devil."

The waitress was at the serving hatch again, where the cook appeared as a wedge of cotton and pink skin. "I don't believe I know the gentleman," Nelson said.

The boy surprised him by leaning quickly forward. "Yes, you do." His black tie bloomed into an enormous knot at his throat. His hair glistened pinkly in the fluorescence. "You know him right well."

The door sighed open and a middle-aged woman entered, also in blue uniform. She scanned the room, and when her eyes met Nelson's, she shook her head in a gesture so hard and quick he wondered if he'd imagined it.

The boy followed his gaze. "Don't mind old Blanche," he said. "I was here last night and we had words, her and me. It's like a body ain't allowed to conduct—" He glanced quickly at Nelson. "My name's Marshall. What's yours?"

Nelson was never rude, though he'd noted with admiration that his father was rude to lots of people. *None of your business* gathered on his tongue, but when he opened his mouth a lone word emerged: "Nelson."

"Nelson." Marshall pondered for a moment. "I'm guessing your friends call you Sonny. That's what I'm led to call you."

"No, no one calls me Sonny."

The younger waitress had donned a sweater and was leaving the diner. Nelson watched through the window as she crossed the parking lot and disappeared.

"Don't mind that one neither," Marshall said. "You got bigger fish to fry." He slapped open a sheet of paper on the tabletop. It was smudged and creased from many foldings and had a black-and-white photograph in its center. "Did you ever go to a freak show at the circus? To see the Lobster Man and whatnot?"

Nelson drummed his fingers. "Sure…I mean, I guess so."

"Read this, then." The boy pushed the paper across. "It'll knock your socks off."

Nelson studied the handbill. The man in the photo was Virgil Lucius Coyle. At five years old he'd lost his right eye to a scratch from a feral cat. His father was dead and his mother a slave to gin, so the boy's grandmother took him to a tent revival in search of a healing. There an evangelist from Siloam Springs, Arkansas, strode into the crowd, plucked the child from the lame and afflicted, and spat into his ruined eye.

From that moment and ever after, the boy saw perfectly through the empty socket.

Now Virgil Coyle traveled the Midwest, preaching the gospel and saving souls. At the climax of his program he removed his glass eye from its cavity and identified any object brought forward, with his left eye—the good one—bandaged shut.

In the photo, Coyle, a barrel-chested man, held a boy in his lap as they read from an enormous Bible. The left side of the preacher's head was wrapped in bandages, his right eye a black gouge beneath his brow.

"Ain't that something?" Marshall said.

"I'm sorry, no. Either the objects are planted beforehand or he peeks."

"Not a bit of it. I seen the show myself two hour ago. They was a nurse there too, to bandage his good eye shut."

"Anyway," Nelson said, making to rise, "I have to go."

Marshall's face went instantly forlorn. "Don't go, Sonny. We just met." He began to cry. "I been so lonely since I left Momma's house in Lebanon. I only happened on this Coyle fella tonight because I didn't know what to do with myself." He brightened and reached for Nelson's arm. "Tell you what. Let's go see him together. You can decide yourself if he's fake."

Nelson paused, moved by the boy's tears. The Froelichs, his father had said, might be better educated than your everyday hayseed in Mount Moriah, but that didn't make them better *people*. He dropped some coins on the table. "I'm sorry for your loneliness, but I have business in town."

"You going to town? I'm headed there myself."

Nelson walked toward the door, stopping when someone called, "Boy!" He turned. The old waitress Blanche was staring at him. "Get home, now."

Nelson gave her a smile and wave, then pushed into the night. A glow on the horizon told him where downtown was, and he hurried toward it.

Shoes scraped the pavement behind him. "Ain't nobody wants to be my friend," Marshall said mournfully. "Ain't nobody got time for Mars." He skipped forward and tugged Nelson's sleeve. "You know what? This way goes right past the show. You can't miss it."

Nelson quickened his pace, but the town's glow receded from him, and he made no progress toward it. Soon, the dark hulk of a tent loomed in a vacant lot ahead—flap open, light streaming from within. He slowed.

"I knew you was curious," Marshall said. "I knew old Sonny was the curious kind."

"My name isn't Sonny, and I'm not the least bit curious," Nelson said angrily. A burst of noise made him peer through the tent flap. He edged closer.

The boy giggled. "No, you ain't a bit curious." He pressed a hand against Nelson's back. "He'll preach a while, and then the fun starts."

Nelson entered to see a crowd gathered in sawdust around a wooden stage. Yellow bulbs dangled from the ceiling. The air was heavy with pomade and sweat and the profane emissions of alimentary canals. Nelson's glasses misted, and he cleaned them on his T-shirt and squinted at the watery mosaic before him. Old women in wheelchairs, a boy with a withered arm, a girl with a crimson birthmark over half her face—all leaned forward to watch the barrel-chested man from the photograph, as he roamed the stage and spoke to them.

"You people," Virgil Coyle said in a voice high and twangy, "you came here to be saved. It ain't for me to save you. You came here seeking the Blood of the Lamb. It ain't for me to wash you in that blood." He shook his head at their folly. "You came to see miracles. I can't show you a miracle what's already been performed."

"I told you he's a phony." Nelson fitted the glasses back on his nose. "He's already trying to weasel out of it."

"Just wait," Marshall said.

"You people," the preacher said again, "if you came for a healing, you'll leave unsatisfied, because I got nothing to share but suffering. That and one thing more." He put both hands over his mouth, and when he removed them his voice trembled. "And it's the last thing a sickly body wants to hear. To be whole again you must first pass through the valleys, the wastelands, the shadows. Like Jonah in the belly of the whale, like Christ hisself when Satan tempted him in the desert, like the children of Israel in the flight from Egypt. And even then"—he pointed a finger and swept it back and forth like a searchlight—"even then, God don't promise you deliverance."

He scanned their upturned faces. "How long did Israel wander before she saw the green hills of Canaan?"

"Forty years!" someone shouted.

"Forty years!" Coyle shouted back. He began to pace again. "How many young men had visions, how many old men dreamed dreams, only to die along the way? How many mommas gave birth, only to lose their babies before sunup?" He collapsed onto a stool, his voice thick with pain. "It ain't for me to tell you nothing, except that narrow is the way to the kingdom, and it goes through a dreadful wilderness. And you people are bound to suffer and die before you get there."

Nelson had never heard a clergyman speak that way. Snow's sermons were filled with hope and comfort, even when he spoke of a final reckoning. God visited justice upon sinners, to be sure, but those were people outside the sanctuary, bearing false witness and coveting their neighbors' wives and oxen.

"What denomination is a pastor of?" he asked.

Marshall stared. "Shoot, Sonny. He ain't a pastor. He's a preacher." He nodded toward the stage. "Watch what happens now."

A stirring came from the crowd as Coyle announced that Esther Wright, an osteopathic nurse from Beaverton, would assist him. A woman climbed the platform, lifted rolls of gauze for all to see, and began to wind them around the preacher's head. When she stepped aside, he sat as Nelson remembered from the handbill, the left side of face shrouded from nose to scalp.

"I will now demonstrate what Jesus done for me by reading from any paper or identifying anything brought up here," the preacher said. "I never learned to read good, but I get the job done." He sat in silence.

A little girl stepped forward, hand outstretched. Coyle leaned above her. "This child is holding a fuzzy doll I believe is meant to be a rabbit. It's white with button eyes."

A woman spoke loudly. "I bought that not two hour ago at Dollar City. He couldn't of knowed."

A man held up a paper the preacher identified as the evening's handbill, a woman a keyring from her purse, another a photo of her dachshund.

"Take it out," someone called. Agreeing murmurs welled from a dozen mouths.

Coyle sagged. "Blessed are they what have not seen."

He rooted at his face, then lifted an object, flawless as a cat's-eye marble, to the light. His empty socket gaped like a puncture wound.

Murmurs welled again, then died.

A man approached, holding a tiny card aloft. The preacher took it and said, "This is the business card of Palmer Gibbs. He runs Gibbs' Body Repair in Mottville." He used the card to scratch the tip of his nose. "You scuff it, we buff it."

The man spun to the crowd. "That's exactly right!"

"Praise God!" someone cried, and an old man with a monstrous shoe, its sole four or five inches thick, knelt in the sawdust to pray.

Marshall slapped Nelson's shoulder. "What you think about that?"

Nelson shook his head. "That man's his brother-in-law or something."

The boy's breath was hot against his ear. "You think you're a smart one, don't you? You think you're better than the likes of these folks."

Guilt touched Nelson's heart. "No, I don't think I'm better than anyone."

"Then why don't you take something up there? I bet you won't lower yourself. I bet you ain't got the hair."

Nelson turned slowly, pulling his driver's license from his wallet. "It's not a matter of lowering myself. I just don't believe—"

The boy grabbed the license, giggled at the photo, and wove his way to the stage. Nelson watched helplessly, empty hand extended, as Coyle studied the document.

"This is the driver's license of one Nelson Froelich," he said. "He's seventeen year old and traveled all the way from Mount Moriah, Indiana, to be with us tonight."

Marshall whirled, "That's just what it says!" He jogged back to Nelson. "I suppose you're going to tell me you and that preacher is cousins."

After several further demonstrations, Coyle announced the show was over. He pointed to coffee cans at the exit and asked that folks be generous, because crisscrossing an unsaved nation was costly. "It ain't just about hiring a tent." He smiled wearily. "A preacher has earthly appetites like anybody else." He climbed down and vanished through a slit in the canvas.

A thought hit Nelson. "Where's my license?"

Marshall gaped. "I bet that preacher kept it."

Nelson looked toward the empty platform. "Nice going, dummy."

"Ain't no worry," the boy said. "He got a trailer out back. Let's go fetch it."

Nelson snatched off his glasses in frustration. He thought he saw the waitress Blanche's blue uniform in the milling crowd, but when he put the glasses back on she was gone.

He followed Marshall through the gap where Virgil Coyle had disappeared.

THE PREACHER'S EYE SOCKET WAS STILL empty when he opened the trailer door. He slapped his forehead when he saw Nelson. "I went and kept your license, didn't I?" The boy nodded, and he laughed and pushed the door wider. "Come on in and we'll dig it up."

Marshall crowded him from behind, and Nelson stepped into the tiny room. A cot rested against one wall, a kitchenette the other. Coyle fell into the trailer's only chair. "Boys your age is always thirsty," he said. "I bet you'd like a ginger ale."

"No, thank you," Nelson said. "I have to be going." He nodded at Marshall. "I don't know about him." He tried not to look at the preacher's face.

"Don't be ashamed," the preacher said. "It's lots of folks don't want to look at me when the eye's popped out. Fact is, it gets swole up in there by nighttime. I leave it out unless they's a preaching."

"That makes sense. Can I have my license now, please?"

Coyle sighed. "It's too many folks in a hurry when their soul's in the balance. Don't you think so, Mars?"

"I do, Virg," Marshall said.

Nelson turned. "You two know each other?"

"I've been here once or twice as I recall," the boy said.

Ripples like butterfly wings touched Nelson's spine. "You didn't tell me that."

The preacher laughed again. "Mars likes to mess with folks, don't he?" He crossed his heavy legs. "Be easy now. All we want is you to have a ginger ale and tell us about your walk with the Lord. It's lots of folks are glad they stuck around, by the time I'm done with them."

Nelson looked at Marshall, busy at a mini fridge. He looked at Virgil Coyle seated between him and the door.

"Well, sure…" He sat carefully on the cot. "I can talk for a minute, but I have places to be."

"Understood, understood," the preacher said. He twisted to scratch a shoulder blade. "What brings Nelson Froelich all the way from Mount Moriah?"

"I'm visiting the university. I might go there this fall."

The empty socket flattened into a frown. "What university is that?"

"Wittenberg, here in Springfield."

"Marsh, did you know they was a college in this town?"

"Didn't know that, Virg."

"Well, I'll be dogged. No wonder crowds is paltry."

Marshall appeared with two tumblers of sparkling liquid. "Drink up," the preacher said, taking one for himself. "You'll want to be getting home." He took a swallow and Nelson did the same, the cold drink a relief in the cramped space.

Coyle belched and wiped his lips. "So, what's Nelson think of my show?"

His father would have dismantled the man's act, piece by piece, as shameless fraud, but Nelson showed the smile he used on Pastor Snow and teachers at school and clerks at the Stop N' Shop when his mother sent him out for cigarettes. "You sure had 'em going, didn't you?"

"How's that?"

"I mean"—Nelson held the icy glass to his brow—"they were eating it up."

Coyle set his drink aside. "If I didn't know better, Mars, I'd say Nelson here is calling me a fake."

"Sounds that way to me, Virg."

The preacher plucked a thread from his shirt and examined it in the lamplight. "Is that what they teach in college nowadays, to deny what your own eyes have seen?"

Nelson's smile faltered. "Well, you…you can't expect me to believe you can really see from—"

Coyle flicked the thread away and covered his good eye. "Clear as day."

Butterflies touched Nelson's spine again, and with them came a crushing emptiness. He longed for the comforts of Pastor Snow and his motel bed.

Coyle lowered his hand and peered at something in the distance. "It warn't my doing, though. It was Jesus done it. They was a dozen worse off folks to pick from."

When Snow talked too much, Nelson found he could tire the old man out by peppering him with questions. He sucked from his drink and nodded. "What was it like when your vision came back? Was it all of a sudden or bit by bit?"

The preacher returned to the moment with a start. "What? Oh, it was sudden. One minute I'm as foul a child as ever was—my daddy dead, Momma drunk all day—and the next, *boom!*, my head blasted clean full of light so's I cried like a girl."

Nelson made a surprised noise in his throat. The room had grown more stifling by the second. He held the glass to his forehead again, but it did little to cool him. "So what happened then? Did you, did you…" He took the deepest breath he could muster, but his lungs refused to fill.

"You know what, Mars?" Coyle said. "That boy seems tired."

"Tired to the bone, Virg."

Nelson set his drink down and stood. "I *am* tired. Could I have my license now?"

The preacher lifted a booted foot and planted it on Nelson's chest. The boy gazed dully at it, then felt himself lofting backward onto the cot. A part of his brain told him he should be astonished and afraid, yet he only studied the ceiling with a kind of mild interest. He heard a familiar giggle. "You ain't going nowhere, Sonny."

In the shadows that followed, and as he was tumbled by many hands, Nelson considered that sentence, deciding he understood every word clearly but the last.

HIS GLASSES WERE GONE. Nelson focused on an object a foot away—the preacher's face. The empty socket looked big enough to reach into and finger at the brain.

"I got a friend what runs a drug store," Coyle said. "You'll be all woke up in a minute."

Nelson tried to move, but his limbs didn't obey. He lay on his stomach on the cot, his wrists bound with nylon stockings to the bedposts. Looking over his shoulder, he saw his ankles were tied likewise. He saw too—the sight stabbing him further awake—that his blue jeans were around his ankles. Marshall sat on the mattress at his feet. When their eyes met, the boy waved.

Coyle was squatted on the floor beside him. "I reckon you know what I'm about."

"You can't...you won't," Nelson said.

"That's right, that's right."

"I don't...I haven't."

"You said a mouthful there."

Nelson squeezed his eyes shut, assembling every gift he had. There were reasons, excellent ones, the preacher shouldn't go forward with his plan, and the boy searched his mind to come up with one. Finding nothing, he heard himself speak in Pastor Snow's voice. "You can't do this. You mustn't. You're a Christian."

Coyle's face darkened. "That don't stop other folks none. Why should it stop me?"

"Because other folks aren't like you. They haven't been chosen by Jesus."

The preacher nodded. "He chose me for certain. It's something I never fussed out. Of all the fruit on the vine, the gardener picks the rottenest."

"You're not rotten. God has a plan for you."

"Oh, his plan for me is manifest, to heal folks and preach the gospel. I do that most every night." The preacher shook his head. "What I ain't fussed out yet is why? Why a scurvy, one-eyed boy from Tennessee? Why Virgil Coyle?"

The man's troubled face filled Nelson with hope. He spoke sternly, this time as his father might have. "There's no 'why' about it. A person who would do this is the worst kind of hypocrite. How can you call yourself a Christian? How can you call—"

Coyle slapped the mattress. "I never called him. I never done nothing." He thrust his face close. "He called *me*! I warn't but five year old. I didn't care two bits about Jesus."

He sat back and gnawed a thumbnail. Tires crunched on gravel in the parking lot, and Nelson stretched toward the sound like a drowning man for the shore.

"I owe him. I know that," the preacher said sullenly. He leaned close again. "But that ain't going to stop me from having a good time."

"I'll tell," Nelson said. "Don't think I won't."

Coyle snorted. "You ain't gonna tell. Nice boys like you don't never tell. What you doing out here anyway? You gonna tell your momma you got bung-holed at midnight by a one-eyed preacher? Your college buddies? Some sweet little girl?"

Nelson thought of his mother and knew the man was right. "I will tell, though. My father's a policeman. He has contacts all over the Midwest."

The preacher laughed. "If I believed that, I'd have to kill your little ass."

Nelson gasped. A torrent of words spilled from his mouth—"but you believe in jesus how can you if you believe in jesus you can't oh no jesus no"—then stopped like a faucet abruptly twisted shut.

Coyle looked at him curiously. "Shoot, Nelson. The demons themselves believe and tremble."

He rose and moved from sight. A straw-colored head bobbed into view. "Just relax," it said. "It don't hurt near so bad then."

Nelson bit at his pillow. He heard moaning sounds and knew the moans were his.

"Holler all you want," a voice said. "I like when they—"

A furious pounding rocked the trailer. "Police!" someone shouted.

The room went dead as three people stopped breathing. The pounding came again.

"Lord God," the voice hissed, "pull up his britches."

Hands scrabbled at Nelson's bonds. Other hands yanked his pants to his waist. In another moment he was sitting upright on the cot, Marshall beside him. Coyle fell onto his chair and stretched to open the door.

The trailer filled with a cold wind, as a large policeman pushed into the room. The waitress Blanche peered from behind him, searching faces until she found Nelson's. "That's him." She pointed excitedly. "He was wearing glasses before."

"What can I do for you, officer?" Coyle said.

The policeman loomed above him. "What's going on in here?"

The preacher smiled. "I, sir, am a preacher of the gospel. Our young friend"—he nodded at Nelson—"attended my revival tonight and later came knocking. Like many boys his age, he sought a closer relationship with the Lord."

Nelson stared mutely about.

"He was right thirsty for it," Marshall said. "Warn't you, Sonny?"

"That yellow hair's the go-between," Blanche said. "He's a spider, lying in wait."

The policeman glowered at them all, as though he'd seen their like more than a man should be required to. He stooped to retrieve a nylon stocking from the floor. "What you doing here?" he said to Nelson. "What's your business with these people?"

Nelson's mouth opened and closed, but nothing came out.

Coyle whispered as if spellbound. "I seen this before. He's struck dumb by the Word, like Zechariah."

The policeman twisted the stocking between his fists like a garrote. "I'll strike you dumb if you don't shut up." He glared down at Nelson. "Get out your butt out of here, kid. Get home where you belong."

Nelson stood, found that he could walk, and squeezed between the policemen and the waitress to the parking lot.

He wandered for an hour, though with his glasses lost, the city lights dimmed, the diner closed, he had nothing familiar to guide him. He roamed the streets, empty as a ghost.

Eventually he found the motel and, after further wandering, his room. He switched on the bathroom light and looked toward the pastor. Snow's eyes flickered open, settled on him briefly, then closed again.

Nelson shut the door and studied the boy in the mirror. He didn't remember screaming, though his mouth was torn at the corners, as though something larger than himself had forced its way out of him.

NELSON AND THE PASTOR ROSE IN PRE-DAWN darkness and drove west toward Indiana. Snow appeared to have slept well, for he immediately began to talk, fervently and at length, about Paul struck blind on the road to Damascus.

But Nelson, huddled against the passenger door and making no effort to appear attentive, was as heedless to his words as he was to the rumor of sunrise behind them, and the promise, the imminence, of light.

Please, Mister, Please

Fulkerson was nearly upon the car when he saw it. A Honda or Toyota, nose-down in an embankment, trunk to the sky. He slowed and peered toward the accident. Steam rose from the ditch, and a full moon and his headlights illuminated two people sitting in the weeds beside the road. He braked and pulled onto the shoulder.

He glanced in his mirror to see a figure hurrying forward. In an instant a young man was staring in at him.

Fulkerson lowered the window. "Looks like you folks had a crackup."

"You might say," the man said. He was bent at the waist, hands on his knees. His chin and T-shirt were dark with blood. "The airbag busted my nose, I think. Karla Jean dinged her shoulder."

Fulkerson was a loan officer, and he relied upon his senses more than his training or a client's credit history. The young man was alert, nervous, and had been drinking whiskey.

"Are you badly hurt? Should I call for an ambulance?"

The man gripped the window frame and rocked the car gently. "You know"—he looked up and down the road—"I've had my nose busted before, and KJ ain't hurt that bad." He grinned. His incisors were large and also rimmed in blood. "An ambulance means cops, and cops is the last thing I need. Know what I mean?"

"I believe so. You've been drinking and have DUI arrests in your past."

The young man chuckled. "Bingo."

Fulkerson looked in his mirror again. He saw a woman stand, then hug herself in clear distress. Her hair was gathered in a knot on top of her head and was pink in the taillights' glow.

"Your wife looks like she needs medical attention."

"That's Dean's wife. He ain't here. He's at work."

"How in heaven's name did you get out of that car?"

The man laughed. "Thing is, I don't remember. One minute we're headed into the ditch. Next, we're sitting by the road, and you show up." He glanced toward the upended car and whistled. "She's not going to be worth much now, is she?"

"Is that Dean's car also?"

The man's eyes hardened. "No, sir. She's mine. I got the papers on her."

Fulkerson looked at the road ahead. Cornfields on both sides made a ghostly tunnel, narrowing as it disappeared into blackness. Insects flickered in his headlamps. Otherwise, there was nothing—no oncoming car, no light from a farmhouse.

"What would you like me to do, if I don't call for help?"

The young man straightened and put a hand to his nose. "She's broke, all right. I can move the sonofabitch all over my face." He laughed again. "Tell you what, if you was to drive us to the ER, I'd be grateful. I'll tell them I ran into a basement door, and Karla Jean fell down the stairs coming to help. Think that'll fly?"

"You know the answer better than I. What about the car?"

"I'll get a tow in the morning, once my head's straight."

"What if the police find it first?"

"That's a chance I got to take, ain't it? I doubt the law gets out here much anyhow."

Fulkerson took off his glasses and studied the man a beat longer. "I will help you," he said at last, "but on these conditions. I'm going to pop the trunk, where you'll find towels, a gallon jug of alcohol, and plastic garbage bags. I want each of you to take a towel and the alcohol and clean yourselves as best you can, then put the soiled towels in a bag and return them and the alcohol to the trunk. I'll take some bags myself and spread them across the passenger seat and in the back. It makes no difference who sits where, though I must ask that, while you're inside the car, you refrain from touching anything—door handles, glass, air vents, anything. When we arrive at the hospital, I'll open your doors. I'll remove the bags you're sitting on after you exit."

"Dang, Mister. What's all that about?"

"I'm what people call a germaphobe. I have a fear of illness and infection."

"Ain't neither of us sick."

"Nevertheless, those are my conditions."

The young man put his hands in his rear pockets and twisted until his spine cracked. "Open the trunk then. You're the only monkey at the zoo."

He walked to the rear of the car, where Fulkerson watched him and the woman talking. She shook her head once or twice, then sagged in a way Fulkerson had seen a thousand times across his desk—the woman, certain better terms were available, yielding to the man.

He released the trunk latch, then fetched a packet of disinfectant wipes from the console and swabbed the window frame where the man's hands had rested. Afterward he stepped from the car and joined the woman at the open trunk. She was wincing as she cleaned her face with a towel, using one arm to do so as she hugged herself with the other. The man was nowhere to be seen.

"How badly are you hurt?" Fulkerson asked.

She scowled, steam from the accident hovering about her shoulders. She was as tall as Fulkerson, himself a big man, and wore a sleeveless blouse, multiple bracelets and leggings that perfectly defined her bottom and thighs. Fulkerson placed her in her early forties, though the young man was barely twenty-five.

"My collarbone's broken," she said. "It doesn't help doing this shit."

"I'm sorry for your troubles. Where's your friend?"

A shout came from the ditch, and her partner struggled up the bank. "I had to get some crap from the car," he announced, holding up a canvas duffel. He looked behind him and shook his head. "Man, she's busted up. I don't know how we're not worse off." He slapped dirt from his knees. "Cheer up, KJ," he said to the woman. "We done been rescued."

"Shut up, Vincent," she said. "You and your happy talk."

The young man bent to the trunk, doused a towel, and began swabbing his face. "I ain't one to look a gift horse in the mouth. Ten minutes ago all was fucked up, and now"—he peered at Fulkerson—"what's your name again?"

"The sooner you're done, the sooner we can be on our way," Fulkerson said. He stood with his hands behind him and watched the pair clean themselves. The woman continued to scowl, while the man—Vincent, she'd called him—chattered and laughed, stuffing the towels into a bag after they'd finished.

"Ready for inspection, sir," he said.

Fulkerson stepped to the trunk and took from it four garbage bags. He walked to the passenger's door and spread one across the seat and sheathed the back cushion with another, then did the same in the rear. He wore a short-sleeved white shirt and narrow tie, and when he'd finished, he smoothed both before turning.

"Off we go, then," he said.

After the two were seated—Karla Jean in front, Vincent behind—Fulkerson closed the doors and took the wheel. Before he put the car in gear, he glimpsed the young man in the mirror. Vincent's face was blank as stone, though when he noticed Fulkerson watching, he winked. "Clean as a whistle back here, captain. How about you, KJ?"

Karla Jean huddled against the door, bad arm to her breast, free hand making and unmaking a fist. "Can we go? Please?"

As they pulled away, Fulkerson watched the upended car diminish and disappear in his taillights. He lifted his cell phone. "Does anyone want to call Dean about his car?"

The woman turned sharply. "What do you know about Dean?"

Vincent snorted. "I might have mentioned it. Chill, babe."

Karla Jean grimaced as she twisted toward him. "You and your goddamn mouth."

"It ain't nothing," Vincent said. Fulkerson felt the man's knee against his seat. "What you doing out this late anyhow, Mister?"

The road widened, cornfields giving way to soybeans. Farmhouses appeared and disappeared. Barnyards were lit by pole lights, though at 4:00 in the morning the houses were dark. "I have insomnia," Fulkerson said. "I find it restful to drive the country roads alone."

"Don't your wife complain?"

"I'm not married."

"There it is," Vincent said to the woman. "He got nobody to talk to."

"That's mostly correct," Fulkerson said. "I live with my mother, who is ninety and has dementia. A nurse stays with her during the day, and I tend to her in the evening. These hours are the only time I have to myself."

"Why don't you put her up somewhere?" the young man said.

"It's my obligation to care for her as long as I'm able. She did the same for me."

Fulkerson turned onto the main highway. The hospital was forty-five minutes distant, and he pressed the accelerator until the speedometer passed sixty. "But enough about me. I've drawn some conclusions about the both of you, if you're interested."

Tires thrummed beneath them. "Shoot," Vincent said.

"I work in a bank," Fulkerson said, "and make a living on first impressions. My clients are often first-time borrowers with little or no credit. They hope I'll take a chance on them, so they put their best foot forward." He felt the woman watching. "It's my belief that the two of you are, as the saying goes, on the run, and that the car behind us is indeed Dean's."

"I said she was mine," came the voice from behind.

"Yes, you did. You even said you had the papers on her."

"Well, there you go."

"The fact that you offered the information without my asking was the first hint you were lying. Your surliness confirmed it."

"Hear that, KJ?" Vincent said. "You ever know me to be surly?"

"What else?" the woman said to Fulkerson.

"Vincent has a tattoo on his left hand—four dots surrounding a fifth. The outer dots signify four prison walls, the fifth the prisoner himself." He returned her gaze. "Your friend has done time."

"I'll be goddamned," Vincent said.

"On that I have no opinion, though Mother believes a virtuous life guarantees one a place in heaven."

"You a preacher?"

"Far from it."

"Then why—"

"Like many men who visit my office," Fulkerson continued, "Vincent tried to win my trust this evening with coarse humor. He even called me a monkey, never dreaming such insolence might jeopardize his chances. You, on the other hand"—he glanced again at the woman—"are above such foolishness. You're always three moves ahead, even now."

She held his eyes before looking away, and Fulkerson heard a sound like a hand unzipping a canvas bag.

"I guess you're calling me stupid," Vincent said.

"Not so. You're clever enough to hitch your wagon to someone with twice your intellectual gifts."

The woman's bracelets jangled as she stifled a cough.

"I'll be goddamned," Vincent said again.

"I only wonder which of you will tire of the other first. She because she knows you're foolish and rash, or you because having the lights off is no longer enough."

"All right, that cuts it," Vincent said. Fulkerson felt a hard object—a pistol, he concluded—against the back of his head. "Pull over, Mister. I'm done with your talk."

"Don't be stupid, Vincent," the woman said.

"It ain't stupid. We'll dump this joker like you said in the first place. Anyway, I don't like that word, Karla Jean. Not from you or him."

"I never called you stupid," Fulkerson said.

"As good as."

Fulkerson pressed the accelerator so the car leaped forward. In an instant they reached eighty miles an hour. "Have you ever considered," he said, "what an odd thing it is to hurtle along in a car at night?"

He felt the gun harder against his skull. "Pull over, I said."

"You did indeed."

"I done murder once tonight. Don't think I won't again."

"I suspected as much about poor Dean."

"Jesus, Vincent," the woman said. "You and your mouth."

"It don't matter now, does it."

Fulkerson sank more comfortably into the seat and put his right hand at six o'clock on the steering wheel. "Vincent's right, it doesn't matter what I know." He reached forward and switched off the headlights, and the night rushed in like water through a breach in a seawall. The road was silver in the moonlight, the soybean fields rumpled oceans of blue. The sky at the horizon had a wan glow, suggesting the lights of a far-off city or a morning sun creeping westward.

Karla Jean gasped, and Vincent shouted, "The fuck?"

"Isn't it odd, even exhilarating," Fulkerson said, "to race across the earth in such darkness?" He swerved gently from one side of the road to the other, letting the tires drop onto the shoulders. "Under a full moon you see how the world must have looked ten thousand, ten million years ago, and here you are in a box of metal and glass, rushing blindly over its surface like a gnat on an elephant."

Karla Jean cried out each time the tires hit the shoulders, and Vincent shouted, "I'll shoot you right now!"

"Oh, Vincent," Fulkerson said. "I'm going eighty, and neither of you is wearing a seatbelt."

The gun left his neck. Hands patted vinyl cushions. "Ain't no belts back here," Vincent said.

"I removed them so I can vacuum more easily. As you noted, I'm a solitary creature. I rarely carry passengers."

Karla Jean's free hand was pressed against the dashboard. She was panting heavily. "Please, Mister, please. Turn the lights on. I won't let him hurt you."

Fulkerson laughed. "'Please, Mister, please,'" he repeated. "When you spend so much time alone, you make the oddest connections. There's an insipid pop song with the same title. Perhaps you're acquainted—Whoa!" A dark shape scuttled across the road, and though he wrenched the wheel a sound came of gut and bone exploding beneath a tire. Karla Jean screamed, and he heard Vincent tumble against the door. The car's rear end yawed crazily before settling.

"I'd say that was a skunk, though it may have been a possum or raccoon," Fulkerson said, easing off the gas. "When I douse the lights they appear like phantoms."

"Please," Karla Jean cried. "Vincent won't hurt you. He does what I tell him."

"As you wish." Fulkerson turned the headlights on and slowed to fifty. "See what happens, Vincent," he said over his shoulder, "when you ask politely?"

"You're crazy."

"I'm not. Or not clinically so. I do have habits you'd find peculiar, though I haven't murdered anyone tonight." He sat erect. "We're at loggerheads, aren't we, Karla Jean? Shoot me and we crash. You've already broken your collarbone, and the way you hug yourself suggests internal injuries as well."

Her voice was hoarse. "Tell me what you want."

Fulkerson inhaled deeply. "Smell that? It was a skunk after all. A friend once told me that a skunk—that faraway whiff on the road—smells like a woman. I wouldn't know, having never smelled a woman besides Mother. When I was a boy, she smelled of Ivory soap and nutmeg potpourri. Now she smells of Depends and gingivitis."

"Ain't nobody cares what your mama smells like," Vincent said.

"Karla Jean asked what I wanted, and that's the first thing that came to mind." He sought the young man in the mirror. "Is it true, Vincent? Does a skunk smell like a woman?"

When no answer came, Fulkerson accelerated and reached for the headlights. "Tell him," Karla Jean cried out. "Tell him what he wants to know."

"I guess sometimes," Vincent said quickly. "Some might smell kind of ripe and randy like that. It's all kinds, though. It's all kinds of women in the world."

Fulkerson lifted a hand to massage his temples. "'It's all kind of women in the world,'" he repeated, "yet even Mother can't hide her disgust when I enter the room."

They passed through a tunnel of corn again, stalks rushing by in a blur. "I have a confession to make," Fulkerson said. "The friend I mentioned a moment ago wasn't a friend at all, but someone I picked up by the side of the road like you. His car was broken down, his phone dead. I was his only hope."

"Did you do your snake-charmer thing on him, too?" Vincent asked.

"If you're asking did I tell him pieces of his story from clues I picked up, yes, I did. I told him his voice suggested Chicago, and he acknowledged being born there. He carried a suitcase that held samples of whatever useless trash he was selling—cleaning products, I guessed, from the piney smell."

"What happened to him?" Karla Jean asked.

Fulkerson paused. "Everything was going smoothly. He asked me to drop him at an all-night garage, which I fully intended to do. It wasn't until he began to entertain me with lewd chatter—skunks and women and how as a boy he'd lost a testicle slipping off a bicycle seat—that things began to go south."

"Like Vincent and the monkey talk," she said.

Fulkerson nodded. "Bingo."

"Dang," the young man said, "I was just yakking."

"When people display such disrespect in my office, I have no choice but to listen," Fulkerson said. "Their abysmal record keeping, their crude jokes, their mountainous lies. My car is another matter. The salesman discussed his genitals and the carnal appetites of lonely housewives. Vincent put his hands on my window frame and called me a monkey." His voice trembled. "I have a right to expect a certain level of decorum on my own premises. I have a right to—"

They drove in silence. The moon had sunk low and shone like a beacon above the horizon. Fulkerson put both hands on the wheel and aimed toward it.

"What's your name?" Karla Jean asked.

Fulkerson looked at her. She was smiling at him, hugging herself with both arms now. "John," he said, though his name was Howard. "My name is John."

Her voice was soft as she leaned toward him. "John, I've always been a man's girl. I know when they're in trouble, I know what they need."

"You do that," Vincent called out.

She leaned closer. "You don't have a soul in the world, do you, John?"

Fulkerson gripped and ungripped the steering wheel. "Do I have a woman friend? Is that what you're asking?"

"That's exactly what I mean."

The road turned briefly to gravel. The tires made a high, scratchy sound like wind through an abandoned house. "No," he said at last. "Besides Mother there's no one."

"Shoot," Vincent said. "You need to get laid, is all."

"No, Vincent," the woman said, her eyes never leaving Fulkerson. "He needs so much more than that." She reached out and rested a hand on his arm. "What say we start again, John. What say we pull over and talk, just you and me."

Fulkerson stiffened. "The moment I stop, you shoot me and take my car."

"No," Karla Jean said. "I'm just like you. I know what it is to have nobody."

"Thanks a heap," Vincent said.

"We can fix this, the two of us," the woman said. "You stopped to help when you didn't have to, when you could have passed by on the other side and gone home to Mother." She touched his arm again. "You're searching for something, baby. It's clear as the nose on your face."

Fulkerson stared forward. A sign indicated the city was five miles distant, and he slowed to forty. "We won't be stopping just yet," he said. "Before long we'll enter a residential area, and I don't believe you'll shoot me there. You already have one body in your wake. You didn't plan for two."

"If you knew Dean…" Karla Jean said, shaking her head. A finger grazed his cheek. "What do you want, John? What are you looking for so late at night?"

Fulkerson breathed deeply. The skunk had faded, and he took in the woman's perfume, a smell like burnt apricots. "Mother broke a hip two months ago," he said, "and immediately developed a kidney infection. I insisted on antibiotics, of course, and the infection subsided."

"Yes?"

"Then the infection returned, and again the antibiotics."

"Oh, my."

"Three times it has happened, and now the doctors are suggesting we hold off on further treatment. Let sepsis overwhelm her. Death is painless."

"And what do you say to that?"

"I—"

"Let the old bat die," Vincent called cheerfully. "Maybe then you can get out and enjoy life." A plastic bag rattled. "Get dirty for once."

"Shut up, Vincent," Karla Jean said.

"I'm just saying—"

"John doesn't care what you're saying."

"Truth be told," Fulkerson said, "your friend has perfectly captured my dilemma. I'm sixty-two years old, and I've never moved out of the family home. I-I've never…"

They'd left the country and were passing through an industrial park. Dark factories lined the road. Storage tanks loomed like abandoned spaceships.

"I know, baby," Karla Jean said. She squeezed his arm once more, then squared to face him. She dropped the arm she'd used to hug herself, then raised the opposite hand and unbuttoned her blouse. Her breasts spilled out—white in the moonlight, whiter than the moon itself, nipples large and dark as the foil-wrapped chocolate dollars he kept on his desk for clients.

Fulkerson's foot left the gas pedal as he peered at her. "Don't be afraid, baby," she murmured. "They won't bite."

"I'm not afraid," Fulkerson said. He massaged his temples again. The car slowed. "You can't know—" he began, but then Karla Jean launched toward him, bracelets and breasts and white teeth flashing, and scrabbled at the wheel.

"Shoot him, Vincent!" she screamed. "Shoot him now!"

Fulkerson hunched and twisted as she clawed at his hands. He had a moment's glimpse of the pistol floating between them before a report went off, and he felt a blow like a skillet against the side of his head. His elbow caught the woman in her broken place, and as the car careened off the highway she screamed again.

FULKERSON WOKE TO THE CLACKING of a crankshaft disengaged from connecting rods. He opened his eyes and stared into a weedy embankment, the weeds so close they tickled the shattered windshield. He looked down at the airbag, drooping like an empty pillowcase from the center of the steering wheel. He felt for his glasses. They were broken in two but pressed so deeply to his face he had to peel them off, one piece after the other. The right side of his head burned, and he fingered a wet crease on his temple where the bullet had grazed his skull.

"I can't feel my legs," a voice said. Vincent was bundled into the space between front seat and dashboard. A silvery light filled the car, and the young man's eyes were round and bright as a child's. "I can't feel my legs," he said again.

Karla Jean had been hurled through the windshield, her upper body suspended above the hood, her lower half still in the car. One arm dangled in the void, limp as a marionette's, bracelets stacked where her wrist widened to become a hand. The way their bodies were piled together reminded Fulkerson of medieval renderings of Hades, and he concentrated fiercely to take in the images and retain them.

"This didn't turn out as I'd hoped," he said, first to himself and then to Vincent when he saw the man was listening. The words came out strangely, and he knew that his nose and perhaps his jaw were broken. Nevertheless, he laughed. "What an odd thing. We began our relationship with an accident and broken bones, and we're ending it the same way."

The young man's eyes followed his lips as they moved.

"I'm not overly concerned," Fulkerson said, "even if you survive. I'm a respectable loan officer, while you two are criminals on the run. A good Samaritan makes an unfortunate choice and pays the price." He stretched painfully and forced a bracelet from Karla Jean's wrist. "I try to keep mementos from these encounters," he explained. "I have a bottle of glass cleaner in my pantry from the salesman's sample case, and I carry a woman's handkerchief in my breast pocket every day to the bank." He shook his head. "What possesses a person, a young woman especially, to hitchhike in today's climate? It boggles the mind."

He glanced at Vincent. "By the by," he said. "Mother is alive and well and lives in a retirement village in Florida, where—can you imagine?—the most common ailments are chlamydia and syphilis."

To his surprise the young man smiled. "Mister," he whispered. He opened and closed his mouth several times, though when Fulkerson bent close, he spoke as if addressing a crowded room. "Ain't nobody cares who your mama's fucking."

He raised the pistol and shot Fulkerson in the face.

Blue Moon

Cam lay in bed and listened to Penny sing in the shower and knew she wasn't singing about him. Sleet peppered the windows, and the furnace rasped from the basement like when Cam was a boy, and his pap woke the house coughing up phlegm.

"Blue moon, you saw me standing alone..."

Penny was singing, he figured, about a guy named Dominic.

Cam was twenty-seven years old, and Penny was his first real girlfriend. She'd moved to Mount Moriah only months before and didn't know about his arrest record, and—though he talked a tough game, though his bearded scowl said he didn't care what people thought of him, though he was strong enough to lift the tail end of her Chevette off the ground—he was desperate to keep it that way.

"You heard me saying a prayer for..."

"Penny," he shouted. "Put a sock in that shit."

She went quiet in a split second, like Ma used to do when Pap was watching *Bowling for Dollars* in the family doublewide. She'd be banging away at the sink when Pap would throw a boot against the wall. "A little louder back there," he'd yell. Ma would let out a squeak and finish the dishes like they were made of buffed leather.

Penny appeared in one of Cam's T-shirts, her head wrapped in a towel. Ordinarily Cam loved when she was freshly showered—skin sweet as strawberries, every surface lotioned and powdered—but this morning he wasn't in the mood.

She slipped under the covers and nestled close.

"Who you singing about?" he said.

"You, sweets."

"Bullshit," he said, but then she unwrapped the towel and shook her hair so droplets rained onto his chest, and he forgot what he was pissed about.

The roads were icy later when they went to the diner, and the sun shone vaguely through clouds like a candle through a bedsheet. When they got there Penny ordered a steak sandwich and only changed it to a tuna melt when Cam gave her the side eye.

She peeked at him over her Sprite. "What's got into you, Cams?"

"Nothing's got into me. Tell me about Dominic."

"He's just a guy at work."

"Is he who you're singing about? The guy you're saying a prayer for?"

She put her lips around her straw so he wouldn't see her smile.

Penny was a receptionist at Waxman Insurance, and while she was always gabbing about her co-workers, when she talked about Dominic she went all hushed and awestruck, like girls Cam remembered in high school talking about boys who'd already graduated, boys who drove their own cars, boys who were home from boot camp and wore their uniforms on movie dates.

That's how it was when Penny talked about Dominic:

"Dom made Agent of the Year two years running."

"Dom says he can cure my migraines with a foot rub."

"Dom says the past and the present are like opposite sides of the same coin."

"Dom reads everything," she said now. "He says we can't believe anything people tell us. Not the government or our parents—" she peeked at Cam again—"or our friends."

"Okay, so how about I don't believe you weren't singing about him?"

Penny laughed into her straw so Sprite bubbled up.

DURING BREAK THE NEXT DAY at Delta RV, Cam sat with his friend Darryl Huckman and told him he was losing Penny to an insurance salesman named Dominic.

The Huckster had fought in Vietnam and lived with his girlfriend and was the only person in town Cam could turn to for advice. "Here's the thing about women, baby boy," he said. "It's all about the cash and prizes." When Cam frowned, he added, "Jewelry and clothes and a great ride. What's old Dom give her that you don't?"

Cam mulled on the question as Darryl described how he used to take one of his daddy's bank receipts to The Pour House—they always showed a balance to make your eyes pop—and when he saw a girl he liked, he'd sidle close and write his number on the back and slip it into her palm. "Call me," he'd say, and before the weekend was over his phone was ringing.

"Cash and prizes, baby boy," he said again, tapping the side of his head. "Take it from the Huckster."

Cam hated when Darryl called him "baby boy," though he never let on. The name went back to when the Huckster was a senior and Cam a junior at Mount Moriah High. Darryl's old man owned the biggest dairy farm in Allen County, and there Cam milked cows before class while Darryl slept in, and again in the evening while Darryl trolled the streets for honeys.

That year the pair led the football team to a sectional championship, the Huckster as quarterback and team captain, and Cam—220 pounds at sixteen, a wall of flesh as dense and foolish as a Holstein on a January morning—a lineman on both sides of the ball.

Then Darryl graduated and got drafted, and, to his surprise as much as anyone's, Cam became team captain himself.

"Every one of these men works his tail off," Coach Roush had said in an assembly the day he announced his choice, the senior boys a hulking semicircle on the gym floor, dusty beams from a skylight bathing them in gold. "But one especially has sweated and bled and dang near died for our team."

He'd then stepped from the podium and laid a palm on Cam's head. "I'd be proud to call this big fella my son."

Cam had never received a grade higher than a B-minus. The guidance counselor at MMHS had gently steered him from algebra to woodshop, telling him the world needed "honest, upright fellows" who worked with their hands.

So, when Roush made his announcement—that Cam would be the team's leader, an example to young men coming after him—the roar from the bleachers pushed his chin to his chest. Tears stained his shirt front.

Two months later the team was undefeated, Cam had begun receiving letters from schools like Indiana State and Butler, and the arrests came.

The case might have ended in a wrist slap—boys in packs engaged in all kinds of mischief, didn't they?—until Cam's court-appointed lawyer told a reporter from Fort Wayne that his client's only crime was doing what had been done to *him*, what generations of underclassmen had endured in the same locker room, and the reporter looked up from his notepad and said, "I'm sorry, did you say generations?"

After that, newspapers from as far away as South Bend and Indianapolis set up camp at the courthouse. Cam and two other boys were convicted and expelled, the football program canceled, Coach Roush fired.

Also, the college letters stopped so fast it made Cam's head spin.

WHEN HIS SHIFT ENDED AT 3:00, Cam drove to the store and bought a pint of Jim Beam, a tin of sardines and a sleeve of crackers, then parked his pickup outside Waxman Insurance and waited for Penny and Dominic to show. He'd seen the man from a distance—company blazer, swirly hair, a real phony baloney—but it occurred to him that the Huckster's question, "What's old Dom give her that you don't?" wouldn't be answered by feeling sorry for himself. Coach Roush had always said, "Any time you're sitting still, you're losing," and Cam believed it was so.

He sucked at the bottle and punched radio buttons and tweaked heater knobs, but he couldn't find a song or a temperature that satisfied him. His fingers were slick with fish oil, crumbs littered his lap, and he imagined Penny laughing at him like she did so often, like she had the night they'd first met.

Closing time at The Pour House, rain like Judgment Day. Penny standing alone beneath the awning, car key in her hand. Cam too shy to speak to her but drunk enough to snatch the key from her fingers and charge into the storm, to find the green Chevette he'd seen her arrive in, to park it under the overhang and drop the key into her palm like a lucky piece.

She'd stared at him—wet, drunk, sure he'd made a fool of himself—then gave an astonished laugh. "You're so sweet," she'd said. "I love a big guy who's sweet."

Cam had been called many names since high school—*Judas* spray-painted on the family doublewide, *squealer* shouted from passing cars, *rat* whispered at the liquor store—but no one had called him sweet before, and hearing it made him go frail and wobbly, like the breech calves he'd yanked ass-end into the world on the Huckman farm, like himself that day in the gym when Roush named him a leader of men.

Five o'clock came and Penny and Dominic appeared. It was snowing, and Dom made a big show of clearing off

Penny's windows. Cam heard their happy shouts from where he sat, the heater turning his pickup cab into a furnace.

About then a song popped up on the oldies channel, the same one Penny had been singing in the shower—*"Blue moon, you saw me standing alone"*—and Cam squeezed the wheel so his knucklebones showed white through his skin.

"Sumbitch," he whispered, as Dom give a final touch to Penny's windshield, a goodbye pat to her rooftop. Cam had made a name for himself knocking such guys on their asses, hearing the wind explode from their lungs. Hotshots like that were asking for it, "cruising for a bruising," Coach Roush had always said.

Cam had been a hotshot once—towel snapper, strider of hallways, headline maker in the *Gazette* for his ferocious tackles—until one day Roush rested a heavy paw on his shoulder before showers. "This team's got no room for a glory hog," the coach had said, kneading Cam's collarbone. "I wonder if our big fella knows that." He lifted his hand to tap his own heart. "In here, I mean."

Then he locked up his office and went home, rather than hang around like usual to collect wet towels and turn off the lights. Darryl Huckman dug a toilet plunger from his locker—it had been passed from captain to captain since Cam's pap played before the big war—and he and the other seniors took it from there.

Later, Cam thought he might murder somebody, but before practice the next day the Huckster had grabbed him from behind and whispered that his wasn't the first butthole to get reamed at MMHS and wouldn't be the last, and Cam could wallow in rage and shame or "use the hurt" to become a better player and a better man.

"I've been there myself, baby boy," Darryl said. "The question is, what you gonna do with it?"

Afterward, Cam saw the Huckster in every rival across a scrimmage line, and the hatred he used to drive that boy into the ground became, over time, a hatred of anyone who was brave and cocksure, as Cam himself would never be again.

THAT NIGHT IN BED HE ASKED Penny straight out, "What's Dom give you that I don't?"

She was curled against him in the way he loved, cheek on his chest and a leg thrown over his thigh. "Oh, you big dumb ass," she said. "Can't a girl have a friend?"

"Darryl says women are all about cash and prizes."

She sat up. "What's that supposed to mean?"

"Cars and jewelry and stuff."

She lay down again, though he felt her jaw working. "If that's what you think of me…" she said, and then, "Screw Darryl. You've been handcuffed to him since high school and what's it got you?" She rolled away. "I'll tell you what Dom gives me. He's good with clients, and when I talk to them like he does, Mr. Waxman says I'm doing a good job." Cam put a hand on her shoulder, but she shrugged it away. "There's an agent opening in sales. A girl can want a better life, can't she?"

"Without me, you mean."

"I never said that. Jeez."

Later, when she was breathing deeply, when the moon shone through branches and made blue shadows on the wall, Cam hugged his pillow and knew and knew and knew he was fucking up and would lose her if he kept going down this road, yet he also knew he was helpless against a jealous wind at his back, pushing him toward the cliff's edge.

AFTER WORK THE NEXT DAY, Cam drove to the Watersville trailer park, where Pap still lived in the family doublewide. Ma had died five years back, from a cancer "down there" she would only say.

He found the old man in his easy chair, a cigarette burned dead in his fingers and a game show blaring.

"What you had to eat today, Pap?" Cam said, and when no answer came, he went to the refrigerator and sliced headcheese over bread and spooned mustard onto it and opened a can of PBR. Penny sometimes came with him to look after the old man, and Cam marveled at how kind she was, how she'd rub lotion on Pap's stump where the prosthetic had rubbed it raw.

"Don't you think it's ugly?" he'd ask later. "Where they cut off his leg, I mean?"

"Not a bit," she'd say. "He's your daddy."

Pap had been a lineman all over east Indiana until thirty years of hauling his ass up and down telephone poles gave him a blood clot in his knee. He ignored the pain for a week, and by then his calf had turned cool with gangrene. Afterward he sat in his recliner and scratched his stump and talked about the torments of parachute school in '44, where a meat-faced instructor had pinned a jump badge to his naked chest and pounded on it until blood ran down his front and soaked his BVDs.

"That sumbitch wanted me to cry," he'd say proudly, "but I never made a peep."

After Pap ate, Cam helped him to the bathroom, where he undressed the old man and soaped his naked body. The scar from the jump badge looked like an ancient dog bite on his chest, the skin wadded and dimpled and brown. He submitted quietly to the bath, though once he looked up and grinned. "I'd like it better if that girly-girl did it," he said.

"She's at work," Cam said. He moved the sponge over his father's chest—once so broad, now watery and loose. A thought came to him, and he said, "You bossed Ma a lot, didn't you?"

"When she had it coming, I did."

"And she never left."

"She knew better."

"Or what?"

"I'd hunt her down."

Cam tried not to react one way or another, but the old man's grin went slack. "That's right, roll your goddamn eyes. Like you was better at minding your affairs." He poked Cam's stomach with a crooked finger. "You was always the soft one."

Pap may have meant Cam's softness for Penny—how he cooked dinner sometimes or washed the Chevette—though he was more likely talking about Cam's senior year in high school, how he'd broken under questioning, how he'd cried and babbled and brought shame to Mount Moriah.

It started with a little sophomore receiver named Spencer Price. Roush rode the kid hard and got sassed in return, until one day the coach pulled Cam aside and said, "What are we gonna do about our Spencer boy?"

Cam felt a sickness in his bones, starting in the marrow and seeping outward. There'd been no incident in the locker room since his own, yet from the moment he'd become captain he'd feared the day would come, and he wouldn't have the courage to refuse. When Spencer mouthed off that same afternoon during wind sprints, Cam waited the rest of practice for the coach's sign.

"This team's got no room for a wiseacre," Roush said before showers, laying a hand on Spencer's shoulder. "I wonder if our young fella knows that?" The locker room was bright, with the yellow smell of old socks and steam billowing from the stalls. The plunger now waited in Cam's locker, and after the coach closed up and left, Cam and two other seniors wrestled Spencer across a bench while the rest of the team gathered like crows around roadkill.

Cam remembered only bits and pieces later, like flashes from a nightmare: the sophomore's howls, the others crowding close, himself gasping, "Just take it, Spence. It don't last forever." The boy fought so hard Cam panicked and twisted his arm behind him until the bone snapped.

After that, Cam drove him to Dr. Tillerman's, where the doc asked how an arm broken in blocking drills might result in bleeding from the rectum.

Spencer's father owned Mount Moriah's only jewelry store, and within the hour the boy's mother had swooped down from the Price family home above town, within the day the marshal's cruiser was parked outside the doublewide, within the week Cam had confessed and ID'd his abettors, and headlines in the *Gazette* took a different slant, labeling him "The Goon from Watersville" who'd got a fine man like coach Franklin Roush fired.

"I had to look t'other way," Pap said as Cam helped him to his chair, "once you commenced to naming names."

OVER THE FOLLOWING WEEK at Delta RV, Cam sat alone during break. Penny was right, he decided. Men like Roush and Darryl had brought him only misery, and, though he was still young, something told him she was his last chance at happiness.

The Huckster let the distance slide until the third day, when he threw an arm around Cam's shoulder and said, "How goes it with baby boy and the insurance salesman?"

Cam shrugged free. "He's Penny's friend, is all. A girl can have a friend."

The Huckster laughed. "What a big-hearted boy you are. You shame us all."

At home Cam was attentive and kind—getting up to fill Penny's water glass and letting her watch what she wanted on television like Pap never did for Ma—and one night he mentioned the position in sales and how went her quest for a better life, and she said Mr. Waxman had asked if it was true she was living with Cameron Goss, and did she know the trouble he'd gotten into in high school?

"I told him high school was a long time ago," Penny said. She was sitting in the crook of Cam's arm as they watched

TV. "And he said, 'A good insurance agent has to think about her reputation,' and I said, 'Friendship is more important to me than any career, and I'll stay a receptionist before I believe ugly old rumors.'"

Cam had gone cold at Waxman mentioning his name. "What'd he say?"

"He said, 'It's not a rumor, dear,' and I said, 'Well, even if it's true, people can change,' and then Dom piped up and said, 'Studies show our lives' paths are more or less fixed by the time we finish high school.'"

"Dominic was there?"

"That was later on, when I was crying in the breakroom." She leaned away. "I told him you were the sweetest man alive, and you know what he said?"

"What?"

"He said, 'Perhaps the rape was an aberration.'"

Cam didn't know what an "aberration" was, though before he could ask, she spun to face him. "Did you really rape that boy and break his arm?"

"It wasn't rape," Cam said. "Rape is with a woman. We were teaching him to watch his mouth, is all." The next words came before he knew it. "Besides, the same happened to me when I was Spence's age, and I'm no worse for wear, am I?"

Penny gaped. In all the nighttime talks they'd had, all the times he'd been free and tender like he couldn't be with anyone else, he'd never told her about his own time in the Mount Moriah High School locker room.

She turned away, and he felt a rush of bitterness. "That's what you get," he said, laughing like it was a joke, "slumming with a boy from Watersville." He went to pull her close again but felt a rumble off her skin, like when a cat has had enough petting and is thinking of biting you.

AFTER WORK THE NEXT DAY, Cam vacuumed the floors and dusted the end tables, then drove to the store and bought makings for Reuben sandwiches and onion rings, both Penny's favorites. He hurried home and worked in the kitchen with corned beef and rye and sauerkraut, pausing now and then to think of Pap and Ma, and how he'd never seen the old man do a nice thing except fetch her ice water near the end.

"Even that half pissed him off," Cam said aloud. "Like she got sick on purpose."

Five o'clock came, and he knew Penny was leaving work, and he set the table and opened wine, though he preferred beer with salty food like Reubens and onion rings.

At 5:30 he stood at the front window, looking up and down the road. The sun was an angry ball behind the trees, and flurries were blowing in.

At 6:00 he let the sandwiches go cold and drove to Waxman Insurance and saw that, yes, the office was closed and the Chevette was gone from Penny's spot.

He'd grabbed a pint of Jim Beam when he left the house, and now he parked across the street and listened to the radio and sucked the whiskey in burning swallows and watched snowflakes slide down his windshield where the heater warmed the glass.

"I guess you're with that swirly-haired sumbitch," he said.

He drove to The Pour House, and before he looked he knew her car was there. He didn't know what Dominic drove, though next to the Chevette was a red Camaro with plastic streamers fluttering from the antenna. He finished the pint and threw the bottle out the window, figuring only a phony-baloney sumbitch would own a hotshot ride like that.

He stepped from his truck, found a wrench in his toolbox, and slouched across the parking lot and through the doors, where music and flashing lights dazzled him. He stood to let his eyes adjust, though when Stu the owner came around the bar to block his way, Cam shoved him aside like he was made of cotton and batting.

"It won't do, big man," Stu hollered after him. "I'll call the law."

Cam walked the length of the bar and across the dance floor, where chairs and tables lined the wall, and people jostled and shouted. He was aware of stools swiveling toward him, of people shrinking to make a path, and he remembered similar scenes from high school, when he'd strode the hallways like a bull, lesser boys glancing off his shoulders, girls holding notebooks tight against their chests.

He spied Penny and Dominic in a crowd—Waxman employees, all—around a table heavy with drinks. Penny was shining, happier than he'd seen her in months, though when she saw him, her face darkened like a room when you switch off a light.

"Cams!" she cried as he pushed into their midst. "It's a birthday party!"

Dom was laughing as he turned, and Cam swept the wrench across the table, sending glass and ice cubes in all directions. Someone screamed, and Cam dropped the wrench and seized Dom's head between his hands like a man trying to squash a melon.

"What's funny, slick?" he shouted. Dom's eyes bulged, Cam smelled his sweet cologne, and then Penny was on his back.

"Babe," she cried wetly into his ear. "Cams. Stop."

Her words reached him, and he loosened his grip, though when Dom nearly escaped, Cam heaved him across the green bloom of a pool table and began to beat him with his fists. Hands grabbed him from all sides, Dom wriggled free, and Cam was himself sprawled across the bright felt, a half-dozen men holding him down and someone pounding his head with the butt end of a cue stick.

He fought but couldn't break free, and he began to roar in a language he knew by heart, though he'd heard it just twice before—once from a boy named Spencer Price and once from his own naked self, pinned to a bench in a steaming locker room.

A HALF HOUR LATER CAM DROVE TOWARD the rental house he shared with Penny. His face was sticky with blood, and his ears rang with shouts and the blows from a pool cue. As men had thrown Cam into the parking lot, Stu the owner had hollered that he'd indeed called the law and Cam's troubles were just beginning. Now as he turned onto his street, Cam saw the marshal's cruiser in the driveway, so he pointed the truck toward Watersville instead. The snow had stopped, and the moon was full, so he turned off his headlights and followed the road, a ribbon of blue in the moonlight.

When he arrived, he half threw himself, half fell through the doublewide's door. "Who's that?" came a shout, and he knew Pap was scrabbling for the pistol he kept in the end table beside the recliner where he slept.

"It's me," Cam said.

"I was set to blow your head off," the old man said. "What business you about?"

Before Cam could answer, headlights swept the tiny room. Brakes squeaked, doors slammed. He stumbled to the window and peered through the blinds. The marshal's car sat in the driveway, he and another man dark shapes against the snow. A voice shouted, "Goss!"

Cam collapsed onto the couch and hugged his knees. His skull pounded like men had been beating it all his life. "It hurts, Daddy," he whispered.

The moon came through the window and shone on the old man's chair. His nightshirt was open, and he was fingering the scar on his chest. "You're goddamn right it hurts," he said, his voice gruff and phlegmy but strangely gentle. "It's meant to."

Man on the Tracks

The train tracks stretched in a faultless V to the horizon, so Perry saw the stranger coming from a long way off. Miles and miles, he decided, though it occurred to him in the same moment that—though he was a mechanic and do-it-yourselfer and understood better than most how the world pieced together—he couldn't recall the laws of distance. How far away might a man-sized object be visible to the naked eye?

He'd known the answer once, but like so much else in his life, he'd forgotten.

The rails shimmered between fields of August corn, and Perry's follower seemed to struggle over a watery surface. They were both traveling west—the man to parts unknown, Perry to a mechanic's job he'd heard about in Olathe, Kansas, but would be a week late applying for when he got there.

He was forty-eight years old. He'd hitchhiked from Fort Wayne before getting into a bar fight the night before in DeKalb, Illinois, and he'd walked the rails thereafter. The last thing he needed was a cop with a stick up his ass finding him alone on the road.

The man he'd fought had been a decade younger than he, with a face like pig iron and ears small and shapely as fortune cookies. Perry had dodged most of his haymakers, but he'd snarled and kept coming. Only after he tripped over a curb, did Perry end things with a steel-toed boot to the chin.

He shaded his eyes and looked back on the route he'd taken. His follower wasn't the man in DeKalb, a pug in a Metallica T-shirt and a rim of white stomach. This one was tall and lanky like Perry himself, with the pink blur of a face unused to the sun.

Also, Perry had hurt DeKalb man bad. He'd be in no shape to travel. After the kick to his jaw, he'd slumped across the curb, his mouth open, his eyes slits of cream. One might have thought him dead, but Perry didn't hang around to find out. He picked up his knapsack and found his way to the railyard. He glanced over his shoulder once or twice—there'd been a dozen witnesses to the fight—but the streets were empty.

His follower was nobody, Perry decided. A lost soul like him. Out of work, out of luck, out of quarters for the slot machine. He would leave the tracks at the next town or the one after that, driven by hunger or thirst.

Perry began to walk again. The ties were sticky beneath his feet. The rails hummed, from heat or distant trains, he didn't know. Thorny scrub poked from the embankments. He remembered reading that certain plants flourished along train tracks, their burred seeds clinging like stowaways to boxcars and shaken loose elsewhere on the line. He fingered his lip, a swollen eye—DeKalb man had landed a punch or two—as he thought how like those seeds his life had become, scattered to and fro by random forces, landing on soil both barren and fertile.

Alice had been a fertile time. Not literally so—they hadn't had children—but their years in Fort Wayne had made Perry wonder if he'd finally found a home. Their rental house had a stash of *Popular Science* magazines left by the last tenant, space out back for a vegetable garden, a La-Z-Boy in front of the TV. The Texaco station where he'd worked had three service bays. Customers asked for him by name—doctors, CPAs, professional men who didn't know cars—when they needed engines overhauled, oil changes, carburetors rebuilt. They leaned against a fender and talked with him as he worked. That Perry was a smart guy, they'd told his boss Mr. Lambert. He could fix anything. He read books. He was no ordinary mechanic.

If it weren't for his temper, he and Alice might have made it work, but Perry had a hair trigger when he felt scorned or belittled, and for a man pushing fifty with grease under his fingernails, both came with the territory. Let a young crewmember laugh when he forgot the timing specs on a Chevy 350, let Evie the bookkeeper challenge the hours on his timecard, and Perry couldn't hold his tongue for the ugliness.

Evie had been the end for him in Fort Wayne. She'd been right about his hours, but she'd been so smug and starchy about it he'd called her a bitch anyway. After Lambert said he'd let it pass if only Perry would apologize, he'd swallowed his bile and agreed, but then Evie smirked when he'd sat across from her in Lambert's office, and the words were out before he knew it: "Evie, I'm sorry you're a bitch."

When he'd told Alice he'd been fired again—the third time since they'd moved in together—she packed a suitcase and left for her sister's place in Shelbyville. He thought to follow, to win her back with a roses and a promise, but he couldn't afford the first and, as to the second, he knew better than to make a promise he couldn't keep.

"Halloo!" A shout made him turn. The man was closer, much closer, as if he'd been jogging to catch up. Blond hair, belt buckle flashing like a mirror, hand lifted high.

Perry pulled a water bottle from his sack. He didn't want a travel partner, but everything in the man's carriage said he wouldn't understand that fact until he heard it straight out. He was still one hundred yards away when he laughed and yelled, "Hold on there, Baba Looey. You got a rocket up your ass?"

Perry hated him immediately. The cartoon nickname, the vulgarity, the presumption that he and Perry were cut from the same cheap cloth. The Texaco guys had been the same. On the first day they'd referred to Alice as his "old lady." In the first week they'd asked how often he stuck his dipstick in her crankcase. He'd taken it in stride as long as he could but finally broke the nose of the biggest of them, and even after Lambert made them shake hands and make up, work became a sullen affair.

"I knowed it was you, Books," the man said as he drew near. "As soon as I seen you jack up that yahoo in DeKalb, I knowed." He pronounced yahoo like yay-hoo.

Perry drained the bottle. No one had called him Books but the other inmates at the Plainfield Correctional Facility in Indiana, where his reading habits had earned him the nickname. "Keep walking, meat," he said.

"Be nice. I'm wore to a nub."

Perry took him in. Sunburned scalp, rotting grin. He didn't recognize the man, but he recognized the type. A June bug, they'd called guys like him in the yard. Someone who would trade his soul for a stick of gum.

He started to walk again. A water tower painted with the name Bethany bulged above the treeline, and Perry knew Bethany to be a fair piece into Iowa. He would stop there for lunch and some shuteye in a park, before pushing on to Olathe.

"You wouldn't be so high and mighty, Books," came a voice behind him, "if you knowed what I know."

"I don't give a damn," Perry said.

"Your DeKalb boy's neck is broke. The law's looking for who did it." The man drew alongside, baring his broken teeth in a smile. "I ain't told 'em, though. I ain't one to rat out a bunkie."

Perry knew him then. Fish, they'd called him on the inside. The years had turned his acne to sallow pinpricks, thinned his ponytail to a string, but he and Perry had once shared Cell #1225 in Plainfield.

If it was true he'd broken the man's neck, he was sorry, though he hadn't started the fight. He'd been playing pool alone when the man had challenged him to a game. "Beer, buck, or fun?" he'd said as he racked the balls, and when Perry answered fun—he was down to his last twenty dollars—he'd laughed and picked at his navel and asked what kind of pussy played eight-ball at midnight for fun?

"I seen you beat somebody like that in the yard once," Fish said. He whistled and shook his head. "I says to myself, Whoo, boy. Don't make Books mad."

There'd been too many fights in too many yards, bars, and parking lots for Perry to keep track of. "I don't know anyone named Books," he said.

Fish frowned and dug something from a pants pocket. "I must of mistook you for somebody else, I guess. It must of been another man who lost this wallet."

Perry stared, then dropped his knapsack and knelt to rummage through it.

"One of them looky-loos took it from your bag during the fight," Fish explained over his shoulder, "and then I took it off him." He shrugged when Perry looked up. "He warn't but a little shit."

Perry stood. "Give it to me."

"Not so fast. Ain't I got something coming?"

"You got something coming all right."

Fish pouted as he put the billfold in Perry's outstretched hand. "Shoot, Books. I didn't talk to the law, I took your wallet off the dipshit who stole it, and then"—he spread his arms to take in the cornfields—"I walked my ass to Bumfuck, Iowa, to return the goddamn thing."

Perry stuffed the wallet in his knapsack. "I'm obliged, but I never asked you to."

The man's pout faded. "It warn't nothing."

"I don't have a dime to spare, if it's money you're after."

"It ain't that," Fish said. "I thought I'd tag along, is all. You was nice to me in Plainfield."

Perry's thoughts went to Alice, how she'd hung the bedsheets to dry outdoors so they'd be cool and sweet-smelling that night, how she'd known not to tease him when he got absentminded, how she'd wince—even when they weren't arguing—if he stood up too quickly from the kitchen table.

"I've never been nice," he said.

"Nah, you're thin-skinned, is all. It's some folks born that way."

Perry chewed on the thought, deciding it was true. He worked hard. He wasn't a drunk. His poor parents had loved him. There was no earthly reason he'd ended up a man on the tracks outside Bethany, Iowa—an ex-con for a travel mate, the law on his tail—except he'd been born that way.

What got him in trouble was, he couldn't abide a bully. He couldn't stand someone, cop or civilian, who made weaker men beg. He hadn't been "nice" in Plainfield, so much as he'd stood between people like Fish and their tormentors.

"I figure you and me should partner up," Fish was saying. He framed an imaginary headline with his hands. "Books and Fish. The law don't know where they went, but it sure as *hell* knows what they took with 'em."

Perry spun. "I'm not Plainfield trash like you."

Fish stammered. "I-I didn't mean nothing. You was such a badass inside, I thought—"

"You thought wrong. I'm no thief."

"Anyway, you and me—"

Perry moved so close he smelled the man's stale breath. "There is no you and me." He jerked his head toward the water tower. "I'm stopping up ahead, and you're going on alone. Got it?"

To his surprise, Fish's eyes welled up. "We was friends in Plainfield, Books. That's why I come after you. I never forgot."

Perry turned away. He listened for following steps, but none came.

THE ROAD INTO BETHANY WAS HOGBACKED, and Perry found it easier to walk its mounded center than its sloping edges. The air was choking hot. The cornstalks writhed audibly in the sun. Far-off thunder made him think he was hearing things. He considered sticking out a thumb when a passing car forced him to the side, but he remembered that the law was looking for him in Illinois, and he didn't know how far the word had spread.

He recalled little about the man in Cell #1225, except that he'd hung close in the yard and always had a spare cigarette. Also, they'd talked at night, Fish telling stories from the upper bunk about a daddy who drank and whaled on him, and Perry asking how it was that a man—even a weak piece like Fish—took such treatment without finding an axe handle and putting a stop to it.

"I ain't like you, Books," Fish had answered with a laugh. "It's some folks born on the bottom rung and only know to stay there."

Another car approached from behind, and Perry veered to the shoulder to let it by. He made out a gas station ahead, a collection of buildings. There'd be food and drink there, and shade for a—

A brown-and-white cruiser passed him and stopped on an angle, its nose almost in the ditch. Perry paused, then made to walk around it. Experience had taught him to keep his head down and go about his business—they were usually just checking him out—but two county troopers emerged, one from each door. They walked languidly toward him, hands adjusting their Smokey-the-Bear hats, dust swirling up from their boots.

"Hey, fella," said the older of the pair. "Where you headed on such a godawful day?"

Perry cut a hard figure, he knew. He hadn't showered or shaved since he'd left Fort Wayne. His left eye was swollen, his lip scabbed. Days on the road had covered him in grime. He dropped his knapsack, hands hanging where they could see them. "Up there," he said.

"Up where?"

"Bethany."

"Mmm-hmm. What's your plans in Bethany?"

Perry sagged. He hated how cops did a man. "I'm opening a greeting card store."

The trooper smiled and glanced at his partner. "That's funny."

"Sorry, dude. I'm beat all to—"

"Where you from?" the younger cop barked.

Perry's legs gave out, and he sat on the hot pavement. "Out east."

"You got any ID?"

Perry pawed weakly at his sack, but the cop barked again, "Show us your hands!"

"Aw, let him be," the older man said. "He's too tired to be a dumb ass."

Five minutes later Perry sat in the cruiser's back seat, a fresh water bottle between his legs and the air conditioner on full. The troopers sat up front, the older one studying his driver's license and the younger trading details with a woman on the radio. Their boy had a record, her garbled voice said, but no outstanding warrants. He'd served his time. He wasn't on parole.

When they'd finished, the older man turned, his beefy forearm resting on the seat back, and said, "You're a bad egg, aren't you, Peter?"

Perry thought to correct him—a judge or two had called him Peter, but nobody else—but he was so grateful for cool air, he only shrugged. "Not so much anymore."

"How'd you bust your face up?"

"Walked into a door."

"Oh, he's bad all right," the young cop said. "Can't answer a straight question, he's so bad."

The older trooper faced forward, drumming his fingers on the wheel. Perry stared at the backs of their heads. He was determined to mind his manners, though the young trooper seemed equally determined to rile him.

"Here it is," the older man said after a moment. "You'll last two seconds in Bethany if you make any trouble." He turned again. "But I guess you know that."

"Yep."

"You can clean up at the gas station, and there's a diner next door." The trooper peered at the sky as he put the car in gear. "Weather's rolling in. We'll drive you there."

"Dang," the young cop said, "whyn't we cut his toenails while we're at it?"

In the men's room at the station, Perry took off his shirt and washed as best he could. There was little he could do for his clothes except beat the dust from them against the toilet tank, but doing so cheered him and made him feel more civilized.

Impact wrenches and shouting voices echoed through the wall, and he thought to ask the manager if there was an opening for a good mechanic. He'd be days late to the job in Olathe, if there even was one anymore. But when he went outside and looked, a half-dozen young men were working the service bays. Most ignored him, though one or two threw him a hostile stare, and the idea of breaking in with a fresh crew of punks filled him with gloom.

Thunder muttered again as he walked across the parking lot to the diner. The booths were filled with the lunch crowd, so he found a stool and ordered coffee and a ham sandwich from a sour-faced waitress behind the counter.

He took measure of his surroundings. Since he'd washed up, not much besides his knapsack and bruises separated him from the other men in the place—farmers, feedstore clerks, working slobs like him—but these differences were enough to earn glances and whispers, and when the waitress put his sandwich in front of him she did so with a clatter.

She crossed her arms and sniffed. "Anything else," she said so loudly the room went quiet.

"No, ma'am."

She blew air from her lower lip so her bangs lifted, and the cook, a big man in a paper cap, leaned to stare at him through the serving hatch. "Eat fast, boy," he said.

Perry caught his own reflection in a mirror over the coffeemaker. He was nothing like the other men in the place. His left eye was purple. His cotton shirt was black with sweat and—though he'd long since lost the ability to tell for himself—he knew he stank to high heaven. He studied his hands. He'd done his best in the washroom, but it had been a lifetime since his nails were clean, since the folds in his knuckles weren't grouted with filth.

He looked at the waitress again, the cook, the men watching openly from the booths. A familiar heat rose in his chest. He hadn't been asking for trouble, but—like a drunk in DeKalb, like seeds stuck to a boxcar—trouble had found him anyway.

The waitress's sour face brought Lambert's Evie to mind. He grinned at her. "Lady, I'm sorry you're a bitch," he said.

She blinked. Her mouth fell open.

He grinned wider as he heard Fish in his head. "It's some folks born that way."

She took two steps back, colliding with the lemonade machine. "Al!" she yelled.

The cook ducked from the serving hatch and in another instant was at the kitchen door, but Perry had rounded the counter by then to meet him, and he broke the man's nose as he'd broken the nose of a guard in Plainfield, an asshole boss in New Carlisle, and his biggest tormenter at the Texaco station in Fort Wayne.

The cook reeled backward into the kitchen, hands grabbing at shelves and cabinets, plates and pans and cutlery falling with him in a great crash to the floor.

The waitress yelled again, a wordless "Yahhhh!" The cook squirmed and bled. The others leaped from their booths. A few advanced on Perry in pairs or threesomes, though when he spun to stare at them they piled together like sheep in a tick bath.

He picked up his sack and walked out the door, the men following in a milling hubbub. Perry froze them with another stare, then turned and ran up the street between shoe shops and bakeries, hardware stores and hair salons. The voices behind him swelled and ebbed, as he ducked into an alley. He thought to make a break for the rails, but train tracks at midday offered no hiding place.

A siren warbled close by, and he sagged against a wall, dizzy with heat and exhaustion. Why not just show himself? He hadn't eaten a bite of his sandwich. He hadn't slept in days. He couldn't keep running forever, and besides, he had no place and nobody to run to. If it came to a fight in the street, he'd land a punch or two at least. He'd have something to smile about later, in the hole where they threw him.

"Books," a voice stage-whispered from across the alley, and there—half in and out of a dumpster, gesturing wildly—was Fish. "Get your ass in here," he said.

The siren warbled again, shouts drew near. Perry grabbed the bin's corrugated edge and heaved his body inside. Fish pulled the iron lid shut, and the two men burrowed through fat garbage bags and soaked newspapers, beer bottles and cantaloupe rinds, to the dumpster floor. There they lay, chest to chest in rot and fetid water.

Fish's breath gusted against Perry's face. "Hush now," he whispered.

Rushing footsteps neared. Someone opened the lid and poked with something through the trash. Another man said, "Anything?" and the man doing the poking said, "Nah," and Perry knew him to be the young cop and his tool to be a billy club.

"He's a stupid greaser. He won't get far," the cop said.

The steel lid tolled shut like a giant bell.

Noises rose and fell. Car doors slammed. Men shouted. Twice more the bin filled with light as someone opened the lid, and twice more it clanged shut. Later the siren wailed in the distance, and Perry figured the cops were racing down the hogbacked road to the railroad tracks.

"Who's stupid now?" Fish said.

With the sour press of garbage on top of him and the sounds of his pursuers fading, Perry felt suddenly, oddly, at peace—no longer hungry or tired. Fish's breath in his face sparked a memory—he'd read somewhere that smells do that to a brain—though try as he might he couldn't hearken up its details.

A crack of thunder rattled the iron box, followed by Fish's whispery laugh. "These yahoos ain't going to chase you in a storm. Come dark, we're home free."

Thunder roared. The skies opened. Rain hit the dumpster lid like gravel from a backhoe. Water rushed through every seam. Fish laughed again, then sang in a soft, twangy voice, "Master, the tempest is raging, the billows are tossing high."

Perry yawned and settled more deeply into the rot. He went to sleep to Fish's crooning voice and the sounds of the rain.

He woke in pitch darkness. Fish had fallen asleep also, head on Perry's chest, and Perry's forgotten memory came to him in all in a piece—crystalline, perfect, like a butterfly preserved in amber.

His last night in bed with Alice. A storm raging then also. Alice was afraid of storms, so he'd held her close as they talked about his meeting the next morning with Evie and Mr. Lambert.

"Promise you'll be good," she'd said.

Perry bristled. "I'm not a ten-year-old."

She flinched as lightning flared. "I mean…she was right about the timecard, wasn't she?"

"She's a bitch. She thinks she's better than folks."

"Perry, I can't—" she began, but then thunder crashed and crashed, and she panted and moved closer. He held her tightly as the tempest rolled across the sky. At last, her panting slowed. She settled more deeply against him, her breath in his face.

When all was quiet, he jostled her. "You can't what?" he said, but she was sleeping, her head damp and heavy on his chest.

There'd been guys in Plainfield—the career types—who were born to rape and steal and set things on fire. Perry wasn't one of those. He was smart and capable. Everyone said so. If it came to holding onto Alice and his job and their comfortable little home, of course he would apologize to Evie. Of course he'd be good.

He'd get things back on track in the morning. Only a fool would throw it all away.

Little Dude

Betty G's been my girlfriend since seventh grade, and there was a time she liked nothing better than getting high and doing the nasty. But lately—like just now in her apartment over the laundromat—she'll smoke a joint and fall asleep, leaving me stoned and forsaken with my dick in my hand.

I think about whacking one out by myself, but then I remember how Lloyd might walk in any minute, so I zip up and light a cigarette. Betty G's in her swimsuit, and I flick the match against her naked back.

She jerks. "God, Mitch, grow up" she says for, like, the fortieth time this week. I'm sixteen and she's eighteen, but before she dropped out we were in the same class, on account of her being in and out of juvie.

I should be in juvie myself, but my dad's the town marshal, so draw your own conclusions on that score. He's tried every which way to civilize me, the most recent being this drug camp outside Fort Wayne, with canoes and rope climbs and fried old hippies explaining why we do what we do.

It starts tomorrow, and Dad says he's driving me there at gunpoint.

So, seeings how in twenty-four hours I'll be up to my ass in stoners jonesing for hit, Lloyd and I and Betty G are headed to Fish Lake today to snag a package at the Hilltop

Inn, where a guy called Zoom sells Dr. Pepper and burgers and weed by the bag if he thinks you're cool.

Zoom wears wifebeaters and flipflops and calls me "Little Dude" because I had rheumatic fever and will never be taller than five-foot-four. He was weird about being my dealer because of my dad, until I told him that *not* doing business with me was the surest way for Dad to find out.

Betty G snorts awake. "We going swimming or what?" A dryer starts up downstairs. The floorboards hum.

"Soon as Lloyd gets here," I say, and just like that the big goober walks in, combed and spiffed after chores. His folks are Amish, so you might think he's a weird match for a fuckhead like me, but he likes drugs and cars and rock and roll better than most people, maybe because he'll have to dump all three once he joins the church.

"Crank it up, girls," he says.

"I smell cow shit," Betty G says.

"Nature's cologne," he answers.

We smoke what's left of the roach, then take Lloyd's car to the lake, me in the passenger seat and Betty G in back, her big feet on the cushion beside my head. She's kind of horsey to be honest—all gums and teeth and a lopey way of walking—but guys like her because she says *fuck* a lot and wears cutoffs so short you can see where her butt starts. She had notions of being a model until she showed up high for a cattle call and had a panic attack when it came her turn on stage.

Later she thought she'd be a stewardess, but now she wants to start a bakery. Everybody likes cookies, she figures, and, besides, the one time she was on an airplane she threw up.

She's three inches taller than me, but outside appearances don't mean anything, she says. We're all butterflies, nestled in our cocoons, waiting for the spring.

I've been around for sixteen springs, I answer, and shit never changes, but she says she's talking about another kind of spring—that place each of us is *meant* to be.

"You'll know it when you see it, babes," she says.

When we get to the Hilltop, I yell in the window for Zoom to get my package together, and we head down to the lake. Lloyd sits on the pier—Amish kids weren't allowed to take lessons at the Y like the rest of us—as Betty G and I swim to the raft. There's a dozen guys out there already, and she stretches among them like a kitten among pit bulls. I float on my back and let the sun cook my eyeballs.

I kind of hate everything, if you want to know the truth.

I hate the sky because it's blue and water because it's wet.

I hate my parents for thinking I'll shape up any day and become a Rotarian.

I hate Lloyd because we both know he's only playing the hoodlum until he marries some chick named Miriam or Etta Sue and starts shoveling cow shit full time.

Mostly, I hate Betty G for being so snotty and adult lately, for telling me to grow up all the time, for flashing her stuff at anything in pants and then saying I'm paranoid for noticing.

After a while I see her yakking with this guy people call Jesus. He has long hair and a beard and a dreamy way of gazing at you, but I know him and his friends to be everyday punks from Churubusco, a town north of here. He's talking to Betty G all warm and thoughtful like he's looking into her soul, when what he's really looking into is the nubby top of her two-piece.

I climb the ladder and ask—seeings how chatty they are—do they have anything to say to me, and Betty G says, "*God*, babes. Can't two people talk?"

Jesus is sitting cross-legged, face level with my waist. His chest is cheesy white, with something like three black hairs per nipple. "Yeah, babes," he says, and I catch him one in the mouth.

Things get fucked up from there. Betty G yells. Jesus's buddies grab me. He punches me in the ear. I fall back into the water like a wounded duck.

Fish Lake is twelve feet deep at the raft, and I sink as far as I can to clear my head. I love going to the bottom. The pale fingers of sunlight, weeds swaying in the muck, a million gallons in your ears…it's peaceful as death. I'd stay down there forever if I didn't have to breathe.

When I come up, Betty G is swimming to the pier, and Jesus is grinning from the raft like he's admiring his own reflection. His look has gone from dreamy to devilish on account of the blood in his beard. "Don't leave yet, babes," he says. "Climb back up here and get your ass kicked some more."

I'm tempted. I got no problem getting my ass kicked so long as I get in some kicking of my own, but including his disciples there are six of them, so I give a wave that means *Another time*, and swim to the pier myself.

There Betty G doesn't say anything about the fight, because what else is new? Once, though, as I'm toweling off, I say "Hey!" real loud, just to watch her jump.

"Whaaaaat?" she says, all falsely accused.

Truth is, I knew I was going to punch Jesus before I climbed the raft, because once I get an itch I can't help but scratch it. Same as when I sliced my hand open in biology class and thought it would be cool to pour ink in the cut. Or the time I figured a buck knife at the hardware store would fit perfect in my pocket, and old Mr. Newell caught me and ratted me out to my dad.

"Christ, boy," Dad said on the drive home, "I'll buy you all the knives you want."

Uh-huh. Tell that to my itch.

We head up to the Hilltop and grab a booth, and after a minute Zoom comes over with Dr. Pepper in plastic cups. He's thirty or sixty—don't ask which—with a bald skull and a string for a ponytail. He's usually half baked, but today he's locked on me like a teacher when it's time for a talking-to.

"Can't be fighting out here, Little Dude," he says. "That shit attracts attention."

"He didn't start it," Betty G says.

Zoom turns real slow like he only just realized she was there. "And you, honey-butt. You can't be twitching your tail and getting the boys riled up. That's the opposite of copacetic, which is how shit needs to be."

This strikes Lloyd and Betty G as the funniest thing ever. They wheeze and hug each other. "Can't be twitching your tail, honey-butt," Lloyd says.

Zoom isn't laughing. "For real, man. Wilkey told me to put the kibosh on troublemakers, or he shuts me down."

I'm not laughing either. My ear hurts, and I'm pissed how la-dee-da Betty G is, seeings how if anybody started the fight, she did. Wilkey owns the Ford dealership and also the Hilltop, and he threatens to close the latter every month or so, on account he's a deacon at Mount Moriah Baptist and has a giant stick up his ass.

"You got bigger problems than Wilkey," I say.

"Like what, man?" Zoom says. His wifebeater rides up to show a roll of cookie dough hanging over his shorts. His eyes look like somebody blew matches out in them.

"Like this," I say, sweeping the cups off the table. Dr. Pepper and ice fly everywhere. "Do what you want with other punks out here, but fuck with me and you get a visit from my dad."

He blinks once or twice. "That's bogus, dude," he says.

"So, get what I came for and I'm out."

"Thing is"—he rubs his belly and glances around—"my guy needs the paper up front. Shit's getting hairy lately."

He knows as well as I do there'll be no paper until drug camp is over. We've had that deal before. "You'll get your money," I say.

"Them's the terms, though. I'm just the messenger."

In the parking lot Betty G hangs on my neck and giggles. "Can't be fucking with Little Dude."

"He'll tell his dad on you," Lloyd says.

I have to laugh. "That's bogus," I say.

We're almost to the car when I hear a yell. I squint down at the water, and there's Jesus waving from the raft. His buddies are gone and it's him alone, rimmed in afternoon sun, skinny as a refugee. "Come back, babes," he shouts. "We got unfinished business."

Lloyd shoves me along. "Not now, Mitch. We got shit to figure out."

He's right. It's only hours 'til drug camp, and I need money bad.

"WHAT ABOUT THE OLD LADY with the wad in her mattress?" I say in the car.

Betty G's in back again, twirling bubblegum on a fingernail. "Who?" she says, though I can tell she knows what I mean.

"Violet or whatever."

"It's *Rose*, and that's not happening."

Rose used to foster Betty G on Milton Street, but now she lives in a place called The Point, where old people sing around the piano and try to pretend they're not almost dead. Her husband was a banker or something, and Rose always had a roll stashed in her bedroom, where twelve-year-old Betty G peeled off a twenty for herself now and then.

She kicks my seat. "I mean it." Rose was sweet, she says, and foster parents are sometimes the opposite of sweet, what with the family being all hard-ass with rules and regs, or the man of the house a tad too pleased having teenage strange around.

"Chill," I say. "We'll just talk to her."

"I've seen how you talk."

We stop at Waffle City, and I lean in with my plan over pancakes and eggs. We visit Rose's apartment. Betty G and Lloyd sit and talk about dead Mr. Rose or whatever. I excuse myself to take a leak and toss the bedroom.

Easy money, in and out. I wouldn't even *have* the idea if Betty G—Miss Conscience all of a sudden—hadn't done the same herself.

Lloyd's lifts his head from his plate like it's too heavy for his neck. "How about we pay her back when camp's over?"

Betty G glances around. Her mood has improved considerably, seeings how she's still in just her swimsuit and a T-shirt, and every man in the place—the waiter, the cook, old marrieds peeking over their menus so their wives don't see—can't get enough of her.

"Can we do that, Mitch? Pay her back, I mean?"

"Sure."

THE SUN'S AN ORANGE BALL BEHIND the trees when we turn into The Point, and right away people are staring from the sidewalks at Lloyd's car, with its bad muffler and spangly shit hanging off the antenna.

Betty G kicks my seat again. "No lake stuff, okay?"

"Right. Like I'm going to punch an old lady."

"Relax, kid," Lloyd says. "I'll mind your boy." He waves at some guy pushing a walker, and after gaping a second the guy waves back.

Rose lives in a building like a dormitory, and as we walk down the hall I get a whiff that takes me back to when my grandpa lived with us, peeing himself in front of the TV. People's names—Myrtle, Wilbur—are on the doors, game shows blare, and I know, without knowing how, that I'll die before I get old.

Betty G knocks at Rose's door, and after about an hour it cracks open and an old lady is peering at us like her last company was when the Mayflower landed. She's wearing glasses, and her head is lit from the inside so her scalp glows through her hair.

"It's me, Mama," Betty G says. "Elizabeth Grace."

Rose stares another beat, and then her face blooms like a flower. "Elizabeth *Grace*. My darling girl."

Betty G kind of shudders. "It's me, Mama," she says again. She and Rose fall into each other's arms, rocking back and forth and crying. Lloyd grins at me over their heads.

"And who are these handsome fellows?" Rose says when they untangle. She's no bigger than an eight-year-old.

"Mitch and Lloyd," Betty G says, throwing me a look. "My best friends."

"And you all came to see me." A door opens across the hall, and Rose yells, "Not now, Margaret." I catch blue hair and a robe. "She's just awful," Rose says.

So, everybody and his dog saw us drive into The Point, Rose knows our names, and awful old Margaret got an eyeful. Real criminal masterminds, us.

"Can we come in for a bit?" Betty G says.

"Mercy, now I'm the awful one," Rose says. She herds us down the hall into a room with a couch and a kitchenette. A bunch of pictures hang on the wall: a painting of a swan on a naked chick's lap, Jesus and the multitudes, a photo of a man seated stiff and angry on a stool, and (maybe?) a young Rose behind him in a dress to her ankles.

Tucked in the photo's frame is a Polaroid of Betty G from junior high. She's all leggy and cute, and I remember how her tongue tasted like Pop Rocks, how we'd smoke a joint before history, how nobody believed a girl like her could go for a punk like me.

She and I and Rose sit on the couch and right away Betty G takes off on how she's going to open a place called Betty's Sweets, how local celebrities—news people and whatnot—will sign photos on the wall, how the scones Rose taught her to make will be the house specialty.

"I've thought hard about it, Mama," she says. "It's where I'm meant to be."

Rose nods, though I can tell she's catching only pieces of what's going on. Her shoulders join her neck in a little hump. Her hands are veins and chicken bones. Her glasses make her eyes huge, grays and blues swimming together like Aggie marbles.

All of a sudden she says to Betty G, "He's like a doll, isn't he?"

"Who is, Mama?"

She puts a hand on my knee. "This one."

I don't know what she means, except maybe because I'm runty and don't shave yet I look nicer than I am.

Lloyd snorts from his chair. "Oh, he's a real Howdy Doody."

"But goodness," Rose says. "What happened there?" She touches my ear where Jesus hit me. It's pulpy and swollen like a boxer's and throbs like a bitch.

"I bumped myself," I say.

"Kenneth does the same. If it isn't one thing, it's another." I glance at Betty G, and she gives me a *You-got-me* look. "But Kenneth," Rose adds, "never considers the consequences. It's hurry-hurry until *somebody*"—she goes for my ear again—"bumps himself."

I hate people touching me, and I lean away. "Easy on the merchandise."

She sways and laughs. "You were always so particular." She turns to Betty G. "Did you know, Elizabeth, that Kenneth visits most every night?"

"He does?" Betty G says, her face both smiley and desperate, like when the carnival ride you're on goes from fun to scary in a split second.

"Oh, yes. He sits where that one"—Rose points at Lloyd—"is sitting right now."

Lloyd nods helpfully. "The seat's still warm."

A crackly voice comes from across the hall. "I won't!" it yells. Another voice rolls in, real patient and firm, and I figure old Margaret's getting a shot or an enema.

"Oh, Mama," Betty G says, "you're seeing ghosts."

"I am *not*." Rose looks at me. "Do you know, Kenneth, how I can tell you're real when you visit? Because when nurse Ivy barges in with my pills, you jump." She smiles, all pleased with herself. "He jumps like he's startled, dear," she says to Betty G. "What sort of ghost does that?"

Everything's quiet, and I get this hum—not a sound, but a vibe—that I know is Betty G pleading we leave an old lady to her spooks.

But like I said, once the itch comes on, it's like a truck rolling downhill.

"I have to go to the bathroom," I say.

"Didn't you go earlier?" Betty G says real quick.

"I have to go again."

"But—"

"Gracious, Elizabeth," Rose says. "Kenneth's a grownup." She smiles at me. "You know where it is, dear. Through the bedroom."

I stand and head that way, and as I pass Lloyd he says, "Don't be long, Kenneth." He says it funny-like, though I can tell he wants to bail too.

"Don't be a pussy," I say.

Rose's bedroom butts up to the toilet, where I switch on a bulb and turn to scope things out. There's a bed and a dresser with a mirror and not much else. I rummage in a side table drawer but turn up nothing but Kleenex and a tobacco tin full of hairpins and buttons and stuff. On the tabletop is a photo of the man from Rose's wall. He looks angry here too, maybe because he's wearing a collar so tight it's a wonder he didn't choke.

I check the bed to be sure—you always hear how old people hide money under the mattress or bury it out back in a Mason jar—but I figure the dresser is my target.

And I'm right. Within minutes of pawing through old lady undies, I find a roll as big as my fist. It's wrapped in a rubber band and looks to be mostly tens and twenties. I heft it, feeling that familiar buzz, when Rose says from the other room. "Do you remember, Elizabeth, how we used to make scones?"

"I do, Mama," Betty G says, like she wants to cry.

"Kenneth loves scones."

You may think I'm bullshitting, but if you were to open my brain and poke around, you'd find soft places here and there. I cried when my dog Rags died. And sometimes when Mom makes me cocoa and toast, I get a tightness in my chest that might be love. And at night, when the wind's rattling the windows and I've gone days without seeing Betty G or Lloyd, I get so lonely I can't breathe, like I'm tangled in the weeds at the bottom of the lake, like there's twelve feet of black water between me and the air.

Betty G's teary voice hits me like that, and I think for a second of peeling off the bills I need and leaving the rest.

But just as quick I think how jizzed she gets lately over other guys' attention, how she played me and Churubusco Jesus against each other, how she and Lloyd are both headed down a road without me—her to her glorious bakery, him into the arms of church and family—and I'm a trashy rest stop along the way.

Who's the pussy? I think. I twist the rubber band, and it breaks and stings me a good one. I say *Fuck!* and put my finger to my lip, and there in front of me is the glowing outline of someone watching everything I'm up to.

I say *Fuck!* again, this time so loud the talk in living room stops.

My fear melts in a second, once I realize the witness is me—a smalltown thief rimmed in bathroom light, in a dresser mirror he'd forgotten was there.

"Is that you, Kenneth?" Rose calls.

I stuff the wad in my pocket and walk back to where everybody's waiting.

"It *is* you." Rose turns to Betty G. "What did I tell you? He comes most every night." She frowns at Lloyd. "You, mister. That's Kenneth's chair."

Lloyd pops up like a Jack-in-the-Box, but I say, "We have to go."

"Oh, but..." Rose pushes to her feet. "You only just arrived." She totters over and hugs my waist. "Until tomorrow then," she murmurs into my face. "We'll make scones."

Like I said, I don't go for touching, but I put my arms around her and squeeze for what feels like forever. Her rib cage swells. Her heart thumps like a bat in a wet paper bag. I let go only when Lloyd says, "Dude," real careful and quiet, like he doesn't want to startle me, like you'd talk to someone playing with a loaded gun.

NOBODY SAYS ANYTHING ON THE WAY to the lake. Betty G sits in back with her knees to her chest, and Lloyd holds the wheel at a perfect ten and two like they teach you in Drivers Ed. He glances at me once or twice, but that's all.

At the Hilltop I step from the car and wait, though when neither of them gets out, I crunch across the gravel to do the deal alone. It's barely nine, but the door's locked and the lights are off, and I figure Zoom closed early and is passed out on his backroom cot.

I go around and try that door, but it's locked too. Peering in, I see the room is empty—even Zoom's cot is gone—and I figure Wilkey has shut him down at last.

I walk to the front and look down toward the lake, its surface dark except for moonlight on the ripples. I imagine how black the bottom must be, like the beginning or the end of the world.

I want to tell you about when Rose hugged me. It might have been the scare I got from my reflection, or because my ear still hurt where Jesus hit me, or because I had a glimpse of how alone I am and was always meant to be, but I got an itch to crush the breath out of that old lady, to feel her ribs break like so many dry sticks, to stop her heart in her chest.

It took everything I had to fight it.

But fight it I did, and for all the ways I'm a bad guy, for all the ways I let my parents down, for all the ways I'll fuck up my future, I deserve credit for that at least.

Lady Liberty

Edmond sat at his desk and listened in helpless outrage as his mother and the girl chattered in the kitchen. The old lady was teaching the child to frost an angel food cake. "Let the knife twirl just so," she said. "Let it *twirrrrrl* just so." The girl giggled and mimicked the lilting phrase, and if Edmond could tell from a distance she was being insolent, why couldn't his mother?

It wasn't enough the child had violated his sanctuary. It wasn't enough she had her eye on his dead father's treasures. Now she was openly mocking the woman who had taken her in, and that was going finally, irrevocably, too far.

He stood, slammed his bedroom door, and turned on the radio. Before the soothing music began, he heard the two go quiet, then break into laughter.

Edmond had quit his bookkeeping job a month earlier at Indiana Tool & Die, moving home until he found something new. If he'd waited for Mr. Chandler to fire him, he could have collected unemployment and muddled along in his apartment, but instead he'd made his own departure. As with every job he'd held, Edmond had seen a multitude of wrongs in how the firm conducted its business and had merely suggested ways to make them right, and if Chandler didn't appreciate him, he would find someone who did.

His mother had kept his room exactly the same as the other times he'd come home, and when he'd opened his suitcase on the bed she appeared with a bowl of Cream of Wheat and insisted he put his feet up while she unpacked. She had good news, she said, and wanted him rested and at full attention.

Edmond ate the hot cereal and watched her hurry about. He was forty years old and shaved his skull clean every morning because he'd found lice in his hair as a teenager and didn't have to be told twice how to avoid a re-infestation. He had no interview that day, but his short-sleeved white shirt was buttoned to the collar, his tie cinched beneath his Adam's apple.

His mother put his socks in the top drawer of his bureau, his sweater vests in the next. She hung five white shirts identical to the one he was wearing in the closet, alongside a spare tie, spare slacks, and a seersucker blazer.

"You were so handsome in that jacket on your graduation day," she said.

Edmond replied he hadn't worn it since then and doubted he could stuff himself into it any longer, and what was her wonderful news?

"Patience," she sang. She put his shaving kit on the bureau top, where photos of Edmond as an Eagle Scout, a clarinetist in the marching band, and a neighborhood watch volunteer were tucked between the mirror and its redwood frame.

Finally, she unpacked her late husband's Whitman coin collection folders and arranged them on the desk, where they'd be in easy reach from Edmond's office chair.

Then she sat on the bed, stretched to clasp his hands, and told him she was taking in a foster child, an eleven-year-old girl. She'd thought long and hard about the decision, but when Edmond called to say he was coming home again, she took it as a sign and had inked the final paperwork that very morning.

"Isn't it wonderful?" she said. "We'll be a family again."

When Edmond received bad news, he removed his glasses and shook his head in spasmodic jerks, as if to discourage an insect from landing on his nose. He asked her to repeat herself. "I'm not sure I heard you correctly. I'm not sure I can trust my own ears."

His mother laughed in a merry way he recognized, when she knew she had a fight on her hands. "Don't be dramatic. Of course, you heard me."

The girl's name was Mary Claire, she said, and was a product of circumstances too horrible to believe. The family mobile home was found by CPS to be without electricity or running water. The girl's mother had committed suicide, and her father was in and out of jail for crimes ranging from bad checks to assault.

Mary Claire was of average intelligence, though her emotional development was stunted, probably a result of her mother's alcoholism. "She drank peppermint schnapps for breakfast," Edmond's mother said. "Can you imagine?"

Edmond felt a stirring like a geyser in his body. "Am I to understand," he said, "that you are bringing a child of crime into this house? A child with no structure or moral guidance? A child whose worldview is centered around the satisfaction of her next carnal impulse? A child who—"

His mother was laughing again, though when she put a hand over Edmond's mouth, she did so with a violence that jolted him. "Just like your father," she said. "Our home is exactly the atmosphere a child like this needs." A combination of healthy food and loving correction would rescue the girl from the abyss. She, his mother, would teach the girl to sew, to launder, to cook Edmond's meals. He, with his professional background, would teach Mary Claire self-discipline.

"She will flourish under your guidance, and you"—his mother eyed him meaningfully—"will have something to do with yourself until you find another situation."

"I won't stand for it," Edmond said. "I haven't worked in a succession of offices where my gifts were unappreciated, only to come home to coddle a waif who will likely steal us blind. I'm here briefly before I set out into the world again, and I intend to pass the time in peace and comfort."

His mother drew upright. She was barely five feet tall, and asthma made her often short of breath, but she had a hard set of teeth in her head. "You have no choice but to stand for it, young man," she said. "This house is in my name."

THE GIRL ARRIVED A WEEK LATER AND wasted no time laying claim to the place. Edmond sat in his recliner and listened to her voice in the living room, asking who the "weird guy" was in the photo on the bookcase. He rose when his mother brought the child to his room, and she shocked him by hugging his waist and looking up at him so he saw a fine crust of mucus around each nostril.

"This is my son Edmond," his mother said. "He has held many important positions in the business world."

"Hi, Edmond," the girl said. Her nose was blunt, and a wide space separated it from her upper lip. Her eyes were brown and alert as a colt's.

"Call him Mr. Edmond, dear. A girl should address a gentleman with respect."

Mary Claire giggled. Her teeth were edged in purple and her breath wafting upward smelled grape-ish and sweet. "Hi, Mr. Edmond."

Later, while Mary Claire played with a doll bought to celebrate her arrival, Edmond's mother whispered that the girl bonded quickly with strangers—men especially, the social worker had said.

"Just what I was afraid of," Edmond whispered back. "She was born to manipulate, and we're her next mark."

"Oh, for heaven's sake," his mother said. "She's just a child."

"I hear *yoooo*," Mary Claire sang. "What are you saying about *meeee*?"

THE CAKE-FROSTING SOUNDS from the kitchen subsided, and the back door opened and closed. His mother, Edmond suspected, was making good on her promise to take the girl shopping for new school clothes.

He sighed and fingered the Whitman coin folders on his desk. They were blue and leathery and smelled faintly of his father's cigar, though the old man had died on a rainy morning two years before.

As always, the scent filled Edmond with a mix of fear and longing. Yes, his father had been cold, even pitiless, but he'd seen things with flawless clarity. The successful life was one of order and simplicity, and his coins were a perfect expression of that view. Bison might have been obliterated from the Great Plains, the Indian nearly wiped out, yet each was represented on opposing sides of the buffalo nickel. A prairie was subdued, a president gave his life to save the Union, and images of both were neatly stamped on the wheat penny.

His father would have ended his wife's crusade, when all Edmond could do was fuss and complain. People got what they deserved, the old man had often said. His wife suffered from asthma because she'd kept cats when she was young. Edmond was a failure because he refused to concentrate his mind. And the girl? His father would say she was a consequence of immorality and sloth, and you could no more contain those two forces than you could halt a tornado.

"The average man gets tied up in indecision," he'd said when Edmond landed his first job after business school. "The exceptional man sees a need and acts upon it."

WHEN HIS MOTHER AND THE GIRL RETURNED, they went to Mary Claire's room, where Edmond heard her squealing over her new clothes. As he'd expected, she fastened like a tick to anything of monetary value. His father's pewter candlesticks weren't interesting when she learned they came over on the *Mayflower*, but they became vitally so when she learned a dealer had offered a thousand dollars for the pair.

"Why don't you sell them?" she'd asked. "You could dump this crappy furniture."

"Some things have value beyond money," Edmond's mother had answered, "and a well-bred girl doesn't use words like 'crappy.'"

Mary Claire rolled her eyes at Edmond, and the realization that she was inviting him to join in mocking the old woman made his blood boil.

"She's making a fool of you," he said later to his mother. "She doesn't care about your manners or your breeding."

"That's exactly why she needs us. She will learn by our example."

"The only thing she's learning is a sucker's born every minute," he said. "And I'd watch those candlesticks if I were you."

She gazed at him forlornly. "Where is your heart? The girl is in the process of being born."

"That process is complete," Edmond said. "Her future was fully determined twelve years ago in the backseat of a Ford."

The old woman gasped. "If I close my eyes, I hear your father's voice."

THE FASHION SHOW MOVED TO THE LIVING ROOM, and Edmond decided that a walk to town was in order. He'd noticed a new chess magazine at the drugstore, and he was desperate for quiet. He looked in the mirror and confirmed that his pate and long face were freshly shaved, his tie knotted perfectly.

As he left the house, Mary Claire called after him. "Bye, Mr. Ed."

"It's Edmond, dear," his mother said as he closed the door, and he heard laughter again.

No one had called him Mr. Ed since high school, when his prominent teeth and a whinnying sound he made when excited had prompted classmates to name him for a talking horse on television. He was certain Mary Claire had come upon the nickname by chance, though there was a slyness about her—a way he caught her watching him, a way she met his eyes when his mother was waxing on about something—that made him feel she'd known him all his life.

He walked the sidewalks in a fury. His neighbor Mrs. Adkins was deadheading her geraniums, and when she asked about the new little girl, he stared at her with such malevolence her mouth fell open.

He passed the barbershop on his way to the drugstore, where the marshal's pickup was parked at the curb. The marshal, a big man named Johnny Baker, leaned against the fender and talked with a pair of idlers sunning themselves on a bench. They ignored Edmond, though Baker nodded. He wore black boots and a khaki shirt with a star pinned over the breast pocket. The pistol in his holster had an ivory handle.

Edmond bought his magazine, and when he came out again he lingered nearby. Johnny Baker had graduated in his high school class and, after a stint overseas during the Vietnam War, had come home to fill the marshal's post after the previous man died. He mowed municipal lawns by day and checked store locks at night. He kept an office in the courthouse basement, where his son and other teenage boys loitered to smoke cigarettes. He had a burly, mocking air Edmond loathed, but he knew everything about everybody and might, Edmond hoped, have something useful on the girl and her family, something to help get rid of her.

Baker looked up and smiled. "What can I do for you, Edmond?" The idlers turned to stare, and Edmond—he'd received curious stares all his life and never had an answer for them—shook his head and hurried away.

When he entered the house, he heard his mother's voice in his room. He stepped to the door, and rage to washed over him like a gasoline fire. The old woman sat in his recliner, Mary Claire squeezed beside her. The two were examining his father's coin collection, one folder open in his mother's hands, the others in her lap.

"And this is Lady Liberty," his mother was saying. "The 1916 Liberty Head dime. It's in fine condition and was your foster father's pride and joy."

"How much is it worth?" came the girl's inevitable question.

"Oh, that varies," his mother said. "Perhaps 3,000—"

"*Whist!*" Edmond said. The old lady flinched, the folders sliding from her lap to the floor. Coins sprang free from their cardboard circles and rolled under the bed.

Edmond spoke with a furious steadiness. "This is my room," he said. "Those folders, those coins, my father left to me." Tears started in his eyes, and his voice rose an octave. "I will not have it. I will not allow either of you in my room without my permission, ever again." He stood over them like a colossus, his legs spread wide and his hands fisted at his hips. "Have I made myself clear?"

His mother had recovered quickly from her surprise. "You might study the terms a bit further, Your Highness," she said. "Everything your father owned must pass through me before it comes to you." She dropped the remaining folder on the floor. "Even your precious coins." She rose, pulling Mary Claire with her. "Come, dear. Let's leave the lord to his manor."

Edmond remained standing as they passed, then fell to his knees to gather the errant nickels and dimes. He heard a giggle and turned to see the girl watching from the door. He stood and closed it in her face.

THAT NIGHT EDMOND LAY IN BED and stared at the ceiling. A shaft from a streetlamp slanted into his room, and as he considered his predicament a shadow blotted the light. He smelled a familiar sugary scent and realized Mary Claire was standing beside his bed.

"I'm on your side, Mr. Ed," she whispered. "A grown man shouldn't have to wait for his mom's permission to have what he wants."

Edmond rose and steered her from his room so forcefully her feet barely touched the floor. He slammed the door, though when his mother knocked a moment later he opened it again and told her he'd caught Mary Claire prowling the house.

"She was no doubt 'casing the joint,' I believe the phrase is," he said, "so she could pass the information on to her criminal relatives."

His mother's asthma worsened at night, and she was clutching her throat and breathing heavily. "You frightened me to death, Edmond. What has gotten into you?"

"The girl was wandering the house in the dark. Even you must admit she can't have been up to any good."

"She was probably having a bad dream. If you'd endured what she has, you'd be troubled too."

Later, the tea kettle whistled, and Edmond heard his mother and Mary Claire talking in the kitchen. He didn't sleep for hours. He turned the girl's words over and over in his mind.

IN THE MORNING EDMOND ROSE AND, as he'd often had to do since the girl's arrival, prepared his own breakfast of eggs and toast, along with a mix of bananas and orange juice in the blender. His mother and Mary Claire had left the house earlier; he'd heard their happy voices outside his window. Lately the old woman had decided the girl lacked exposure to the arts and had begun taking her to the library and the children's museum in Fort Wayne.

"Honestly, Edmond, she soaks it up like a sponge," his mother had told him. "She wants to be an astronomer."

"You're the one with stars in her eyes," he'd answered automatically.

After breakfast he tried to read his chess magazine, though he couldn't stop thinking about what Mary Claire had said the night before: "A grown man shouldn't have to wait for his mom's permission to have what he wants."

Was she suggesting he take what was rightfully his? The house and his mother's estate were likely worth hundreds of thousands of dollars. What could he do except wait for the day when all came to him?

What would his father do?

When his mother and Mary Claire returned, the old woman tapped on his door. "May I enter these hallowed portals?"

Edmond groaned and tossed the magazine aside. His mother sat on the edge of his bed and peered at him.

"I've been doing a lot of thinking," she said. "Your father ruled this house with an iron hand. He kept me from my parents and was jealous of my friends, and in the years he's been gone I've behaved as if he were still at the kitchen table, barking that his coffee was cold." She straightened her skirt, and Edmond saw that her fingernails were painted the same bright hue he'd seen on the girl's nails recently. "But I was wrong. He's dead and gone, and, God forgive me, I'm glad."

She leaned forward. "I don't expect you to understand this, dear, but for forty years I lived like an Eskimo huddled around a campfire, fearful of polar bears and the howling wind." She smiled. "I know better now. Having Mary Claire in this house has shown me how wide and beautiful the world can be, if only I choose to embrace it."

Edmond stared. His mother had never been particularly religious, but her face glowed with saintly fervor. "Let me understand," he said. "After a month caring for a coarse, ignorant child, you've discovered life's meaning, something that eluded you your first seventy years?"

"I expected as much," she said. She leaned back and folded her hands in her lap. "In any case, I've made some decisions." She took him in sadly. "Edmond, I was always so proud of you—your discipline, your educational bent, the positions you've held—but I believe that's because I had no one to compare you to. Now that I have someone else in my life, I see you and your father for what you are, small and miserly and mean." She shook her head. "All those years…all those wasted years." She sighed and the glow returned to her face. "I'm sorry to speak so harshly, but I've been set free."

"You haven't any idea what you're—"

She reached to cover his mouth but drew back quickly as if he were poisonous. "First of all," she said, "I want you to know you'll be taken care of, whatever happens. Second, I am going to sell the Liberty Head dime at auction and place the money in a college fund for Mary Claire. In seven years, it will have grown substantially."

Edmond took off his glasses and twisted his head like a man being strangled. "You will do no such thing. He meant those coins for me."

She smiled again. "Whatever his faults, your father was wise enough to dig a moat between you and his treasures. I intend to sell the lion's share and do some good with the proceeds."

Edmond whinnied like an old mare. "This is madness. That girl will never go to college. By the time she's eighteen she'll be in jail or pregnant with her third whelp."

His mother stood. "Every word you speak justifies my decision further."

After she'd left, Edmond sat for a long time and stared out the window. Then he rose, tightened his tie, and left the house.

He walked to the library where he found a book and studied it for an hour. Then he went to the hardware store and, for the first time in his life, tucked an item under his arm and left without paying. Finally, he walked to the town square, where Johnny Baker leaned alone against his truck, picking his teeth with a chicken bone.

"Hello, Edmond," the marshal said. "Back so soon?"

Edmond said he had a matter of importance to discuss. Did the marshal know about the girl staying with them?

"I sure do," Baker said. "It's a fine thing, your ma taking her in that way."

Edmond edged closer. "How much do you really know? What do you know about the family?"

The marshal looked at him humorously. He peeked over each shoulder and then leaned forward. "I know the mama's dead and the pa's in a halfway house. The girl's name is Mary Claire. She's eleven years old, and guess what?"

"What?"

"She's been seen gadding about with an old lady," Baker whispered. "I think they mean to overthrow the commonwealth." He laughed and slapped Edmond's shoulder.

Edmond waited for the man to settle himself before he spoke again. "I'm afraid of her. Mother and I both are."

The marshal blinked. "How do you mean?"

"My mother and the girl are at each other's throats day and night. Mother has notions about how a young lady should comport herself, and Mary Claire…she has her own ideas. It's a mix that doesn't bode well."

Baker twirled the chicken bone in his fingers, then tossed it away. "Edmond," he said, "this sounds a bit far-fetched."

"Am I wrong that her mother was an alcoholic and her father's a career criminal?"

"The family's a sad case, for certain," the marshal said, "but I'd be hard-pressed to call the dad a career criminal.

He's dabbled in marijuana and bad checks, but he's not a bad Joe. Just unlucky and dumb."

"Wasn't he convicted of assault?"

Baker fished a Pall Mall from his pocket. "A judge sentenced him to six months for possession with intent. When the bailiff led him from the courtroom, the dumb ass jerked his arm away, the bailiff stumbled, and the judge saw it all." The marshal lit the cigarette and blew a plume of smoke toward the sky. "Like I said, he's unlucky."

Edmond was used to being taken lightly by Johnny Baker and his kind. He had a sudden memory of the man as captain of the baseball team and himself a hallway monitor, demanding Baker's pass.

"You may think this is all a joke," he said, "but Mother and I don't. Valuable items have gone missing. The girl has tantrums. I believe she's capable of violence."

Baker turned slowly to face him. "Nothing in her history suggests such a thing, Edmond. And don't tell me I don't take my job seriously."

"Be that as it may," Edmond said, "I have gone on record with my concerns."

EDMOND'S MOTHER TOOK ILL THE FOLLOWING Wednesday and died the Monday after that. Her first symptoms were stomach pains, followed by blood in her urine and a ravening thirst. Though Mary Claire begged to help, Edmond made himself the old woman's caretaker. He gave her hot broth and served her fruit drinks from the blender. When she complained about the bitterness and grit of the latter, he told her he used chopped guava seeds in the mix, because they contained the highest concentration of vitamin C in the natural world.

"What do you think is wrong with her, Mr. Edmond?" the girl asked. He was surprised by the roundness to her eyes, the fear in her voice.

"If you'd lived here more than a month," Edmond said, "you'd have seen this before. Her asthma begets a variety of ailments, this time a bad case of flu."

"I had the flu once. My nose didn't bleed."

It rained the morning his mother died. Edmond found her in bed, the blankets tight beneath her chin as if to ward off an icy wind. A cold gripped his heart as he stroked her hair, but he told himself she hadn't suffered excessively. In the end, her tiny body and weak lungs hastened a quick and merciful end.

"What's the matter?" Mary Claire cried from the doorway. "Mama! What's wrong with Mama?"

The ambulance came, followed by Johnny Baker in his pickup. The EMT and the marshal spent a half hour in the old woman's bedroom, then zipped the body into a bag and wheeled it through the rain to the ambulance. A social worker arrived, packed Mary Claire's clothes, and took her away. The girl stared at Edmond as she left the house. Her smirk was gone, and he was struck by how young she seemed.

When they were alone, Edmond and Baker stood in the living room. The marshal crossed his arms over his chest, his eyes never leaving Edmond's face. "It's a bad thing, Edmond," he said. "A very bad thing."

Edmond was more troubled than he'd expected to be by the morning's events, but he pressed forward. "I believe you'll find this wasn't a natural death," he said.

"I had a look at the body," Baker said. "That's how I read it."

"Mother and I thought it was the flu," Edmond said. "She told me not to call anyone, because there's nothing to do but let it run its course. I was going to call today, even so." He took off his glasses and rubbed a hand over his skull. He felt a fine stubble there and realized he had yet to shave that morning. "Now it's too late."

"Edmond," Baker said, "I'm no coroner, but your mother's bleeding gums and blotchy skin tell me she was poisoned."

Edmond cupped his chin in his palm and twisted his head so his neck popped. "I told you it was bad between them."

"But why, Edmond? After our talk the other day I sniffed around. I watched them myself. Everywhere they went—the store, the library—they were laughing, talking, having the time of their lives. Why would the girl do such a thing?"

Edmond returned his glasses to his nose. "Why do her kind of people do the things they do? Their hearts are deceitful and wicked."

Baker stared so long that noises from the outside world seeped into the house: birds in the trees, shouts of children, the whisper of cars on wet pavement. "We're not finished here, Edmond," he said at last. "Not by a long shot."

After the marshal left, Edmond went to his room and sat in his recliner. The quiet was new to him. When his mother and the girl had left on errands, they were gone only a short while, so any tranquility was fleeting. Even when he was alone in his apartment, he'd heard thumps and muffled conversations from tenants above and below.

Of course, Johnny Baker was right. There would be an investigation, an autopsy, a search warrant. They would find the yellow box in the garage, a breakfast spoon the girl had handled with dusty residue in its bowl. They would find the same bluish residue on a pair of gardening gloves in her closet, along with a set of pewter candlesticks.

As he sat, Edmond allowed himself to mourn his mother's passing. Until recently, she had believed in him when no one else did. In the end, though, she'd lost her way. Now he could re-establish peace and order to the house. His father would approve.

A slapping sound startled him. When he realized it was the day's mail tumbling through the slot and onto the hardwood floor, he scolded himself gently, then went to the front hall and gathered the letters and bills. The cold touched his heart again when he saw a gardening magazine addressed to his mother. She had taken up the hobby recently in hopes of teaching the girl the joys of rose cultivation. He would cancel the subscription.

He took the pile to the kitchen table and thumbed through it. Besides the magazine, there were other savings to look forward to. The water bill would be reduced considerably, as would electrical usage. When he saw the return address of his mother's attorney, he shoved the other pieces aside and tore the envelope open. He scanned the document quickly, his mother's revised will. Just as she'd threatened, the Liberty Head dime would seed an educational fund in the girl's name. Otherwise, the house and its contents were to be liquefied upon his mother's death, and the estate, just over 200,000 dollars, would go into a trust. A fifth would go to Mary Claire after her first year of college, a second fifth after her second year, and so on. The remainder would go to her upon the completion of her degree.

A codicil awarded Edmond a cash payment of 3,000 dollars and the remainder of the Whitman collection. His mother's signature adorned the final page, in the carefree, swooping style she saved for Christmas and birthday cards.

JOHNNY BAKER HAD BEEN A MILITARY POLICEMAN in Guam during the Vietnam conflict, and—between the boozing and fistfights, sewage in the gutters, old men's noses eaten up by leprosy—he'd seen enough ugliness to last two lifetimes.

Then he'd come home to Indiana, and, though the landscape was different in countless ways from an island in the Pacific, in other ways it was no different at all. A farm boy suffocated in a grain bin; a drunk frozen solid confusing a snowbank for his bed; a country woman who'd shot her dog and then herself, their bodies wedded in putrification to the mattress where he'd found them.

There wasn't much that troubled Johnny these days, yet he couldn't shake how tiny the old lady's body had been, how her hands remained clutched beneath her chin even after he'd pulled the blanket from her fingers.

He was certain Edmond had murdered her, and he was hungry to break the man, to watch him sob and puke and confess. He drove from the house, but instead of continuing to his office he circled the block and parked again at the curb. It was a method the previous marshal had taught him: ask your suspect to tell his story a second time, a third, a fourth. Nobody keeps a lie straight forever.

He stepped from his truck and walked to the house, nodding to the mailman coming the other way. The rain had stopped, and the sun warmed his shoulders as he climbed the porch. He was about to knock when he heard a noise from inside. It was a strangled whinnying, a frenzied rise and decrescendo that repeated itself over and over. He couldn't tell if the person was laughing or crying, but the sound curdled his blood.

Johnny Baker made it his business to know everything about everybody. He'd stood outside countless doors and, despite the ugliness waiting within, had never shied from knocking. But now he backed down the steps and climbed into his truck, where he sat until he'd calmed himself.

Edmond wasn't going anywhere. Johnny had plenty of time to get what he was after.

Her Precious Things

Joetta woke from a dreamless, midday nap to a knock on the door, and the first thought that came to her was, *The grass isn't mowed.* Visitors to the Thatcher home were rare, but like the woman traveler who wears clean clothes in case of an accident, Joetta believed a house's tidy exterior promised a respectable life within.

On the other hand, with bills to pay, with the Indiana heat stifling, with Mother sick in bed upstairs, the last thing Joetta needed was company.

She rubbed her eyes and limped to the front window. A young man in a corduroy jacket stood on the porch. Joetta didn't know him, though she decided he wasn't a Jehovah's Witness. Those people carried tracts and Bibles, not manila folders under their arms. Also, they had a smile at the ready, while this one—he knocked again, then mopped his face and checked his watch, all in the same harried motion—had difficult business before him.

She thought not to answer, but she figured someone compelled to be there would feel compelled to return, so she opened the door slightly and peered over the safety chain.

"Is that Mrs. Thatcher?" the young man said.

Joetta had never been anything but *Miss* Thatcher, despite having recently turned fifty. "Who's asking?" she said.

"Am I addressing Dorothea Thatcher?"

"Mother is upstairs and not well."

He stooped to take her in. His eyes were blue, his lashes nearly white. Perspiration beaded his smooth upper lip. "You must be the daughter Joetta then."

That was more familiar than Joetta was obliged to tolerate, and she closed the door firmly. She put an ear to the wood and listened for departing steps, and when they didn't come, she knew the young man was still standing on the other side.

"Miss Thatcher," he said, as if two inches of cedar weren't between them, "I'm Leonard Weeks, from county code enforcement. I'm here to talk about the cabin."

Joetta suffered from various ailments—an enlarged heart from a childhood bout with rheumatic fever, a withered leg from polio—but her memory was sharp as ever. The last time a county man had visited to talk about the tumbledown wreck at the rear of the property had been a July morning like this, five years before. The day had been hot then too. Mother had made waffles for breakfast.

"We have no business with Allen County," she said loudly. "Our taxes are paid."

"This isn't about taxes, ma'am."

She figured as much. The cabin had deteriorated steadily in the decade since Joetta's father Reverend Thatcher had died, and with its decline had come attention from local government. The building was an eyesore, a safety hazard. Pigeons in the rafters spread disease. Teenagers were breaking in to smoke marijuana.

That last complaint had prompted Joetta to hire a man to board up the door and windows. Otherwise, she'd let the old place—all but invisible from the main house, a grim shell in a stand of ancient oaks—fall in on itself.

"Miss Thatcher…"

"We have no business with Allen County," Joetta said again.

"Joetta," Weeks said not unkindly, "our next talk might include the sheriff."

Joetta stayed for a moment with her ear to the door. Its two coats of shellac were sticky in the heat, though it had been years since Papa had applied them. Previous county men had also promised visits from the sheriff, but those threats had come to nothing. Boarding things up had been enough the last time, knocking down the remains of a privy and filling in its hole enough the time before.

"What do you want?" she said.

"To talk a bit, ma'am."

She cracked the door again. Leonard Weeks was blond, skinny as a fence post. He'd taken off his corduroy jacket and slung it over his shoulder. Moons of sweat rose from his armpits and met beneath his tie. He brought his face close. "Might I trouble you for some ice water?"

It was a ploy to gain entry, Joetta knew, but, though she'd long abandoned her father's faith, she still lived by his dearest biblical maxims: clothe oneself in modesty, give without thought of repayment, welcome the thirsty stranger in.

"Make it snappy, then," she said, undoing the chain and stepping aside. "You'll get nothing from me but cold water."

At the kitchen table, Weeks held an icy tumbler to his cheek and told her he'd been with the code office in Fort Wayne for a month. His job, as best he understood it, was to pester folks. "For this"—he laughed ruefully—"I got my social work degree."

When she didn't answer, he put down his glass and fixed her with a smile. "You told me at the door, Joetta," he said gently, "that Mother's not well?"

"I also told you," she said, "you'd get nothing from me but water. That includes permission to use my Christian name."

He laughed again and lifted his palms. "I'll state my business, then."

"We have no business with—"

"Of course." He opened his folder, his eyes not leaving her face. "You must know, Miss Thatcher, that the cabin is an important county landmark. Its provenance dates to your great-great grandfather Joseph, back to when the Miami Indians roamed the hills."

"I'm aware of its history."

"But its condition has sparked three complaints this year alone. The roof is eaten away, the foundation's crumbling…" He nodded to take in the bright kitchen. "As nice as you keep the main house, Jo…ma'am, you'd think you'd want—"

Joetta stood. "Finish your water, Mr. Weeks."

"Miss Thatcher, please."

"This conversation is over."

He left soon after, though not before dropping a letter on the kitchen table. She'd accomplish nothing by burning it, he said. He had plenty of copies.

When she'd closed the door behind him, Joetta thought to climb the stairs and check on her mother, but her bad leg ached, and she was short of breath. Instead, she fell onto a chair and pondered her circumstances.

Papa was ten years gone. Mother was nearly eighty and, aside from a halting trip to the toilet every day or so, hadn't left her bed in weeks.

Otherwise, there was only her brother Alex, though Joetta hadn't seen him in a lifetime. Adopted when he was four and Joetta an infant, the brilliant Alex Thatcher was everything his sickly baby sister was not. Dark-haired and handsome, a genius on any stringed instrument he touched, he'd gone directly from Purdue to the Chicago Symphony, until whispers of scandal made their way east in the years thereafter—a rich man's wife, cello lessons where there was no cello—and for all Joetta knew he lived in Timbuktu by now.

She pushed to her feet, catching a glimpse of herself in the toaster's reflection. She was nice enough looking, Mother had sometimes said, despite being childishly thin, but a girl who lurched around like a sailor in a windstorm, a girl who read every book in the library but never picked up a hairbrush… well, a girl like that should set her sights on other dreams, because she could forget a husband or children.

Joetta had tried her best. She could name every state capital by the time she was six. She'd been a champion speller in junior high school. She'd missed being co-valedictorian her senior year with a single B-plus, while Dennis Frederick got all As.

But when a scholarship invited her to follow her brother to Purdue, when she imagined chancing upon Alex—him by then a senior—on a campus sidewalk at night or in an empty lecture hall, Joetta knew that home would be her vocation. She would cook, clean, manage the bills, and, when a decision was beyond her, look to her parents to decide.

She climbed to the upstairs bedroom, where her mother lay swaddled in blankets like a child. The room was ripe with soiled linens and an odd, new stink coming off the old lady's skin. Joetta wanted to throw open the windows and let in light and air, but Mother was cold—she'd always been cold, even when she wasn't sick.

Joetta sat and smoothed her hair until she jerked and moaned. "Quit your petting," she said, her voice like rats' feet over dry leaves. Her daughter lifted water to her lips, but Mother covered her mouth with a hand. "What was that business at the door?" she whispered when Joetta had set the glass down.

"A man from the county. About the cabin."

Phlegm rattled in the old lady's chest. "I'll speak to the reverend about it."

LATER IN BED, JOETTA READ THE LETTER Leonard Weeks had left behind. The county had run out of patience, it said. Though the Thatcher cabin had been built before the Civil

War, it had most of its original timbers and was clearly salvageable, if only the family would look to its restoration. But the time for discussion had passed. Under Allen County's powers of eminent domain, the structure would be purchased at a fair market price, taken apart log by log, and reassembled near the Lincoln Library in Fort Wayne.

"Future generations," the letter finished, "should LEARN from such a piece of history, not watch it fall apart before their eyes. We pray you'll agree."

Joetta examined Weeks's signature. Its prim, formal loops suggested an educated man, its closing flourish a cocky one. She turned off the lamp and lay with the letter open on her breast. Besides a shared handsomeness, the county man hadn't resembled her brother Alex in the least, yet there was something in each that recalled the other.

She grappled to say what that was, but only as she'd begun to drift off did the answer come. Other men—the grocer, the meter reader—looked past her as one might a broom leaned against a wall. Leonard Weeks, like Alex before him, had studied her closely, smiled at her demurrals, pushed for things she wasn't willing to give.

IN THE MORNING, JOETTA PULLED on Papa's boots and began to cut the grass. Mother had insisted on doing the job until a stroke two years before, the mower propping her up like a walker at a rest home, but these days she couldn't snap beans without getting tired.

The sun was hot, and soon Joetta's leg was throbbing. Her path went back and forth between the house and the cabin, where each time she took in its broken chimney, oak trunks crowding its outer walls, foundation stones that, Papa had told anyone within earshot, Joseph Thatcher had hauled to the site behind a mule called Cygnus.

"Why would he name a mule after a star?" Alex had asked once when he was fifteen and Joetta twelve.

"Cygnus isn't a star," Reverend Thatcher had answered. "It's a constellation, vast beyond our imaginings."

"So why name a mule after a constellation?"

"Because God's grandeur is in all of us. Even the lowliest creature."

Alex giggled, pinching his sister's bottom. "Even Joetta?"

Joetta looked to see if her father might scold him for the cruelty, but, as he did with all her brother's misbehaviors—cheating in class, fights on the ballfield, spying on Joetta in the bath—the reverend only laughed and tousled the boy's hair. Alex was a "rascal," Papa would say, but rascals had a way of growing into city managers, businessmen, even ministers of the gospel, once their rough edges were smoothed.

Joetta had cut half the yard when she needed to rest. She killed the mower and sat heavily on the porch steps. A flagstone path stretched from her feet to the cabin. Once perfectly edged, it was all but lost in the grass.

She couldn't keep up, was the truth of the matter. Mold in the cupboards, water in the basement. Rot and collapse were always impending; even the strongest person couldn't keep them at bay forever.

She stood to return to work, but found herself instead in Papa's tool shed, where she dug through rakes and shovels until she found a crowbar. She walked to the cabin and pried loose the boards nailed over its doorframe. The door itself had swelled and shrunk so often in the seasons it was stuck fast, but she put her shoulder to it until it broke free with a kind of scream.

She stepped inside and groaned aloud.

The main floor, once so tidy under her father's care, was a shambles. Fingers of sunlight struggled through holes in the roof. Cobwebs hung from the windows like ghostly curtains. An animal scuttled overhead in the loft. The plaster walls had crumbled, littering the floorboards with dust. The reverend had used the space to store hymnals, tithing envelopes,

Sunday School readers tied up with string, and these—soaked by rain, hardened by drought—leaned together in calcified piles.

"Ah, me," Joetta said in the fusty quiet.

The stairs to the loft had collapsed before she was born—its pieces still lay where her father had piled them in a corner—and a ladder leaned in their place. Joetta followed it upward with her eyes, just as two pigeons flew through a window and perched on a rafter. They fussed and cooed, their feathers teal or pearl or salmon, depending how the light hit them.

Joetta rested a boot on the ladder's bottom rung, found it solid, and lifted herself one step and then another. When she and Alex were young and Papa had given permission, they'd used the loft to play hide-and-seek, to tell secrets from school, to spread quilts and have a sleepout, moonlight flooding in, their naked feet pressed against timbers.

Now she climbed to the loft for the first time in thirty-five years. There she found a spot mostly clean of bird waste and sank to the floor. The pigeons had fluttered away, but wasps floated from their nests to study her.

She was exhausted, sweat dripping off her nose and a taste like burnt pennies in her throat. Her bad leg was thinner by half than the healthy one, and she squeezed it and panted until the room stopped swirling.

After a time, she crawled on hands and knees to a corner, where broken chinking made a niche. There she pushed a hand through spider webs and mouse leavings until she found a wooden cigar box. She undid its clasp and emptied the contents into her lap:

A blue ribbon from the Allen County spelling bee.

A Morgan silver dollar.

A tintype of her grandfather Joseph Thatcher, for whom she'd been named.

A magnifying glass in a leather pouch Papa had given her on her sixth birthday.

A letter, crimped and fragile as a moth wing. Joetta unfolded it and read:

> *Daughter...*
>
> *I feel badly for what I said. Your father reminds me that we have all sinned and fallen short of the glory of God. Your sin is forgetting your chores. Mine is a sharp tongue. You and Alex each have your own gifts, and comparing you to him was wrong.*
>
> *— Mother*

Joetta folded the letter again, wondering, as she always had, why it deserved a place among her precious things. She returned it and the rest to the box, until a single object, a jewel case like a sleeping bird, remained. She clutched to her chest and listened—to the gentle hum of the wasps, to a breeze in the oak leaves, to the thudding of her own heart—when a voice called from below.

"Is that Miss Thatcher?"

She dropped the case into the cigar box and returned all to the nook, then crawled to the loft's edge and peered down to see Leonard Weeks looking up at her. He'd taken off his corduroy jacket again in the heat and held it in one hand as he spread his arms.

"What a grand old place this must have been, hey?"

"What do you want?"

"I have good news."

Joetta was in the long skirt Papa had insisted she wear for outdoor work. "Stand away, please," she said, putting a foot on the top rung.

"Yes, ma'am," he said, moving to a wall.

When her feet touched the floor, Weeks was examining the grooves in an exposed beam. "Did you know, Miss Thatcher," he said, "there's a cave painting in France of bison and rhinoceroses, where the artist signed his work with a palm print?" He shook his head. "Your grandfather's axe marks will strike future historians the same way."

"Adze marks," she said.

"I'm sorry?"

"He shaped the timbers lengthwise with an adze."

He nodded. "Adze marks. Of course."

"Also, the Chauvet artist may have been a woman. Scholars disagree."

He looked at her in surprise as men had always done when she knew things they didn't. "I stand corrected, Joetta," he said, bowing slightly at the hips.

She nearly scolded him again for using her first name, but he'd said it with such good humor she let it go. "That's kind of you, Mr. Weeks, but the cabin stays put. We'll burn it down before we let the county take it."

"Who is 'we,' exactly?"

"Mother and me."

"Mmm-hmm." He studied the beam some more. "What about your brother?" he said, as though the thought had just occurred to him. "Alex, I believe his name is."

Joetta's heart froze. "What do you know about Alex?"

"Only what my digging tells me. He's fifty-three. He lives in Battle Creek. He—"

"My brother is none of your business, sir."

"Actually, he is, ma'am."

"What do you mean?"

"Alex inherited half this property when your father died." He looked at her curiously. "Surely you knew that."

"It's a lie."

"It's not, Joetta," Weeks said. "We talked on the phone just this morning. He's coming south to help with this cabin business." He smiled. "That's my good news."

MINUTES LATER, JOETTA STOOD IN THE house's front room and watched the county man walk to his car. His back was turned, though the looseness of his stride, the tilt of his head, told her he was whistling.

She went to the kitchen, where she poached an egg and heated a cup of broth, taking both upstairs. Mother had faded visibly in twenty-four hours, her skull adamant beneath her flesh, the skin shrunk from her teeth. She groaned as her daughter lifted her, and when Joetta put the broth to her mouth she twisted away.

"Be*have*," Joetta said, but she lowered the old lady to her pillow again, then sat in the wing-backed chair and watched the sun through window shades change from late morning to early afternoon.

Alex lived in Battle Creek, two hours to the north. The same heat scorching Joetta was no doubt scorching him as well. They looked at the same stars at night. She had imagined him roaming the world like a lion, seeking someone to devour, when he and Leonard Weeks had talked on the phone that very morning.

She heard a rustle and saw that Mother had rolled to a side and was watching her, eyes bright in her gaunt face.

"Want to eat something?" Joetta said.

Mother worked her tongue before she spoke. "Not hungry."

Joetta leaned forward. The old lady's flashes of awareness came and went these days like heat lightning above a far tree line. There might never be another. "I need to know some things," she said.

Since her stroke, Mother's eyes moved independently from each other. Now one fixed on the wall and the other warily on Joetta's face. "What sorts of things?"

"Did Papa leave half the house to Alex?"

Mother coughed drily. "It's what folks do," she said.

"What is?"

"Leave their worldly goods to the son."

"What about me?"

"What about you?"

Joetta stretched to take her mother's hand, holding it tightly when the old lady tried to pull away. "Didn't I give my whole life to this place?"

Mother sighed. "You did your best. I always said so."

Joetta sniffed deeply. The stink off her mother's skin was like spent marigold blossoms, dead flies on a windowsill, milk left out overnight. "What did Alex do to… to deserve so much?" she whispered.

Mother smiled and closed her eyes, as one remembering a dream. "He was the answer to a prayer."

Joetta dropped her hand and sank back into her chair. The dark room pressed in from all sides. The air was foul. She wanted to rip the curtains down, smash the windows with her fists.

"But wasn't he a monster?" she cried aloud. "Didn't he hurt us and bring us shame? Didn't he take and take and take without a thought to anyone else? Wasn't he the opposite of what Papa preached every Sun—"

Mother was writhing from side to side. "He had no choice in how God made him. The morning star only knows how to shine. He… he…" Her chest swelled with a great draught of air, and when she released it she was dead.

AN HOUR LATER JOETTA SAT IN THE KITCHEN. A better daughter, she knew, would have washed Mother's face, crossed her arms over her breast, called Mr. Labuzienski at the funeral home. But Joetta had left the upstairs room in haste, and now she only sat and traced the whorls in the wood table with a fingertip.

She remembered Labuzienski's oily condolences as he'd zipped Papa into a bag and wheeled him to the hearse. She remembered neighbors appearing soon after, hands bearing walnut bread or pies, eyes famished to know who had been on the gurney.

She remembered Mother in the days that followed, looking up from her needlework in a kind of stunned confusion and saying, "I'm a widow," as though the change from one existence to the next had been too abrupt to take in.

"I'm an orphan," Joetta said to the quiet house, trying to generate a like astonishment, but all she felt was emptiness, like a child's pumpkin scraped out at Halloween. She went over and over her mother's final words:

The morning star only knows how to shine.

She'd been almost sixteen when Alex came home from his first year at the university. He'd taken up smoking and was banished to the porch when he indulged, and there he'd regaled his sister with stories of the brilliant people he knew, the parties he attended, the music and poetry she'd only read about in books.

Inevitably, his talk turned to Joetta's place in the Thatcher house. She was no longer a child, but a young woman. His dormmates had remarked on the family photo he kept at his desk, how fragile and pretty his sister was.

"Aren't you tired," he'd said, lighting his third cigarette in half an hour, "of being Miss Goody Two-Shoes? Of hanging onto that old gasbag's every word and jumping whenever Mother calls?"

Yes, Joetta had acknowledged, she supposed she *was* a little tired, but what other life was there for a girl with a bad leg and bad heart and not a friend in the world?

"Whatever life you choose!" he'd answered. He jerked his head toward the indoors, where Papa was writing his sermon and Mother embroidering a pillow. "It's positively wicked to raise a daughter in a swamp of superstition and involuntary servitude. Those people—those pious good-for-nothings—are the worst kind of criminals. Degenerates during the week and money changers on Sunday."

"How are they degenerates?" Joetta had asked softly.

"By treating you like a scullery maid," he'd nearly shouted, "fit for cooking porkchops and paying the water bill."

Joetta wanted to protest—Papa was forever kind, Mother could be sweet when the house was running smoothly—but she held her tongue. Her brother was exceptional. Everyone said so. He'd gone places and seen things she'd only dreamed about.

Alex had been home a week when he suggested moving their talks to the cabin. It would be like old times, he said, and besides, there were tales from university life that weren't suitable for the porch.

When Joetta asked their father's permission, the reverend clapped his hands and agreed. It was a fine thing, he said, having his children under the same roof again. "God's in his heaven," he proclaimed. "All's right with the world."

And that night in the loft—the spring air cold, owls in the trees—Alex had produced a silver flask from his jacket and sucked from it as Joetta huddled beside him, and between swallows he'd described how sophisticated life was beyond the Thatcher walls, how men and women drank wine and smoked hashish and traded partners like ordinary people lent out magazines.

"It's always been that way," he said, his voice soaked with contempt. "The Greeks passed slave boys back and forth. Ben Franklin had"—he made quotes in the moonlight with his fingers—"'intrigues' with prostitutes. Even the sainted Joseph Thatcher married his first cousin Belinda."

Joetta was shocked by the flask—tobacco was an abomination, Papa often said, but whiskey was the devil's brew—but she knew all about great-great-grandmother Belinda. Cousins marrying cousins, the reverend had explained, was once a common practice. Men and women didn't always have the luxury of choice. Adam and Eve's children "most certainly" had connubial relations, given that they were Creation's first people and God had commanded them to be fruitful and multiply.

"Papa told me about Grandma Belinda," Joetta said. "He—"

Alex silenced her with a barking laugh. "Of course, he did. He was covering his ass." Joetta was shivering, and he pulled her to him. His large teeth gleamed. His breath was hot against her face. "Do you doubt for a minute, my naïve Joetta, that our parents slept together before God sanctified their union?"

"I don't know," Joetta said. "I—"

"Ah, baby sister," he said, pressing her to the floor. "You're so adorably stupid."

She wasn't stupid, but when she tried to say so, he was suddenly kissing her with his whiskey-tasting mouth, the first time—the only time, as life would have it—that Joetta Thatcher would be kissed by a man.

THE PHONE ROUSED JOETTA FROM HER THOUGHTS. She looked at the clock above the sink. She'd been sitting for an hour. Folks rarely called the house, and she thought at first it must be Leonard Weeks, but after the phone had rung five times, ten, twenty, she knew it was Alex.

He was calling from a gas station on the road, from the county man's office, from the house across the street. Soon he would walk up the sidewalk and turn a key he'd never gotten rid of in the front door. With every tick of the clock, he was drawing closer.

The phone went dead as she climbed to Mother's room, where she opened the curtains and threw the windows wide. The old lady's face in sunlight—eyes staring, mouth in angry mid-utterance—was dreadful, but Joetta combed her hair and tucked the covers beneath her chin, then closed the door and went downstairs.

There she found Weeks's letter and pinned it to the wood tabletop with a boning knife. She thought to write something caustic at the bottom of the page, but instead she took the egg she'd poached and smeared it with her palm across the county man's signature.

The phone began to ring again as she was washing her hands, so she dried herself and went outside. There she paused to survey the house she'd lived in for fifty years. The siding was faded but clean. The windows were sparkling, the flowerbeds tidy.

Any passerby would assume that decent people lived within.

The interior was spotless as well, but for a dead woman upstairs and an egg congealing on the kitchen table. These could be easily remedied—one by a call to Mr. Labuzienski, the other by a dishrag and some cleanser.

She walked to the cabin and pushed open its door. Afternoon light slanted through boarded windows. Pigeons cooed from the rafters. Papa's hymnals and envelopes and church readers leaned in mummified stacks against the plaster.

Joetta studied the stacks for a time, then found the crowbar where she'd dropped it the day before and pried a bundle from the wall. It broke apart as it fell, spilling its moldy guts about her ankles. She did the same to the stack next to it, and the one next to that. Soon she was striding back and forth like a reaper, slashing at the piles, splitting their skins, scattering pages in her wake.

In ten minutes, paper covered the floor. Joetta thought to rest, but evening was upon her, and there was more to do.

She walked to where Papa had stacked pieces of the ruined staircase, and these she pried apart with the crowbar, stuffing church litter between them until she'd assembled a small mountain of paper and wood.

When she'd finished, she stepped back and examined what she'd built. Some of the pages were damp but most were not. The staircase boards had escaped rain through the roof. She was satisfied all would burn when she asked it to. She fussed with the pyre a bit longer, then climbed the ladder to the loft. There, she fetched the cigar box from its hiding place and took from it the sleeping bird jewel case.

SHE NEEDN'T WORRY, ALEX HAD SAID when he was finished, leaning against a timber and draining the flask. He'd pulled out at the last moment. Also, they weren't really brother and sister. Also, it wasn't possible for a girl to get pregnant her first time, and tonight—he'd laughed out loud—was clearly her first time.

When Joetta didn't answer, his voice turned cold. There was no sense telling Papa or Mother. They wouldn't believe her. She'd only be making trouble for herself.

He was right, of course, and the next day when the reverend asked why she was so quiet, Joetta said she was getting sick, perhaps from spring air in the cabin.

And she *was* getting sick. By sunset she was feverish, and she woke in the middle of the night to throw up. A muffled heaviness settled over her in the days that followed, so she could barely do her chores. After a week of this Mother suggested that she was playacting for sympathy, that Alex being home meant she wasn't the queen bee any longer, that her change in status galled her.

As for Alex, he breezed in and out, visiting old classmates, playing softball at the park. Soon he left for Camp Interlocken in Michigan, where'd he'd won an eight-week fellowship teaching music theory to gifted teenagers.

With her brother gone, Joetta could almost breathe again, but then the nausea returned. She found herself crying at odd times. She couldn't bear the smell of her own cooking. When she missed a period, she told herself that she'd never been regular, that Alex had promised she wouldn't get pregnant, that Reverend Thatcher's God couldn't be so cruel as to give his daughter a child by his adopted son.

Her fears were realized and put to rest on the same August morning—nine weeks after the loft, only days before Alex was to come home from Michigan—when furious cramping drove her to the toilet. There she crouched and sobbed as her insides splashed in pieces large and small into the bowl.

HER BABY HAD BEEN PINK as a newborn mouse when Joetta scooped it from the toilet, but thirty-five years wrapped in a tinfoil shroud had hardened it like a worm baked on the sidewalk. Even so, she made out its nubby fingers and toes, its rounded spine, its bulging face curved inward, as if to study the thing it would never become.

She clutched it and lay on her side, listening to the snapping of the fire below. She wasn't afraid. She'd read every book in the library, and she knew that children upstairs in burning houses or women burned at the stake as witches were almost always dead before flames touched their flesh. The oxygen around them was used up. They slipped away, passed on to whatever—

The heavy door crashed open beneath her, and then Leonard Weeks was shouting, "Miss Thatcher! My God, Miss Thatcher!" An older man's voice joined him, in a roar that demanded obedience. "Joetta, show yourself!"

Joetta didn't hear. The loft had filled with smoke, and she was unconscious, her only child tight against her breast, a smile on her face like a woman remembering a dream.

A Vigorous, Mostly Happy Couple

By the time the raccoons appeared, Mickey had run out of excuses. The apple tree had fallen in a summer storm and he'd left it sprawled across the yard for days, until the masked creatures appeared and began feasting in the rot. They stared toward the house in the daytime and climbed the deck at night to peer in the sliding kitchen door, scaring the bejesus out of Mickey's wife Kate and their chocolate lab Bosco.

Kate had pestered him time and again to clean up the mess, and why had he insisted on buying the new Husqvarna only to leave it sitting spotless in the garage when there was finally an actual reason to use it, and would he at least show her how to start the damn thing so she could do the job herself?

She'd do it herself. Checkmate.

Mickey and Kate were a vigorous, mostly happy couple. He coached high school football and taught freshman algebra. She sold ad space for a local radio station. He played golf every weekday over summer vacation. She batted cleanup in a women's softball league. On Saturdays, they mowed the yard and weeded the garden, then sat on the deck to toast the rising moon.

All was well between them, but for the speed with which Mickey acted on Kate's wishes: taking out the trash or calling the gas company about a confusing bill or, these days, cutting a fallen apple tree to pieces and hauling it away.

Mickey was sitting in his basement den, watching a ball game on television, when Kate came down the stairs to remind him again.

"I'll get to it"—his eyes didn't leave the screen, but he lifted a meaty paw to trace a clockface in the air—"when the big hand reaches twelve."

She answered that the tree was on her list, and she couldn't relax until it was off her list, and his stubbornness was something she'd excused while they were dating—who would make dinner reservations, who would buy a card for *his mother's* birthday—and now wished she hadn't.

Like Mickey Mantle, the Yankee slugger he'd been named for, Mickey was an affable, careless man. If there was anything he liked better than a perfectly struck four iron or his after-dinner scotch, it was jousting with someone—his students, opposing coaches, referees. Giving as good as he got.

Now he stood and put his hands on his wife's shoulders, gently shaking her. "You're acting kind of nuts, aren't you?"

He was clearly being funny, but Kate squirmed free and punched his chest—she a big woman, the blow not without heat.

In truth, her impatience puzzled him. Why would a woman whose batting skills led her softball team to championships, who climbed the roof on her own to hose out the gutters, whose job at the radio station earned twice what he made in the classroom—why would such a woman fuss over such petty things?

A confusing bill? Do like Mickey's father did and wait a month. If the man wants his money, he'll make himself clearer next time. Birthday cards? If fake words written by failed poets are your ticket to happiness, God help you.

When Kate answered that Mickey's mother adored receiving cards, he reminded her that the old lady was so fretful she vacuumed the living room every day and, when Mickey was a boy, had insisted he take a square of Saran Wrap to the movies to put between the seat and his head, for fear of ringworm.

He put gas in the car when the needle neared Empty. He saw a dirty sock and dropped it in the hamper. When the semester ended, he calculated student scores and entered them in his book. No lists required. The gas gauge told him when to fill the tank. The calendar announced when grades were due.

The apple tree had fallen only days before. Stumbling among wet branches with a chainsaw seemed like a tragic adventure. He'd get to it.

"Show me how, then," Kate repeated, noting that the last twenty-four hours had been sunny and dry, while the raccoons had only gotten bolder, staggering drunkenly among the fermented apples, lurking so close to the house Bosco that had begun pooping on the kitchen floor. "I'll do it myself."

They both knew that wouldn't happen: the man going to the garage, gassing up the shiny new saw, perhaps yanking the cord if she lacked the strength to start it cold, then returning to his ballgame while the woman tackled the difficult chore.

Instead, Mickey went to the backyard and hadn't been working more than a minute or two when the tip of the saw pinched fast in the hardwood and kicked upward, cleaving his face from scalp to chin.

He stumbled and sat against the privet hedge separating his and Kate's yard from the neighbors'. His head spun with dull surprise. Blood thrummed down his front, soaking his T-shirt and pooling between his legs.

I'm in trouble, he thought.

Other thoughts followed, these mostly wordless and centered on forgotten, tender places: *Something important has happened. Everyone will be horrified and gather around.* He'd had the same feelings when he tore a ligament in his knee during pickup basketball and lay writhing on the asphalt, or the time he'd wrecked the family car and had to call his father, himself a coach and teacher, out of practice with the news. Despite his pain and fear he'd felt an odd lushness in his chest, a twitching thrill. *People will be reminded how much they love me. They'll be sorry for the times they mocked me—my stammer, my soft body.*

The saw burbled where he'd dropped it, and when he leaned to turn it off his bulk carried him prone into the grass. "Kate!" he shouted, though the word came out like a drunken man's. His nose was clogged with blood, his teeth moved independently from his jaw. "Katie!" The back door opened and in the next instant Bosco was licking his face and whining frantically.

Time compressed and expanded at once. He heard Kate scream, then felt neighbors Emily and Chase Butler in the yard. People turned him over and covered him in a blanket. Someone applied pressure to a place on his neck, he was aware of the sun moving across the sky, twice he raised a hand to brush a fly from his cheek. Soon he heard sirens, though the hospital was a half hour distant, and in the next instant men were struggling to lift him. One called him "Mick," and the other said "Oh, Jesus" as they laid him on a stretcher and into the darkness of an ambulance. A needle stabbed his arm and they were speeding away, light and shadow flitting across the ceiling.

Mickey's head ached, though he knew worse pain was coming. He heard the EMT say "Oh, Jesus" again and felt a familiar urge to deflate the moment. "Who are you to make such a fuss?" his old man would say when Mickey dared to cry. When he'd hurt his knee, the pain so bad he'd wanted to throw up, he'd whispered to his buddies, "You should see the other guy." He said it now, the words mangled, the men too busy to respond. Another needle, and he drifted off to a warbling siren.

"You're a lucky man," an elderly doctor said a week later in the hospital. "You could have severed an artery and died on the spot. You could have blinded yourself."

Mickey sat fully dressed on his bed. The accident had broken most of his front teeth, split his face from top to bottom, breached a sinus cavity. The wound had required one hundred and thirty stitches to close, though pink drainage soaked one gauze pad after another he held to his nostrils. He would be released in half an hour and had yet to look at himself in a mirror.

He glanced at Kate across the room. "Hear that?" he said, the words whistling through a lacerated septum. "I'm lucky."

She looked back, her brave smile telling him his appearance was ghastly.

As a boy Mickey had been pudgy, shy, a late bloomer, though by thirty he'd grown into himself. His body hardened, the whiskers on his jaw went from silky to coarse almost overnight. In the classroom he learned to speak in his father's voice—the fun teacher, the long-suffering coach—and his stammer disappeared. Girl students openly flirted with him. Kate dragged him from parties, him shouting jokes over his shoulder.

"You're like a kid in a candy store," she'd say, and she was right. For the first time in his life, people found him attractive.

"You are lucky," the doctor insisted. "You must remind yourself every day." In one short year, following surgery and laser treatments, Mickey's scars wouldn't prompt a second glance on the street. "Before then," the man continued, "I suggest you begin the psychological healing straightaway. I recommend that you and your wife stand together, this moment, and assess yourself in the bathroom mirror."

"Assess myself?"

"Look at your face. Without fear or hesitation."

In the days since the accident, Mickey's humor had taken a caustic turn. He'd asked his nurses if the racket they made when he was sleeping was deliberate or mere sloppiness. He'd asked the old doctor if the tufts of hair in his ears obstructed his hearing. Now he caught Kate's eye, lifted the gauze from his nose, and squeezed it so pink droplets ran down his wrist. When she gasped, he snorted and walked alone into the bathroom.

When Mickey was a child, there'd been a boy next door with a cleft palate, a "harelip," people called it then, and as he gazed at himself in the mirror that boy emerged from the glass like a hobgoblin. The blunt, purple nose. The flesh above his lips bunched into a wad, as though the surgeon had pulled the torn ends together and stitched them hastily before they sprang free in his hand.

He ran a finger along his sutures. Chin to scalp they made a zipper, his secret self hidden inside. He was a child at Halloween, safe behind a terrible mask.

Kate's face pressed against his shoulder. "I did this," she said.

He stared at her reflection. "What? How?"

"If I hadn't badgered you. If I'd let you do the tree when you wanted…"

He made to pull her close but instead touched his face again. His eyes were black, his cheeks lopsided. He felt the same twitchy lushness in his chest. The harelip boy came to him once more. Wheezy, belligerent, daring you not to pick him for your team. He stuck out his tongue and licked the tip of his nose.

THE TREE WAS STILL DOWN WHEN Kate tucked Mickey into a chaise lounge on the deck, though returning to the task anytime soon was out of the question.

"Rest for a bit," the doctor had said, winking at Kate. "Let your better half pamper you."

"School starts in a month," Mickey had answered.

"So you have a goal. Rest until classes begin, then restart your life with gusto."

In the days that followed Mickey sat in a narcotic haze while his wife was at work, and when she came home he watched her bustle about. And though the old Kate might have fetched him a beer if she was already up, now she bought him milkshakes after his dental procedures, rubbed his feet, dabbed vitamin E on his stitches.

He submitted to her care as he had from nurses in the hospital. Being fussed over was new and delicious. He wasn't about to refuse it.

Alone he studied his face and recalled again being a boy in a Halloween mask. He remembered other children, even his bullies, peeking shyly at him, not knowing his name, his intentions, where he was looking through dark, latex eyes. With his teeth wired shut, his big voice was silenced, and in that silence he discovered a world untethered to politics or creed. His mind blossomed. His senses grew keen. At night he felt himself romping a thousand, ten thousand feet above the earth. In the silvery morning he decided that rain in the trees sounded like a roar of applause. He drank the pineapple milkshakes his wife brought home and took in not just the taste, but the heft and color of the fruit. He watched Kate rush this way and decided her guilt was like a cloud of moths that followed her about, settling on her shoulders the moment she stood pat.

His first visitors were neighbors Emily and Chase Butler, she bearing a pot roast, he a dozen golf balls.

Emily threw her arms around his neck. "I will never forget," she said, "seeing people wrestle that dog from your face."

Chase Butler was a volunteer fireman, and he recalled scenes he'd witnessed: car crashes, accidents in woodshops, attacks by pit bulls. "You wouldn't believe how quick those folks were back on their feet."

Mickey had taken to wearing a hooded sweatshirt, and he gazed at his visitors through the fleecy tunnel, his mouth in a tight-lipped smile. "Thank you for your kindness," he wheezed. "I'm sure you have your reasons for bringing a roast to someone who can't consume anything but liquids."

Chase laughed, while Emily—she'd never "gotten" Mickey's humor—said the food was for Kate more than him, she now breadwinner and caretaker both.

At twilight the couples went to the deck, where the others drank wine and Mickey sucked scotch through a straw. The summer evening arrested his newborn senses—the sky an indigo dome, the moon a twice-bitten cookie—though the others chattered and laughed, ignorant to anything beyond their noses. Mickey sat in his hooded cave and listened to their familiar laments—the Butler boy's aversion to his cornet lessons, Kate's difficult clients, Chase's putting woes—and decided that his wife and friends were foolish people, skimming like ducklings over life's surface, blind to the dark and awful truths lurking beneath.

Emily, with her flip-flop earrings and store-bought tan, had built a shrine to her own fading summer. Chase had reached the crest of a modest hill—he owned an insurance business and had recently been named chief at the firehouse—and was beginning his slow, inevitable tumble down the other side.

Kate, for all her pluck on the softball field and in business, was as fretful and foolish as Mickey's mother had ever been.

"Goodness, look at that," Emily said, pointing to the yard. A family of raccoons had emerged from the hedge and was perched on the fallen apple tree. Their masked faces peered toward the deck. Their paws gripped the branches like human hands.

"They're here every night," Kate said. "That's why I pushed Mickey out there in the first place." She shuddered. "I'm scared of them."

"Oh, honey," Emily said, "you're not scared of anything."

"I am, though. They carry rabies. I'm scared they'll bite Bosco."

Mickey snorted. "Bosco won't go near those creatures. He's as stupid and domesticated as"—he glanced at his wife—"the rest of us." He dabbed at his nose. "I'll get to the tree when I'm better."

"Over my dead body," Kate said.

"I could give it a go," Chase said. "I know my way around a chainsaw."

Mickey blew air through his nostrils with a sound like a toy train's whistle. "Did I stutter just now? I still speak English, don't I?"

The Butlers left soon after, and Kate asked Mickey why he'd become so hateful.

"I was being funny. No one has a sense of humor these days," he replied.

She was loading the dishwasher, and she stayed bent to the task for so long he thought the discussion had ended. "I know this is a hard time," she said finally. "But your sense of humor is killing me, and now it's driving away our friends." She straightened. "Where did my happy husband go?"

Mickey flipped the hood from his head and bared his ruined teeth. "He didn't go anywhere. This is side B."

She turned to leave, pausing to say she'd hired a tree service to clean up the apple tree. "They'll be here tomorrow," she said.

"Like hell they will. I said I'd get to it."

For the first time since the accident Kate laughed. "Like hell they won't," she said, and though her hands were on her hips Mickey had a sudden image of her squaring herself at the softball plate, daring the pitcher to throw a fat one.

THE TREE CREW WAS A FATHER AND SON, the older man wielding a chainsaw twice the size of Mickey's, the younger dragging branches to a woodchipper parked on the street.

His path took him near the deck, where Mickey sat gazing down at him, deciding he resembled boys at the high school: sullen, shallow, soft.

Before he got hurt, Mickey would have chatted up the pair, followed them around, gotten in the way. Now he watched the tree trimmer's son come and go and enjoyed knowing his face made the young man uncomfortable. He looked forward to the semester beginning, to restarting his life, in the doctor's words, with gusto. The old Mickey had hungered for love and approval. The new one would be fearless and true. He would call a spade a spade.

The accident was the best thing to ever happen to him.

When the tree was gone the men fetched rakes and scoured the grass clean of apples. Later Mickey heard the father and Kate in the kitchen, settling accounts. Afterward she said the man had discovered a hollow in the tree trunk, the raccoons' lair.

"He said they were watching through the hedge," she said. "Like they were waiting to come back."

"Nonsense," Mickey said. "There's nothing to come back to."

WEEKS PASSED. SCHOOL NEARED. Mickey's stitches came out. With a crusty seam now dividing it, his face was like two halves of an apple carelessly joined with glue. His eyes were still dark, his mouth gleamed with silver. He spent his days in his basement den, assembling his lesson plans.

Kate found him there one evening. "They're back," she said. Bosco trailed in her wake—panting, pressed against her legs, eyes wheeling around.

"What are you talking about?" Mickey said.

"The raccoons. One of them, anyway." She gestured vaguely toward the backyard. "It's out there now."

"What do you expect me to do about it?"

"Can't you scare it away?" She stared mournfully at him.
"Mickey, I can do everything else. Literally every other thing this house asks of me, but I can't—"
"I'm sure it'll be gone soon."
"No. You don't understand. It's been there for hours. Bosco and I have been watching all afternoon, and now that it's almost dark. It goes back and forth from the hedge to the center of the yard and squats there watching the house." She hugged herself. "It stumbles around like it's sick. It gets closer every time."

Mickey glanced at his papers. Though he started each planning session with enthusiasm, the words before him inevitably swirled into nonsense. He wondered if he was losing his mind. He nodded at the cowering dog. "How is it that a descendent of wolves has evolved into something so timid and afraid?" A truth came to him, and he spoke it. "You've raised that dog in your image, haven't you?" He turned away. "I'll be done in an hour. If the animal's still there I'll deal with it."

"No." She began to weep. "I'm sorry as can be for what happened to you. I'm sorry for my part in it. I'm sorry you've gone from the silly oaf I loved to this creature you've become. I'm sorry to ask anything of you, but I want you to stand up right now and get a rake or something and chase that devil away. If you do I won't ask anything else. I'll wait on you hand and foot for the rest of your goddamn life. I'll—" She put her hands to her face and sobbed, and Bosco whined with her.

Mickey looked back and forth between them, then stood so his papers scattered to the floor. He climbed the stairs and went outside, pausing on the deck to fetch a shovel Kate used for Bosco's poop.

The backyard was golden in the evening light, shadows long and fingery. He walked to its center, realizing he hadn't been this far from the house since the accident. The ground was squelchy beneath his feet, and there was a cidery taste to the air—apple waste, he decided, though he'd watched the men carry the fruit away weeks before. He heard a sound and turned, expecting to see a masked face staring from the gloom, but instead saw that Kate had followed him. She clutched an aluminum softball bat and was clearly terrified, her face pale even in shadow, her eyes rolling this way and that like Bosco's.

"I said I'd deal with—" he began, but she gasped and pointed. He whirled as a flash of gray disappeared behind the hedge. He gripped the shovel and ran after it.

The sun hadn't fully set, but the hedge blocked its glow, and Mickey was immediately plunged into darkness. He stood to let his eyes adjust, his senses alive and quivering. He took in the cider taste again, and now he smelled the raccoon as well—a feral sourness that spoke of rage and musk and rot. He heard a low, rumbling moan like an angry cat.

Another man might have been afraid, but there was no creature stirring tonight more fearsome than Mickey. He laughed and pounded the shovel on the ground. The flash came again, as the raccoon burst back through the hedge where his wife waited.

"It's coming your way! It's coming your way!" he shouted. He stooped to squirm through the gap the animal had taken, and there Kate met him full between the eyes with the softball bat.

She was a big woman. She gave it everything she had.

Wicked Heart

I may get better grades than Kenny Cross at Mount Moriah Elementary, but his dad died in the war and his mom serves drinks at The Pour House, and I guess he thinks those two things—along with him being held back and a year older—make him smarter than me in the ways of the world.

His sloppy grin tells me so, every time we play together.

Like the time I found a frog at the creek under the railroad trestle. Its legs were wrapped around a gooey mess of eggs and its eyes were half asleep, and Kenny said it was a mother frog, too dazed from fucking to be scared.

"Like a woman gets," he explained, rubbing his soft stomach.

The same thing happens when old Pete comes back to town. I see him behind Yoder's Market, stuffing rotten apples into a sack. I see him coming out of the abandoned pumphouse behind the creamery. He scares a neighbor lady half to death when he looks through her backdoor screen, begging aspirin for the misery in his mouth.

His right knee is hinged funny, so his ragged shoe flies forward with each step and slaps the sidewalk. When I tell Kenny what my folks said—that Pete had polio when he was little, that he went crazy locked up in an iron lung—his smirk tells me how stupid I am.

"It's a fake leg, dumb ass," he says. "The real one got shot off by a Nazi."

I ask at the supper table if that's true, and Dad says I need new friends.

It's meatloaf night, and Mom forks a slice onto my plate. Kenny Cross is a sad case, she says, without a man in his life to look up to, but Pete back in town gives her the creeps. No good will come of it.

Dad groans and shakes his head. Pete hasn't misbehaved in ages, he says. He's sick. Used up. The years have cleansed his heart of its afflictions.

"I'll believe that when I see it," Mom says.

"Let it be, now."

"He's so foul, Punk."

Dad's real name is Abe, but people call him Punk because he grew up runty on account of his asthma. He owns Mount Moriah's feedstore and is a deacon at the Church of God, and once he starts spouting scripture you know he's had his fill of a subject.

"We're all of us unclean, Sally," he says, whopping his workpants so corn dust blooms. "Our righteous acts are as filthy rags."

Mom sniffs. "Even so, Isaac Hawkins, stay clear of that man. You hear?"

"Yes, ma'am," I say.

"The last thing we need is Pete at our back—"

Dad sets his cup down so hard coffee sloshes out. "Let it *be*, I said." He sops up the spill with a napkin, frowning at me like I'm to blame. "He wouldn't hurt a fly."

Kenny Cross says otherwise. Pete looks up Linda Adkins's skirt when she's on the monkey bars. He peeks in bathroom windows. He keeps naked pictures in his sack.

"He showed me at the pumphouse. I got all hard, too."

I get hard in the morning when I have to pee, and sometimes when I'm looking at Mom's underwear catalogue. The first is nice enough, but the second—the underwear kind of hard—is wicked and curious and something else altogether.

When I ask Kenny if Pete will show me the pictures too, he says I'm too young and chickenshit. I'll feel guilty about it later and tattle to my folks.

My face gets hot. "No, I won't."

"Yes, you will."

MOST KIDS EXCEPT THE AMISH go to summer Bible school at the big church in the park. There we learn about David and Goliath or Daniel in the lions' den, and afterward we make pictures of the stories by gluing Indian corn—orange kernels for skin, blue for sky, red for blood—to construction paper.

At recess we eat cookies and drink Kool-Aid and play games like kickball or Drop the Hanky on the church lawn near the cannons.

One morning Pete wanders over to watch. His face is lard-colored except for his eyes, which are pink and runny. When I drop the hanky behind Linda Adkins and she chases me around the circle, he starts lurching along beside her, bad leg swinging, mouth open in a noiseless laugh.

Mrs. West steps in and heads him off. "That's enough, Peter," she says. "You go off and play by yourself."

She was my teacher in first grade and wears the same katydid pin on her blouse every day, and the way she puts her hands on her hips and says "Peter," the way he sticks out his chin and sulks off, I wonder if she was Pete's teacher too, a thousand years ago.

After class lets out, Kenny and I find Pete on a bench across from the courthouse, the two of us sitting on either side as he spits bloody tobacco on the sidewalk. His sack, a filthy thing of cotton with black letters, rests between his legs, and I recognize it as the same one my mom buys sugar in for cakes and pies.

I'm hoping Kenny will ask to see the pictures again, but he brings up Mrs. West instead. "She's a crusty old witch, ain't she?"

Pete spits some more. "You know that bug she wears on her tit?"

"That cockroach, you mean?"

"It's not a cockroach," I say, happy to know something Kenny doesn't. "It's a katy—"

Pete shows me naked gums in a smile. "She sticks it in her pussy at night, like Punk Hawkins does to your ma."

Kenny almost falls off the bench laughing. "Look at Ike go red," he says.

AT LUNCH, DAD EATS HIS BOLOGNA SANDWICH without a word, but afterwards he wipes his mouth and says, "I drove by the park earlier, boy."

"What about the park?" Mom says, where she's washing dishes at the sink.

"The boy knows what I mean." He pokes my wrist with the butter knife. "What business did you and Kenny Cross have with old Pete?"

"Oh, my." Mom dries off and sits, giving Dad a *What-did-I-tell-you?* look. "Florence Adkins called not half an hour ago. She said Pete was bothering Linda at the park this morning."

I want to tell them what Pete said, but I know there'll be a huge fuss. Dad will get up that minute and hunt Pete down. Mom will tell Kenny's mom. He'll be right about me being a chickenshit tattletale.

Worst of all, I'll never see Pete's pictures for myself.

"He didn't do anything," I say. "He just ran alongside her, is all."

Dad grunts and puts the knife down. "Ike, Pete's not someone to play with like you do your other friends."

"We weren't playing. We were—"

"Never you mind. Your mother said to stay away from him, and you disobeyed."

"How does he know you?"

"What's that?"

"He said your name. Punk, I mean."

Everything goes quiet, like when you hold your breath between lightning and thunder. "We grew up together," Dad says finally. "Of course he knows me."

"Like Kenny and me?"

He doesn't answer at all this time, so Mom jumps in. "Like Kenny and you, yes."

LINDA ADKINS ISN'T AT BIBLE SCHOOL the next day. Kenny says her mom called Marshal Baker, and Pete's locked up in the courthouse jail until he learns to behave.

"He never touched her," I say.

Kenny giggles. "Only 'cause she's faster."

After class Kenny says we should ride our bikes to the back of the courthouse where the Amish tie their horses and there's a window to the basement cell. We'll talk to Pete through the bars, pass him a cookie from snack time, maybe even steal a file at the hardware store so he can saw his way free.

"Pete's my friend," Kenny says proudly. "It ain't right, him locked up that way."

I've never stolen anything. Also, I figure breaking someone out of jail would mean a whipping, something Dad doesn't do very often but lays on hard when he does.

It's almost noon, the sun burns high through the trees, and the jail window is boarded up. I park my one-speed and wander in circles as Kenny explores the steps to the basement room, and all of Mount Moriah seems to crowd close. "Fifty-thousand miles, my ass," a man says just yards away at Conoco station. A woman comes out the side door of Yoder's and stares at me before putting her groceries in a car. I walk to the hitching rail and stroke the noses of a sorrel and a big black, as if petting Amish people's horses was my reason for being here all along.

"Ike, the door's open," Kenny whispers all of a sudden, and sure enough, the door to the cell room is ajar and he's motioning me from halfway down the steps.

I climb after him to a stone landing, where the air is cool and mossy, and a black beetle as big as my thumb waves its pinchers at me from a corner.

"Pete?" Kenny says through the crack in the door. "You there?"

A scratching comes from inside, a cough. Kenny pushes the door wider, and there's Pete on a cot, rubbing his face inside a cell no bigger than a broom closet.

"Goddamn," he says, "can't a body get some sleep?"

We squeeze into the entryway, Kenny first and me at his shoulder. Spikes of sun poke through the boarded window, and the smells—a bucket on the floor, something else like when our cat had an abscess and died in the garage—make my eyes sting.

Pete blinks at Kenny. "You're the fat ass from yesterday."

Kenny looks at me and laughs real hard, so I know it's a joke. "We felt bad for you," he says.

"For me? It's all hotdogs and sodee-pop in here."

"You never touched that girl."

"I seen her panties though."

"Anyway, we was just—"

"Looky there," Pete says, his gaze lighting on me, "it's the Hawkins boy again."

"That's Ike," Kenny says, like he doesn't think much of the name. "He's not even ten yet."

Pete's leg makes a rachety sound as he swings it to the floor. "Step over here, Ike Hawkins. Pete's eyes ain't what they was."

I elbow in front of Kenny and stand at the cell door. Flies buzz around the bucket. Kids' voices float through the window. A dog barks. Pete's sack lies at one end of the cot like a pillow.

His gums gleam in the half-light. He reaches a finger through the bars and pokes my stomach. "Little shit like your daddy, ain't you?"

I swallow and take a step backwards. "Can I see your pictures?"

His eyebrows bunch into a frown. "My which?"

"The naked ones you showed Kenny."

He frowns some more until Kenny giggles desperately behind me. "That's me, Pete. I told you so at the pump—"

The door crashes open and Marshal Baker fills the room. He's twice as big as my dad, with a khaki shirt tight across his belly and a pistol at his hip. "What's going on in here?" he yells.

Pete laughs. "We was playing hey-diddle-diddle, constable, like boys do."

The marshal scowls at Kenny and me. "You idiots get home."

Kenny scrambles past him up the stairs, and I'm doing the same, when Pete shouts after me, "Come see me again, Ike Hawkins. Punk won't mind."

"Enough with that horseshit," I hear the marshal say.

"Pete doesn't really want to see you," Kenny hisses as we pedal back across Main Street. "He was just being nice."

THE PHONE RINGS THAT NIGHT when I'm in bed, and after a minute my door opens and Dad's standing there, black against the hall lamp. I think to pretend I'm asleep, but he crosses the floor and drops beside me so the bedsprings squeal.

"I'm very unhappy, boy," he says. "Very unhappy indeed."

"It was Kenny's idea."

"I don't give two hoots about Kenny Cross. It's my own foolish son I'm worried about." His body crowds me on one side of my little bed, and the wall on the other, so I'm trapped like a bug in a matchbox.

"I didn't mean to."

"Right there. That's the foolishness I'm talking about." His hand snakes under the blanket and finds a soft place above my knee, grinding until I squirm. "You didn't *mean* to dishonor your parents? You didn't *mean* to follow Kenny down to Pete's cell?" He grinds harder. "What demon possessed you then?"

"Pete called you a little shit."

He lets loose in an instant. I feel him staring in the dark. "Why did he say that? What'd you ever do to him?"

He faces forward like before, hugging himself and rocking. "I told you we were boys together, Ike," he says. "Doesn't Kenny pick on you? Doesn't he call you names?"

"This is different."

"How is it different?"

"Pete's a grownup."

He spins like he's going to grab me again but instead leans so close the words gust on my face. "He's a moron. He's got no more sense than a dog."

I lie as still as I can, my eyes flitting about the dark room. My clothes across a chair are a boy my age, huddled into the cushion. A mirror on the wall is a window to another world. My jacket hanging from a hook is old Pete himself, his sack of naked pictures slung over a shoulder.

I flinch as Dad's hand finds my knee again, but he only rubs it gently. "I'm sorry, son," he says. "I hurt you. I'm ashamed."

He never apologizes. The most he'd do after yelling at Mom is bring chocolate home from Yoder's. The most he'll do after a whipping is pull me against him later and explain how sparing the rod only spoils the child. I don't want to make him mad again, but I've been troubled all day over a last thing.

"Guess what else," I say.

He pauses his rubbing. "What?"

"Pete said I should go see him again. He said you won't mind."

He's quiet for so long I almost repeat myself, but then he stands, mutters "shitfire," and leaves the room. I hear his and Mom's voices rising and falling in the kitchen. They're still talking when I drift to sleep.

DAD'S STILL HOME WHEN I GET UP in the morning, and he and Mom sit me down at the kitchen table and say there'll be two changes in my life going forward.

First—the one I expected—I must never talk to Pete again.

"Your ma was right about him, and I was wrong," Dad says, staring into his coffee. "It pains me to say so about one of God's children, but it's true."

"How was she right?" I say.

He and Mom trade glances. "He's broken, unredeemed. From the time we were boys, he's succumbed to every temptation. When there was a clasp knife to steal at the hardware, he stole it. When there was a…a—"

"When there was a Linda Adkins to chase," Mom finishes for him, "he chased her. When there was a smaller boy to –"

"That'll do," Dad says quickly, putting a hand on her arm. "I don't know if it was the illness that ruined him, Ike," he says, "or if he was born with a wicked heart, but Pete's the same as he ever was."

I stare at them back and forth, waiting to hear the other change they have in store for me, when Mom says, "So, we're clear? You won't go near him again?"

"Yes, ma'am."

"Now," Dad says, "something else. Your ma called Mrs. West last night, and she agreed to give you and Kenny Cross a time out from each other."

I'd half expected this too, but I make an indignant face. "Why?"

Dad gets kind of gray and sad. "He brings out the worst in you, Ike. We're concerned about the boy you're becoming."

AT BIBLE SCHOOL, MRS. WEST PUTS me on one side of the classroom and Kenny on the other, where he sits glaring at me for two days. At recess she makes sure we're on separate teams, but once during kickball, he veers into me and knocks me down, though I'm nowhere near the action.

"You tattled," he whispers as we get up in a tangle.

"No I didn't," I whisper back.

On the third day, he corners me in the boys' room. "Pete wants me to bring you to the pumphouse later," he says sullenly. "He says he'll show us the pictures."

"I thought you saw them already."

He crowds me into the sink. "Shut your mouth, or I'll tell him you're too scared."

I spend the rest of class building Noah's Ark out of popsicle sticks and considering my circumstances. I *am* scared. The pumphouse sits behind the creamery north of town, and I'll have to pass Dad's feedstore to get there. Also, you never know when the marshal might be nosing around. Also, when Pete reached through the bars and touched me, I almost peed myself.

But I'm pretty sure by now there aren't any naked pictures, and I can't wait to see Kenny's stupid face when he looks in Pete's sack and finds nothing but rags and bad apples.

We meet behind the church after class and set off on our bikes, but when we get to Warren Street I split left. I'm heading into the country, I yell. I'll do a big block and come in above the creamery, so I don't have to pass the feedstore.

"You're chickening out, you mean," Kenny yells back.

I wave and pedal west on Warren, then north on gravel roads. Pebbles sting my ankles above my sneakers. The sun beats down without mercy. I pass Amish farms, where pale dresses flutter from clotheslines like headless ghosts. Soon I'll turn south onto the main road into town.

I feel strangely free and happy in the moment, away from Kenny and my folks and anyone else who thinks they know who I am or what's best for me. I remember how in adventure stories boys sometimes run away from home. They join the circus. They wind through the Yukon with just a dog for company. They make their own way.

But I'm not even ten yet, so at the crossroads I turn right and pedal back toward Mount Moriah. In a mile I pass the city limits sign and swing into the creamery. Fresh butter and stale milk fill my nose as I follow the lane to where the old pumphouse squats, gray and forgotten in a thicket of scrub.

Kenny's Schwinn leans against the oak door, ajar like the door to Pete's cell was. I sit astride my bike and catch my breath. The noon whistle blows at the fire station in town, and I know Dad will be locking up soon and heading to the house for lunch.

I'm thinking of doing the same—going home to my sandwich and milk, bearing up later under Kenny's jabs—when Pete's voice comes from inside, low and raspy like he's half asleep. "Hey-diddle-diddle," he says.

"Don't, Pete," Kenny answers, sobbing like a five-year-old. "Please."

There comes a laugh and a slap, and then, "Hey-diddle-diddle" again.

I listen a minute longer, then get off my bike and walk it carefully back up the lane. Dad's probably still at the feedstore. The marshal keeps an office in the courthouse. It's noon in Mount Moriah, grownups will be everywhere. I'll flag down the first one I see and report the goings-on behind the creamery.

At the main road, I climb onto the seat and race for town. My head hangs low over the handlebars, my tires hum. Shame fills my throat, and I even throw up a little, the mess dripping from my chin to my shirtfront, because I know why I lingered at the pumphouse door.

My wicked heart had liked it, hearing Kenny cry.

Tell Me About Bobby Kennedy

The night Barack Obama was elected president, Roger Sinclair and his family gathered in his living room to watch the results come in. And there, Roger—lifelong Democrat, city councilman, local party chair—drank a bottle of Merlot and elbowed his granddaughter Emily in the face, breaking her orbital socket.

Before the incident, the evening had been a happy one. Roger's son Joel and daughter-in-law Colette were as rapt as he by the momentous events. All agreed that John McCain (a patriot, to be sure) was mired in the past, while the young candidate from Chicago—his beautiful family, his dazzling smile—represented an optimism the country hadn't seen in a generation.

"It's a return to Camelot," Roger said, lifting his glass, though Joel's and Colette's puzzled faces told him they missed the reference.

But when the hour grew late, when her parents remembered Emily had school in the morning, when Roger's wife Gail began tidying up, a deep loneliness came over him. Soon the young folks would drive away, the cheerful hubbub go silent. To salve his melancholy, he began to wrestle with his son.

Roger was fifty-eight years old and drove every day from his comfortable home in Mount Moriah, Indiana, to the

Toyota dealership in Fort Wayne, where he roamed the new car lot, prospecting for customers. He had a large head and quick, birdy legs, and when he talked with you, he leaned forward and trapped you in a smile until you couldn't help but smile back.

Joel was taller by half a foot and in his early thirties, yet he'd never objected to roughhousing with his father.

The bout escalated as the men rolled to the floor. Roger's head was pinned beneath his son's arm, his fist about to drive into Joel's gut, when he felt a small body leap onto him from behind. Gail later said Emily only meant to join the fun, though something in the attack—the silence of it, the abruptness—made Roger think otherwise. She was almost seven and, for reasons he didn't understand, had never warmed to him.

His fist drew back as Emily leaped forward and his elbow struck her above the right cheek. The blow, damp and splintery, shocked him to his core. His granddaughter tumbled away and began to scream, and Roger stood in the center of the room crying, "Oh my goodness, oh my goodness."

It was all he could do. His tongue slurred over the word "goodness," so it came out minus the "d," and in that moment he knew, of all his life's embarrassments—like when Ronny Nussbaum had pulled his pants down during a school trip to Chicago, or the time he'd walked in on his mother-in-law naked on the toilet—hurting Emily would haunt him to his dying day.

"I'm sure she'll be okay," he said as Colette hurried the girl to the kitchen, where Gail was filling a bag with ice. He glimpsed Emily's face, her cheek already beginning to swell. "I'm sure—" he began again, but a quick glance from Joel stopped him.

At the hospital, Roger and Gail waited while Joel and Colette disappeared with their daughter into an examination room. Tortured by the silence, Roger announced he'd seen a similar injury when he played basketball in college. "The guy was back on the court in a week," he said. "You just have to give it time." He noticed a young couple watching from across the room, and he rolled his eyes theatrically. "You won't believe what I just did," he called, but stopped when his wife's fingernails dug into his wrist.

Soon a doctor appeared and asked to speak to Roger and Gail privately. "Your daughter-in-law told me what happened," he said when they'd found chairs in his office. He was Indian or Pakistani, with mournful eyes and a lilting, diffident way of speaking. "You understand that an injury like this, to a child I mean, requires I follow a certain protocol?"

"Of course," Roger said. He leaned forward and fixed the doctor in a smile. "You should know I'm a city councilman and close friends with Chappy—I'm sorry, Dr. Charles Lantz—the chief of thoracic surgery here."

The doctor looked at his notes. "Your granddaughter has a fracture of the lower eye rim. The break is not severe and will heal itself in a short time."

Roger buried his face in his hands. "Oh, thank you, thank you."

"Now, please. I've been told that you and your son were fighting when the injury occurred?" Roger lifted his chin and stared. The doctor's eyes were unblinking. "It is required that I ask."

"We were roughhousing," Roger said. "Like fathers and sons do."

"I'm sorry. 'Roughhousing' is?"

"Wrestling. Play-fighting. Maybe that's not something people do where you come from, but we were play-fighting."

"And you were drinking also?"

Roger sat erect. "Yes, I'd had some wine, but that has nothing—"

"Excuse me," the doctor said. "This is my colleague Mrs. Wilson."

A woman had entered the room and stood at Roger's elbow. She was short and square-bodied, with close-cropped gray hair and a sweater made of many colors of yarn. Her earrings were tiny dolphins.

"Now, Mr. and Mrs. Sinclair"—Mrs. Wilson sat and opened a notebook—"how did Emily come to be hurt?"

"IT'S OUTRAGEOUS," ROGER SAID as Gail drove them from the hospital. "Did you hear that woman asking the same questions over and over, like she was hoping I'd slip up?" His wife held the wheel rigidly and said nothing. "Can you believe Colette told them Joel and I were fighting, that I was drunk?"

"Both are true," Gail said.

"Ah, right on time with the support. The loyal helpmate. Et tu, Brunhilda."

"And invoking Chappy Lantz was inappropriate. He's my father's friend, not yours."

"That is demonstrably false," Roger said. "Dr. Lantz greets me whenever I see him. We play in the same foursome often. We ate lunch in the clubhouse just the other day."

In truth, he and the old surgeon played golf together at their country club only when the starter's clipboard happened to pair them, and they'd shared lunch a single time, when Gail's father, in a rare moment of beneficence, waved Roger to their table. Lantz might nod when they met on the practice tee, though he showed the same heavy-lidded courtesy to everyone, from the board president to Abner the locker room attendant, eighty years old and the grandson of Louisiana sharecroppers.

"I only know," Gail said, "that the instant we find ourselves alone you choose to caterwaul about your treatment instead of worry about Emily."

Roger twisted, his face close to hers in the darkening car. "God in heaven, don't you dare. I feel awful about what happened." He turned and huddled against the window, his breath making a tiny oval on the glass.

The road followed railroad tracks on their right, and soon a train overtook them, its rusty bulk rocking between pavement and rising moon, the final car identical to the one before. Roger had always loved the caboose, before technology erased it from the scene. The men in the windows—the rumpled jackets, the pipe smoke, the waves—had always reminded him of his father, who'd died when Roger was a boy.

"I'll never get over it," he said, his voice catching, "hurting someone like that."

"Your granddaughter," Gail said. "You hurt your granddaughter."

AT HOME, ROGER SAT IN HIS OFFICE and watched Obama greet supporters at Grant Park in Chicago. Reports estimated the crowd at one hundred thousand, and as the camera swept the kaleidoscope of faces, the banners proclaiming hope and change, it found a grizzled and weeping Jesse Jackson. The civil rights leader had been with a dying Martin Luther King on a Memphis balcony forty years before.

"You're remembering his dream, aren't you?" Roger whispered, and as he dwelt on old men and their dreams he began to weep also. He thought of his own hero, Bobby Kennedy, martyred that same awful spring, the young senator's stirring plea for calm the night King was shot.

"Even in our sleep, pain falls drop by drop upon the heart," Bobby had told a grieving Indianapolis audience, "until, in our own despair, comes wisdom…"

Roger had listened to those words on the radio with a girl he'd just met, and he never thought of Bobby Kennedy without also thinking of her.

Her name was Frances, though he'd always called her Franny. They'd been divorced for a lifetime, and he doubted she would recognize him now. Yes, he'd become heavy and gray, but more than that, she'd known him *before*, when he was.... He dabbed his cheeks, struggled for the words.

She'd known him when he was a better man.

He padded down the hall and listened to Gail's snores at the bedroom door, then returned to his desk, where he twice picked up the phone and dialed a number he hadn't used in years. Both times he hung up before the call went through. He dialed a third time, and when Franny answered he hung up so quickly he knocked the phone to the floor.

He bent to retrieve it and banged his temple on the desk, then held his head in his hands and rocked back and forth. Yes, he'd been reckless and wanting tonight, but weren't recklessness and want the fires that drove him? Hadn't it always been so?

Franny would understand.

THE NEXT DAY WAS WARM for early November, so Roger took off work and went to the golf course. He sat over a Danish and coffee in the crowded clubhouse and listened to dark mutterings from other members about the election. Roger was one of only three Democrats at the club, and he recalled similar talk from his youth, how Joe Kennedy's boys—John, Bobby, and young Ted—were more beholden to a pope in Rome than they were to the U.S. Constitution, and anyone who thought differently was an idiot.

His thoughts were interrupted by the starter asking if, because Roger was a single, he might round out a foursome with Dr. Lantz and two of his attorney friends. Their usual fourth, the starter said, was with his wife on a river cruise in France.

Roger agreed and, as he joined the group on the first hole, he sang out, "How ya gonna keep 'em down on the farm, after they've seen *Paree*?" The other men smiled, though Chappy Lantz was preparing to hit his opening drive by then, and he straightened and examined the stitching in his glove until Roger was quiet.

Though Roger's handicap had crept upward as he'd aged, he was still a capable player. He couldn't hit the ball as far as he once had, but his first shot usually found the short grass. Today, though, contact between clubface and ball sent a shock into his elbow and recalled Emily's cheekbone breaking. He began to flinch with each swing, and his shots sailed wildly off target or didn't leave the ground at all. He followed his mishits with laughter at first, but after receiving no like response from his partners, he played grimly on.

Dr. Lantz was famously taciturn on the golf course, though once as they waited for a fairway to clear, he nodded at Roger before addressing the whole group, "I gather our local councilman considers last night a decisive blow for racial equality."

Roger didn't take the bait. Republicans bought Toyotas too, he liked to say, and the world was big enough for everyone.

After the round, he escaped to the locker room and dropped off his golf shoes for Abner to clean. The course was wet from overnight rain, and he apologized when he laid the muddy things on the attendant's counter.

"Shoot, that's my job, Mr. Sinclair," the old man said, ignoring once again Roger's appeals to call him by his first name.

"And you do a damn fine job of it."

Abner spoke in a heavy Louisiana patois, and, though Roger despised it when club members loudly mimicked him to his face—"How you doin', Abner? You fine as frog hair today?"—he found himself doing the same, *sotto voce*, when they talked alone.

"Your boy sure kicked butt last night," he said, leaning heavily on the counter.

Abner looked up. "What boy is that?"

"Obama. I bet you're tickled."

"I'm always tickled to be on the topside of the grass, Mr. Sinclair."

Roger laughed, then ground the heels of his hands into his forehead. "I fucked up last night, Abs. Oh man, did I fuck up." He told the attendant about Emily.

Ordinarily Abner sympathized with Roger's troubles—his putting yips, Gail's tempers, endless council meetings—but today his rheumy eyes grew wide. "Damn," he said. "You broke that baby's nose?"

"Her cheekbone." Roger slapped the countertop. "What a dumbass, right?"

Abner frowned as he hunched over his rag and saddle soap.

"It was an accident," Roger said.

"I get it. But damn, were you drunk?"

Roger felt a stirring in his skull, like a beetle gnawing into rotten wood. He'd always scoffed when Gail suggested he was too familiar with the attendant, that their frequent chats hurt his standing at the club, that Abner was hustling him for tips.

"That has nothing to do with it," he said coldly. "Joel and I were wrestling, she jumped on my back, I didn't see her coming." He found a tee in his pocket and pointed the sharp end at the old man. "You wouldn't have either."

Abner's face went instantly blank, a mask he wore when club members thronged his station, piling filthy shoes on the countertop. "I expect not, boss," he said. "I expect I wouldn't have at that."

"I mean it, goddammit. Don't get all self-righteous with me." Roger flicked the tee away and stood panting heavily. "I'm sorry, Abs," he said. "She came out of nowhere. I feel terrible about it."

"Well of course you do, Mr. Sinclair," Abner said, though the mask remained.

ROGER LEFT THE CLUB AND DROVE to Walmart to buy a gift for Emily. Gail usually shopped for the child, and he wandered the gaudy aisles in a daze, like the monster trapped in the glare of the villagers' torches. He chose the pinkest, most expensive doll he could find, a suckling infant that made burping sounds, and lurched to the cash register.

Later, he sat on Joel and Colette's sofa and held out the doll for Emily. She approached him warily, her cheek a purple outrage and both eyes laced with red.

"What do you say to Grandpa?" Joel said, and the girl mouthed a thank you, though she only took the doll when her father nudged her forward.

"We try to avoid gender-specific playthings," Colette explained. "We don't think girls are any more nurturing than boys"—she appraised Roger coolly—"or boys any more rough-and-tumble than girls."

Joel and Colette began to prepare dinner, though they took turns coming and going, never leaving Roger and Emily alone. He brooded over the Diet Sprite Colette had pressed into his hand and asked his granddaughter about school (the boys were mean), what her favorite subject was (she didn't know), if she was mad at him for making a big mistake and hurting her cheek (no). When it became clear he wouldn't have a seat at the table, Roger stood and put on his jacket, motioning for Joel to join him in the foyer.

"This isn't necessary, you know," he said at the front door.

"What do you mean?"

"This song and dance, making sure I'm never alone with my granddaughter."

Joel groaned and looked at the ceiling. "It's what they recommended at the hospital, Dad," he said. "The CPS people, I mean. They said they wouldn't pursue things any further as long as you and Emily took a time out from being alone together."

"What do you mean, 'pursue things any further'?"

"Charges, Dad. Misdemeanor abuse, or something like it."

"Oh, hogwash," Roger said. He noticed Colette peering from the bright kitchen. "Hogwash!" he shouted at her.

"Calm down," Joel said fiercely. "They were on me at the hospital too. I was part of the fight, I'd been drinking. We have to go along."

Roger sagged, then flipped up his collar to protect his neck from the night air. "It's a sad day when a father and son can't engage in innocent horseplay."

"That's just it, Dad." Joel reached to cover Roger's hand on the doorknob. "We can't do that anymore."

"Can't do what?"

"Wrestle like that. Colette hates it. Mom hates it."

"But you love it. You have since you were little."

Joel's face clouded. "I used to, yes," he said, "but you want to do it all the time, especially when you've been—" He shook his head. "It's different now, Dad. It's like you mean it, somehow."

"What are you talking about?" Roger cried out. "I don't 'mean' anything. I love you. You're my big, handsome boy." He lifted his arms clumsily to embrace his son, but Joel shied away, palms in the air.

"I'm a man, an adult," he said. "What you're doing upsets my wife, and now you've...now *we've* hurt my daughter." His voice turned husky. "I'm sorry, Dad, but whatever it is you want from me, I can't be that guy anymore."

TRAFFIC WAS HEAVY AS ROGER DROVE HOME, and he hugged the bumpers of cars in front of him, no matter the speed. Twice drivers hit their brakes to warn him off, but he persisted, passing them in a din of honking. A cold rain was falling, and his cataracts lent a rainbow halo to oncoming headlights that made him sick to his stomach.

He recalled the night before: Colette's betrayal, the foreign doctor who didn't smile back, the woman with the dolphin earrings and a dozen questions. He thought of today: Abner's frown as he hunched over his tools, Joel stopping him at the doorway.

"It was an accident!" he shouted, pounding the hard plastic console between the seats. He gasped instantly as dizziness washed over him. He looked at his hand in the dashboard light and saw his third finger and pinkie were misshapen. "There you go," he said. "Dumbass."

When he got home, he went to the kitchen and filled a bowl with ice water. He plunged his injured hand into it and with the other poured a juice glass full of vodka. He called for Gail, but his voice echoed through an empty house. He welcomed her absence. It would give him time to collect himself. He'd either broken or dislocated his fingers, but a trip to the same emergency room was impossible. All would keep until he saw their family doctor in the morning.

He sat on a stool and nursed his drink and then saw Gail's note on the counter.

Roger,

I'm staying with my sister for a while. I'll call when I'm settled.

I've begged—yes, begged!—you to seek help about your alcohol use and your erratic behavior, but you ignore me.

I think you're hugely selfish, despite the affection you claim to have for other people. Only a selfish man would fail to notice how unhappy I am, but you never ask me what's wrong.

I'm appalled by what happened to Emily, but it may finally make you think about others before you act. I pray it does.

Gail

P.S. – Remember to change the newspaper in the birdcage.

Roger read the note several times. Gail knew better. He thought about other people all the time and tried to make them happy. What she didn't know was he had spoken to their doctor recently about his mounting anxiety, his jitters when he drove on busy highways, his fears that his best days were behind him.

"Your goblins are creeping up on you," the doctor had said. "It happens to many of us as we age." He suggested tranquilizers, but Roger dismissed the idea. He wasn't some old woman, with "spells" and "episodes."

As for asking Gail what was wrong, Roger had avoided the question for much of his life. To ask was to invite an answer, to ring a bell that couldn't be un-rung. When he was a boy, he'd asked his mother what was wrong, and she told him she was divorcing his father. He'd asked his father what was wrong and heard that God was a cruel trickster, bent on man's misery. He'd asked his basketball coach and found he was cut from the varsity. He'd asked his boss and learned his customer list had been divided by half, the remnants to be distributed among a fresh crop of salespeople.

The last time he'd asked Gail what was wrong, five years before, she told him she'd met someone else. After the affair ended and she came home again, she stared at him over dinner one night with torment in her eyes, and he nearly asked the question once more, but instead he stabbed a slice of pot roast and filled his mouth with meat.

THE GRANDFATHER CLOCK CHIMED 11:00 as Roger sat at his desk and dialed the phone. He held his injured hand above his head, astonished by the electric pain thumping down his arm and into his shoulder.

He and Franny had spoken twice in thirty years—once after he'd lost a job, once during Gail's affair—but when she answered, he said, "It's me."

"Well, well," she said after a long moment. "Forgotten but not gone."

He enunciated with great care. "I'm just checking in."

The line rasped with a snort. "Had a few?"

Roger restrained an urge to snarl. "What are you up to?"

"No, what are you up to? Was that you calling last night?"

He imagined her sitting in the darkness, wearing the mocking smile he remembered like yesterday. "Where's your husband?"

"Out. I don't know. It's none of your business. Jesus."

Roger leaned his head against the chair cushion, his hand throbbing, his breath seething in and out. "Franny, I'm in trouble."

"So naturally you call me?"

"I didn't know what to do. I'm a freak and a danger to everyone else, it seems."

"Oh, for heaven's sake." She made her voice comically forlorn, like a ventriloquist's dummy. "'I'm a freak and a danger.'"

"I mean it. I have nowhere else to turn."

She was silent, and he was surprised to hear a dog barking in the background. She had never liked dogs and their ceaseless wanting, preferring the haughty otherness of cats. "What is it?" she said. "What's wrong?"

He took in a great lungful of air, and the words came in a tumble. "Tell me," he said, "about the first time you ever saw me. Tell me about that time."

"No, Roger. You have other people for that stuff. Ask them."

"Please," he said. "Tell me about Bobby Kennedy. I'll never ask again, I promise." He winced as he pressed his injured hand to his eyes. "Franny, please."

He knew she hated when he begged—for love, for forgiveness, for money when his car was repossessed. "You're demeaning us both by what you're asking," she said.

"I know, I know. Please."

She didn't say anything for a half a minute, and when she spoke at last her voice was gruff. "It was April 1968. I was seventeen, a senior at North Side in Fort Wayne. Bobby Kennedy was running for president, and we were all crazy about him. I don't know why, except he seemed so young and hopeful, like he was one of us. Nixon and Humphrey were old gasbags as far as we were concerned, Tweedledee and Tweedledum."

"That's it," Roger said excitedly. "That's just how it was."

"We heard he was making a stop at Notre Dame, and the principal said the four of us in honors history could skip class and drive up to South Bend. I didn't know it then, but you lived fifteen miles away in Mount Moriah, and your school did the same thing."

"They let the senior boys go. Just the boys. We had two carloads."

She sighed. "If you'd like to tell the story, I'll just sit quietly."

"You're right. Not another peep."

"Anyway, the drive took two hours, and when we got to the campus, we found out he was going to speak in this weird-looking building like a spaceship, where the roof went almost to the ground."

"The Stepan Center," Roger said, then bit his lip.

"If you say so. The place was so full we couldn't get in, so they had loudspeakers on the lawn, and when Bobby showed up everybody went wild. His wife Ethel was with him and that baseball player Stan Musial, and I remember being amazed by how gray Bobby's hair was, how short he was next to the Secret Service guys. We were waiting on either side of a roped-off walkway for him to go into the building, and the next thing you know I looked up and saw this maniac on the roof."

Roger sat perfectly still, phone tight to his ear.

"The cops saw him and started shouting—this was five years after Dallas, yet I swear nobody thought it could happen again—and the guy laughed and flashed peace signs with both hands. He was skinny with wild hair and his shirt tied around his waist, and he made his way to the archway where Bobby was going in, and he lay on his stomach and reached down as Bobby passed beneath, and the two slapped hands like God and Adam."

"What happened then? What happened to the guy then?"

"The cops wrestled him off the roof, and the crowd was screaming to turn him loose." She laughed sadly. "The sun was bright, and the sky was empty of clouds, like a big, blue dome over everybody: the kids, the cops, Bobby. It was the best day." She paused. "Six weeks later he was dead."

Roger found himself smiling hugely, tears streaming down his face. "What did you think of that guy when you first saw him, Franny? That guy on the roof?"

"No, I've done what you asked. You got your fix."

"Tell me," he wept. "Tell me."

He heard ragged breathing, as though she'd climbed a steep hill and was gathering herself for a final push over the top. "I thought...I thought he was a beautiful madman," she said. "The kind of boy I wanted." She spoke so faintly he barely heard. "The kind of boy I might love."

Elation flooded Roger like a narcotic. "Oh, Franny, I love you. I was crazy to hurt you like I did. There's never been anyone but—"

The line buzzed. She'd hung up.

A light tapping made him turn to the window. It was still raining. He watched the droplets run down the glass, and the elation drained from him as water seeps through sand. He turned on the news to a report about Grant Park the day after Obama's victory party. The expanse was empty now, save for an army of faceless custodians, pushing brooms and barrels, sweeping gaudy litter into piles. It was raining there too, and the workers' shoulders were hunched against the November cold.

The rain grew heavier, rattling the windowpanes. It was raining all over Indiana, the TV report said, and would continue through the night, before changing to snow.

The Half Hour

Maizey Bates was twenty-three years old and lived with her mother on Crawford Street, while most of her friends had husbands and babies. She was six feet tall and had a rash on her elbows that never went away, so her prospects for love had thinned to a few bachelor farmers or the mortician's son, a boy who wandered the sidewalks of Mount Moriah and talked to people his father had embalmed the week before.

She was skeptical of things improving. Then one July night she came home from The Pour House to find her mother Colleen waiting on the porch swing with news.

"The oddest thing happened," Colleen said. "A man stopped by the salon for a shampoo and cut." Most men went to Bickel's or had their wives give them trims at home, but this one—his name was Presley Hill—told her he loved a woman's fingers in his hair.

He was a pharmacist and had moved to town to take over for Mr. Delacroix, who had retired from the drugstore to Florida. Presley was tall and single and had the most lustrous hair Colleen had ever seen. "Like spun gold," she said.

"Not interested, Ma," Maizey said, sitting on the porch at her mother's feet. At The Pour House that night, every man and his dog had asked her friend Vicki Ragsdale to dance, but their eyes had passed over Maizey like she wasn't there.

"Would it change Her Highness's mind to know he bought the Delacroix house?" Colleen said. "That's 3,000 square feet and a pool."

"He'd never look at a stork like me."

Her mother sniffed. "An attitude like that guaranteed your father's place on the bottom rung." She pressed a knee into Maizey's back. "You're on borrowed time, girl."

Colleen owned The Pretty Girl Salon and liked to say a woman has a half hour to make her mark on the world. That half hour, she said, comes somewhere between seventeen and twenty-two, when the freshness of a girl's face, the perfume of her hair, the curve of her hips, are like catnip to men.

Maizey remembered little of her father Billy—quarter-blood Potawatomi, dead from the lung cancer—though her coppery skin and strong nose showed the lineage he'd passed on to her. She'd gotten mostly As and Bs in high school and been a star on the volleyball team, but afterwards she hadn't found any like success, and now she cashiered at the Stop N' Shop during the day and went to The Pour House at night, where she watched everybody couple up but her.

"You're too smart, is why," Vicki Ragsdale told her once.

Colleen blamed the rash, saying Maizey should bake it away under a sunlamp.

Maizey had tried a sunlamp, but it only made her itch all the more. Besides, her mother didn't want her any darker, did she? Colleen Bates had been seventeen when Maizey was born, making her just forty now, and her pale, Irish beauty—blue eyes, strawberry curls, rowdy laugh—were the stuff of Mount Moriah legend.

Maizey was the exact opposite, though in school the girls had insisted she was "handsome" or "striking," with her long legs and black hair to her waist. For a while she thought she had a real boyfriend in Vicki's brother Harold, captain of the basketball team and one of the few boys in class taller than she. They'd had sex her one and only time on graduation night, steaming up his Mustang so he wrote their names in a window.

Harold & Maizey, it said, with a heart and an arrow through it.

Later she learned he'd been making fun of her with the arrow, and also that he told the other senior boys her pussy hair was itself shaped like an arrowhead. He mentioned the rash too, but only to say you couldn't see it in the dark.

He joined the Marines after high school and went to Iraq and, though she could have asked Vicki anytime about his adventures, the years piled up and she never did.

Tonight, she promised Colleen she'd keep an open mind about the new druggist.

"Just think," her mother said, "he'll know all about bad skin."

OVER THE NEXT WEEK MAIZEY worked her register and kept watch for the mysterious Presley Hill. The Stop N' Shop was the only grocery store in town, and, unless he bought his food twenty miles east in Fort Wayne, he'd have to make an appearance sometime.

On the third day a man came in, and by the looks of his hair—wavy, flecked with light—she knew it was him. He was thirty-five or so, wore a sweater over his shoulders with the arms tied around his neck, and smiled at everyone he met.

He was the handsomest man Maizey had ever seen.

Then, wouldn't you know it, he chose the other register. The cashier, a high school girl named Crystal, fumbled so much with his purchases she had to start over, and when the drawer popped open it hit her in the stomach so she gave out a little squeak.

"You're doing fine," Presley Hill said. He smiled at Maizey, and she turned so the scalier of her elbows was pointed away from him.

After he left Crystal sighed and said, "Pinch me."

From then on Maizey wore long sleeves to work, though Indiana summers were beastly. She'd glimpsed what the man had bought that first day, and it was all eat-right-now choices—chicken and cantaloupe and fresh bread from the bakery—so she figured she'd see him again.

In four days, he was back, and this time he chose Maizey's station. As she rang him through, he hummed, pausing to say, "You have autumn tones."

When Maizey stared, he added quickly, "That's a compliment." He'd studied interior design as an undergrad, he said, and had especially liked working with colors. Autumn shades like brick and cinnamon made the best combinations, while spring hues were too inevitable, and the whites and blues of winter—her mother's tones, Maizey thought—were, well, cold.

"What's your name?" he asked.

"Maize," she answered. "Maizey."

He nodded. "You're a Wyeth painting, aren't you? Fall corn beneath a September sky."

No man had ever spoken to her like that, and Maizey found it hard to breathe. On the other hand, she figured "fall corn" meant "Indian corn," and she remembered Harold Ragsdale's arrow in the steam.

"Don't make fun of me," she said.

His smile froze. "I can be too forward if I'm not careful." He offered a hand. "I'm Presley Hill."

She kept her hands at her sides. "I know who you are."

"I've gotten off on the wrong foot, haven't I?"

"My mama does your hair, that's how I know."

"Colleen Bates is your mother?" And then, sure as Monday follows Sunday, "You don't look a thing like her."

"Like I never heard *that* before," Maizey said.

Presley gathered his bags like a man escaping a burning hotel, and after he left Crystal looked over and said, "Could you be any weirder?"

Maizey shook her head. A girl learned to be gun-shy.

When she got home that evening, a huge bouquet sat on the hallway table. The flowers were yellow roses and daisies and butterscotch chrysanthemums, and Maizey wouldn't have been surprised to see live goldfinches nesting in the stems.

Colleen appeared from the kitchen with a card in her hand. Her eyes had the glittering, famished air Maizey recognized from when she hit big at the casino or had drop-dead gossip from The Pretty Girl.

Maizey took the card and read:

Maize, What I meant to be a friendly exchange turned into an awkward moment for both of us. Please accept my apology and my invitation to dinner – Presley Hill.

When she looked up her mother was glaring. "What do I take from this? A man pays attention to you, and you drive him away?"

The flowers and card had again made it difficult for Maizey to breathe, but she whispered, "He said I looked like Indian corn."

"So, what, for goodness sake? Do you think you're a great beauty?"

Maizey stiffened. "He asked me out, didn't he?"

Colleen turned back to the kitchen. "You can't afford to be choosy, girl," she said over her shoulder. "Your half hour has come and gone."

PRESLEY HILL CALLED THE NEXT DAY and Colleen answered, and when she handed the phone to Maizey her eyes had the same famished glitter as the day before.

The druggist's voice was higher than Maizey remembered, and he bit off each word with great care, as if eating something that threatened to drip down his shirtfront. "It's Presley," he said. "Did you receive the flowers?"

"Yes," Maizey said.

"I asked for an autumn blend."

Maizey felt her mother watching and struggled for the right thing to say. "They're beautiful. Nobody ever gave me flowers before."

Colleen sighed and threw her hands into the air, and after Maizey hung up she said, "In other words, no one else finds you pretty enough for roses."

Maizey didn't answer. She was wondering what a girl wore to The Steak and Ale.

AT WORK THE NEXT DAY SHE RANG UP the same jar of olives twice and dropped a carton of eggs and called Doris Froelich "Dolores," and finally old Mr. Kozlov came around and said, "You okay, kiddo?"

"I'm fine," Maizey said. When breaktime came she went outside and lit a Virginia Slim.

Today was Wednesday, and she and Presley were going out Friday night. He'd made reservations for eight o'clock, though Maizey and her mother usually ate supper in front of the TV no later than six. "Eight is when those people eat," Colleen explained, and Maizey wondered how she'd made it this far in life without knowing such things.

She smoked and watched people across the street pass the barbershop, Mercy's Shoes, the hardware.

Farther on was the drugstore and The Pretty Girl, where Maizey made out a customer in the window, reading beneath a hair dryer. Between the two storefronts was a tiny park with a gazebo, and sitting on its bench were a man in a lab coat—the golden hair could only have been Presley Hill's—and a strawberry-blonde woman in a smock.

Maizey tossed her cigarette aside and walked toward the pair, shading her eyes and squinting. Mr. Kozlov hollered after her that breaktime was over, but in the same instant Presley gestured as he said something, and the woman rocked back and forth, then bent to touch his knee.

Maizey was eighty yards away, but her mother's laugh was unmistakable.

When she returned to her register, Crystal said, "You look like death."

Maizey's mind was a confusion of old wounds and outrages, though it settled on a long-ago volleyball game. The other team's star was a towering blonde the newspapers called "the Swede" for her last name, Bjorklund, and her golden ponytail. The duel was hyped from Muncie to Churubusco, and everyone, even Colleen, came to watch. She sat in the bleachers with Maizey's boyfriend Harold and spent the whole time—every time Maizey looked anyway—squeezing his arm or pressing her cheek into his shoulder, and by the match's end Maizey's team had lost in straight sets and she'd sprained a thumb on one of the Swede's two dozen kills.

Afterward in the rainy parking lot as she and Harold walked to his Mustang, two things happened at once: Harold said, "If I didn't know better, I'd say your mama wants to fuck me," and the Swede came out of the gym and shouted, "Nice game, Pocahontas."

Maizey reached into Harold's back seat and found a hammer in his toolbox, then walked across the wet pavement and invited the big blonde to say it again.

The Swede stood her ground for a moment, her teammates clustered behind her, but then all recognized their hopelessness in the face of Maizey's wrath, and they melted into the team bus. As she watched them go, Maizey felt something she'd never felt before and wouldn't feel again until today at The Stop N' Shop—the capacity for violence, the will to wreak terrible harm.

When she looked again the gazebo was empty, the woman beneath the hair dryer was gone, and people passed back and forth on Market Street as before.

At the end of her shift, she went to the office and called the drugstore, and when Presley Hill came on, she told him Friday was off.

"But why?" he said.

She looked at Mr. Kozlov's bulletin board, where her life was scheduled months into the future. "Because I'm not a joke or a charity case. Find yourself another girl."

"You misread my intentions, Maize. I only meant to make up for—"

"It's Maizey," she said and hung up.

At home Colleen knew everything. "Explain this hogwash," she said, following Maizey upstairs to her room. "Rich, smart and funny isn't good enough for you?"

Maizey turned in her doorway. She'd been taller than her mother since she was fourteen, but Colleen's tongue was as daunting as her beauty, and when her face went white with anger the strongest man backed down. "How do you know he's funny?"

"From when I washed his hair, of course. We talked up a storm."

"Are you sure it wasn't today? Your date in the gazebo?"

Colleen blinked. "I was singing your praises. God knows you won't." She chewed on a thought, then spat it out. "You're as useless as your father. Success falls from the sky, and you open an umbrella."

Maizey's eyes went to a shelf by her door, where an array of trophies gleamed. She reached for the tallest, a volleyballer stretching for a kill, and lifted it clear. She held it at her side—the figurine in her hand, the base resting against her thigh—as she'd held a hammer in a distant parking lot.

"I never had a boy look twice at me but what you stuck your nose in," she said. Tears sprang to her eyes. "As for my daddy, if he was still alive, he'd be proud of me. Mr. Kozlov said so."

Colleen gaped, then turned and went downstairs. When Maizey returned the trophy to its shelf, her hands were shaking.

ON FRIDAY, MAIZEY WENT TO The Pour House with Vicki Ragsdale instead of the Steak and Ale with Presley Hill, and she felt just fine about it. As a girl she'd attended teen revivals at Mount Moriah Baptist, but she'd never answered an altar call. She was suspicious of the swooning and crying and the notion that one might—from one moment to the next—become a reborn person.

But her faceoff with Colleen was like stepping into a new country, where trees were heavy with strange fruit, and a strong, young woman was free to sample what she wanted.

After she and Vicki found chairs and she'd told her friend the whole story, Vicki waggled her eyebrows and said, "Harold's home on leave."

Before Maizey could answer, a big man in a flannel shirt detached himself from the shadows and walked across the dance floor, and it was Harold himself.

"My, my," she said when he loomed above her. "The dead have arisen."

"Maizey Bates." He'd filled out in the shoulders from the boy she remembered and had a scar on one cheek like a giant fishhook. "You look good enough to eat."

They danced once and again, and the second time Maizey buried her face between his neck and collar and took in the heat off his skin, the way his chest rumbled as he hummed to the music, and it came to her that the last time she'd been in a man's arms was Christmas two years before, when she'd surprised Mr. Kozlov with a box of cigars.

Harold put his lips to her ear. "I thought about you every night I was gone."

She tried to pull away, but he held tight. "You were a shit to me," she said.

"I was a shit to everybody. I'm grown now."

He had the same Mustang—he'd parked it in his daddy's barn during his deployments—and later he and Maizey drove the country roads. He wasn't home on leave, as Vicki had said, but home for good. The scar on his cheek came from shrapnel that had peeled a flap of skin away so it looked, the flap and the bloodied place, like an open Valentine's Day card, until the docs sewed him up and left the fishhook scar behind.

Being a Marine in Iraq, he said, was like family. The man to his left and the man to his right would have died for him. But the noise and the grit and the never knowing had gotten so bad he'd longed for home every night.

They parked at Little Indian Creek, where he turned and said, "I wanted things back to regular, where the woman walking up didn't have an AK in her burka."

"You came to the wrong place," Maizey said. "I've wanted to kill you for years."

He pulled her to him with his big hands. "Now's your chance."

THE NEXT DAY MAIZEY TOLD HER MOTHER she was moving out, and the day after that, Sunday, she quit the house on Crawford Street for Harold's apartment above the butcher shop. The bed was a mattress on slats, the stove a single hotplate, and the closets pitifully small, though Maizey didn't have much to put in them anyway.

Colleen met the news with the same face she'd shown when Maizey lifted the trophy from the shelf. "I can't tell you what to do," she said, "but that boy's trouble."

Maizey was packing a bag in her bedroom, and she stretched to her full height so her fingertips grazed the ceiling. "You're right," she said.

"How's that?"

"You can't tell me what to do."

Colleen turned away, and Maizey, though she hadn't had a drop, felt drunk and grand like when she was a senior and received a perfect set in volleyball, and the girl across the net was a ninth grader.

Harold had a job in the flooring department at Windsor Mobile Homes and came home every night smelling like sawdust and linoleum glue. For the first month the meals Maizey cooked went cold because she and Harold couldn't stay out of bed.

Afterward they walked to The Chief for ice cream or watched the Amish boys play softball under the lights or sat on a bench and tried to catch a breeze, and before long Harold joined a softball team himself and was gone two and three nights a week.

At work Maizey looked every day toward the gazebo, and it was a rare afternoon Presley Hill and Colleen didn't meet there at least once, and Crystal said people had also seen them at the movies or drinking wine at The Steak and Ale.

One evening in September she and Harold were sitting outside—he in his softball spikes, waiting for a ride—when Presley walked by, stopping to say he hoped Maizey was happy in her new arrangement.

"Your mother hopes so too," he said in his precise, smiling way. "She misses you. She asked me to tell you."

He was wearing shorts and loafers without socks and the same sweater she'd first seen him in, its arms looped around his neck, and after he'd walked away, Harold said, "Who's the flit?"

"Mama's boyfriend," Maizey said.

He snorted. "He might be a boy and he might be her friend, but he ain't her boyfriend."

Maizey had heard the same from Vicki and the girls at The Pour House. Colleen, the story went, had first imagined Presley Hill as a son-in-law and then later a bedmate, but when she discovered he wasn't suited for either, she'd settled for friend and companion. Presley was no Billy Bates in the love department—he was good for a cuddle, nothing more—but he liked dancing and dinner and didn't smoke like a chimney.

Presley was happy too, folks said. He was a new businessman in a small town, and having a local beauty like Colleen on his arm tamped down talk about his private life.

That night Maizey lay alone and mulled on Presley's words—"She misses you. She asked me to tell you"—and loneliness came over her as raw and sudden as an ice bath. She remembered her room on Crawford Street, the gossip she and Colleen had shared as they sat together on her bed. She remembered how they would laugh together over a TV show, or in wintertime read magazines under the same quilt.

"I miss my mama," she said to the empty room.

HAROLD DIDN'T LIKE CONDOMS, and Maizey couldn't imagine buying birth control pills at the drugstore, so she kept track of her periods and made him pull out when the time was risky, and by October she was pregnant.

"Harold will be thrilled," Vicki said, but Maizey wasn't so sure. Lately he'd been telling her his softball teammates were like the guys in his platoon, where sweat and blood and loss made a bond only men could understand.

Otherwise, he didn't say much besides "Pass the salt" at supper, or "Leave that shit alone" if he caught her scratching an elbow. He'd wolf down her casserole and head out the door, and she wouldn't see him until midnight, when he'd come home and fall into bed like he was shot.

So, she doubted he'd be thrilled by her news, and a day after learning it herself, she walked to The Pretty Girl where Colleen was finishing a rinse on Doris Froelich.

Maizey pulled her mother aside and said she had something to tell her. Colleen's blue eyes went wide—the two hadn't spoken since Maizey moved out three months before—and she dried her hands on her smock and sat opposite her daughter among the ficus trees and schefferas in the sunny waiting area.

"I'm going to have a baby, Ma," Maizey said and fell into her mother's arms, weeping like her heart was breaking.

Colleen hugged her back, and when they broke, she was crying too. "We're going to make this the happiest baby in the world," she whispered.

Doris Froelich gawked from her chair, and Maizey figured she'd best tell Harold soon, because Doris never met a martini she didn't drink nor gossip she didn't pass along.

Harold took the news that night as she'd expected. He hugged her roughly and murmured in her ear, "I thought you were taking care of that stuff."

BY FEBRUARY MAIZEY'S FEET HURT from standing all day at the register, and her stomach bumped the counter when she turned to make change. Harold had joined a winter bowling league, so she found herself more and more at her mother's house. There Colleen cooked meals of fish and spinach—pregnant mama food, she said—and Presley Hill stopped by with little gifts from the drugstore: vitamins or foam inserts for her shoes or Palmer's Tummy Butter for when her belly began to itch.

He brought cream for her elbows too, though the bigger she got the more her rash cleared up, and Presley said hormones did that to pregnant women sometimes.

As the blush of their making-up faded, Colleen began to speak to Maizey in the old way, teasing her for her ugly maternity tops or her swelling ankles or how Harold drove a flashy car while Maizey walked everywhere.

"Leaving already?" she said one evening when the three of them had eaten together and Maizey rose to leave. "Does Bluto need his shorts washed?"

Maizey's face went hot, both from her mother's tone and because she *did* have a load to do, and the laundromat closed at ten. "I like taking care of someone, Ma," she said.

"He barely knows your name. If you weren't there to clean up after him, he'd find somebody else before you said boo."

Maizey opened her mouth to sass back, but Presley said, "Colleen, that is so inappropriate. The girl's an adult."

"I'm only saying a boy like Harold doesn't care who—"

"Maizey isn't interested in what you're saying. My goodness, the mouth on you." He winked at Maizey while Colleen looked at her hands, and on her walk home Maizey smiled to think that Presley Hill, of all people, might be a friend.

Her pleasant thoughts turned to gloom when she found Harold in a foul humor. He'd bowled badly that night and came home expecting cocoa and a grilled cheese. "Where is it you live exactly?" he said. "Here with me or at your mama's place?"

"Here with you."

"I suppose Nancy-boy was there too?"

Maizey thought of how Presley had hushed Colleen with a wink and a word. "He's nice," she said. "Nicer than you'll ever be."

What came next was more a shove than a slap—she'd suffered worse bumps on the volleyball court—though it was the first of half a dozen that winter.

SHE COULDN'T TELL HER MOTHER. Colleen would nod like she'd expected this all along. She couldn't tell Vicki. Harold was her brother. She couldn't tell Mr. Kozlov. He'd find a baseball bat and charge out to Windsor Homes, and he was seventy years old.

She thought of telling Presley, but he was slim and gentle while Harold had only gotten bigger, what with all the beer he drank and the plywood sheets he flung about at work.

In the end Maizey kept Harold's shoves to herself and marveled how short the jump was between frying pan and fire.

HER BABY BOY APPEARED IN JUNE, and Maizey named him William, and soon everyone was calling him Billy as they'd called her father Billy. And though the birth certificate gave his last name as Ragsdale, she called him Billy Bates when it was just the two of them alone.

"Does Billy Bates want to eat?" she'd sing. "Does Billy Bates need a diaper?"

His skin was brown like hers and he had an amazing shock of black hair, and when he suckled at her breast his dark eyes followed her face.

Harold tried at first. He skipped ballgames to put his son to bed and treated Maizey with a tenderness recalling earlier days. He even took her shopping at the mall in Fort Wayne, where he carried Billy in a sack against his chest and smiled back when other young parents smiled at him.

"He's a different man," Maizey told Presley who, but for the occasional weekend "holiday" in South Bend or sometimes even Chicago—absences that left Colleen miserable and short-tempered—had all but moved into the house on Crawford Street.

"Maybe he's growing up," Presley said.

Maizey looked to see if Colleen agreed, but her mother was sitting on the rocker with Billy in her arms, and she only smiled and nuzzled her grandson's brown cheek. "It's like I'm holding you all over again," she said.

"Say the rest," Presley said. "Tell Maizey what you told me."

Colleen shook her head as if surprised by what came next. "I wish your father was here to see."

BILLY WAS A MONTH OLD WHEN the nighttime crying began.

"I know it's eight o'clock," Maizey told Colleen, "because that's when he starts."

"You were the same," her mother said. "It drove your daddy nuts."

It drove Harold nuts too, though Maizey thought it best not to say so. Billy's ragged wails would begin mid-evening and last for hours, and nothing gave him comfort.

"You're fed, you're dry," she'd sob into the hot face. "Tell me what's wrong."

She took Billy to Dr. Ambrose, who ruled out colic or earache or anything else medicine might fix. "Growing pains," he finally said. "It's a new world for your little man. Give him time."

After that, Maizey was able to relax and wait things out, knowing if Billy's cries began at eight, they'd be done by ten, and in the morning he would be cooing and happy and grabbing at shadows in his crib from leaves outside the window.

Harold was a different story. He stayed away as much as possible, bowling or playing softball or going to The Pour House, but when he was home he stalked the tiny rooms—eyes red, jaw muscles popping, casting accusing looks in her direction.

The baby's cries, he said one evening, were like incoming mortar fire, and he'd "never signed on for this shit."

She answered that she'd told him the fateful night was a risky one, but he'd always been selfish about sex, and their son's presence was more his fault than hers. "If you thought with your brain instead of your dick," she said.

He slapped her, and Billy stopped crying in his crib at the crack of flesh on flesh.

Maizey put a hand to her face, where her lower lip had already begun to tingle. Harold's other blows had been cuffs to the head or shoves against walls, and neither Colleen nor Presley nor anyone else knew she'd had a hand laid on her in anger. Now she would be like other women people talked about in Mount Moriah, the ones who stayed indoors to hide their bruises or walked the streets—how else to buy groceries or take a child for a haircut?—for all to see.

She turned to the crib and grasped its rail, and her son, when she came into view, pumped his legs like a man underwater, kicking toward a pond's surface.

In an instant Harold's hands were on her shoulders. "Sorry, babe. When you piss me off like that, I can't—"

She spun and drove a knee into his crotch. Having a baby had added ten pounds to her middle and made her tired all the time, but she was barely twenty-four, as tall and strong as the girl she'd been on the volleyball court. Harold shouted and fell into a heap, pulling his knees to his chest and holding his vitals in his hands. His breath whistled through his teeth, and his face went so gray the scar on his cheek turned crimson.

Maizey picked up her baby and, without extra diapers or a stitch of clothing besides the onesie he wore, ran from the apartment and through backyards and alleyways to Crawford Street. There she held a bag of frozen peas to her lip and rocked Billy to sleep, while Presley drove out for Pampers and baby food, and Colleen fetched her dead husband's pistol from the bureau and sat on a chair in the front hall in case Harold came crashing through the door.

MAIZEY DIDN'T HEAR FROM HAROLD FOR DAYS, and then one late afternoon she was on the porch rocker with Billy in her arms, when he appeared on the sidewalk below. He'd quit his job at Windsor Mobile Homes and was re-enlisting, he said. His temper since he'd come home had surprised him as much as her, and he'd decided to take it where it might be useful.

"I never meant to hurt you, Maizey," he said. "I'm sorry as can be."

She'd just gotten Billy to sleep and didn't answer.

"Maybe another tour will bring me around," he said. "Get the poison out of my system." He made to step onto the porch, then seemed to think better of it. "Maybe when I come home again, we'll get married and make a real home together."

Again, Maizey didn't speak, her silence an answer they both understood.

The afternoon sun touched his face, and she was surprised to see tears glisten there. "So long, then," he said. He stretched to glimpse his son. "Goodbye, little man."

As he walked away Maizey's heart chased after him, but only for a moment.

Billy was sleeping soundly, so Maizey stayed where she was as the sun sank behind the trees, and the September sky turned indigo overhead and honey-colored in the west. Soon her mother and Presley came out, Colleen sitting on the porch swing and Presley on the step beneath her, where he rubbed her feet as they talked. The smell of burning wood and tiny bits of ash drifting down spoke of a fire somewhere.

The baby stirred and began to fuss, so Maizey pulled up her shirt and offered him a breast. The rhythm of his sucking sparked a like rhythm in her lower parts, as her body tightened and repaired itself from childbirth.

Later that night, her son would begin a cough that would soon turn to croup. In a week, Mr. Kozlov would have one of his spells, this time a heart attack that would land him in the hospital. In two months' time, word would come that one of Mount Moriah's sons, Harold Ragsdale, had gone missing during a night patrol outside Baghdad.

But tonight, in the half hour between dusk and full darkness, Maizey Bates listened to murmured laughter from her mother and her friend, and smelled a fire she could not see, and watched the setting sun paint Billy's face and her breast in the same amber light, so it was hard to tell where her own skin ended and her son's began.

The Devil's Age

Johnny Baker had been there himself, a hundred years ago. All fire and meanness and no sense at all. Throw him a sideways look, and he raised his fists. Put a bat in his hands, and he couldn't help but take a cut. Ball or strike, it didn't matter.

He'd made his share of mistakes, but, like a man does if he's lucky, he'd outlived their costs.

"Every boy goes a little crazy," he said, but his wife Helen—she hadn't uttered two words since the call came—buried her face in her palms. He stabbed out his Pall Mall so the ashtray clattered to the floor. Normally she'd have dropped to her knees in an instant to clean up the mess, but now she didn't move. Like everybody else, she was waiting to see what Johnny would do next. Nobody asked—they were all too chickenshit—but if they did, he'd say the boy had to face the music. A marshal's son was no different.

Mitch was seventeen, raw and spiky as barbed wire. Sixteen, and you're still wet behind the ears. Eighteen, and you're out looking for a job. Seventeen is a no man's land, the devil's age. Anything can happen.

"But I guess you'd rather moon around," Johnny said. He wasn't one to raise a hand to a woman, though he wanted to grab Helen's wrist, make her admit her coddling was to blame. Instead, he rose and went to the back deck, where he lit another cigarette and surveyed the October morning. A frost had come down hard overnight, and the trees at the edge of the yard were ashy white on their bottom branches. He sucked in the smoke and let the cool poison do its work.

He'd fix this. Give Johnny Baker a problem and, like his father before him, he found the cause and bent it to his will.

He walked to the pole barn where his pickup was parked and his tools overflowed the work bench. A wood plane with a burled walnut handle, a sledgehammer from his job on a rail crew. In the empty stall a Chevy engine block hung naked from a chain. It was just back from the machinist, and it gleamed like the day it left Detroit. Eight cylinders bored to 5,000th of an inch clearance, head milled so clean the surface flashed like a mirror.

Johnny had planned to teach his son to rebuild the engine top to bottom—pistons, rings, valves—and together they would drop it into the teal '57 Bel Air.

The car, if accounts were to be believed, Mitch was driving the night before.

Johnny pushed the block so it swayed gently, casting a shadow like a giant horse's head on the wall, then climbed into his pickup. He was fifty-three years old and tired to the bone. His shirt stretched tight across his belly, the plantar wart on his heel hurt against the clutch. He yanked the truck into reverse and backed onto the road.

A crowd of loafers had gathered in the alley between Newell's Hardware and the bank, when Johnny pulled onto Main Street. One of the store windows was covered with plywood, the pavement littered with broken glass. Chet Newell had a replacement pane coming later that morning, and with his man in the hospital he'd need help with the install. Johnny made a note to be there when the new window arrived.

Until then he had things to do. Ahead was the courthouse, with a hitching rail behind for the Amish. There

Moses Troyer and his son Vernon waited by the family buggy, Mose's big red sorrel tied fast and blowing steam.

Johnny parked and descended the steps into his basement office, where he fell into his desk chair. Only then did he look at the Amish man and his son, who had followed and stood with their hats in their hands. Mose was ruddy and barrel-chested and, though it was Wednesday, dressed in a formal straight coat. His eyes were fiercely blue, and his bald pate gleamed where the sun rarely touched. His beard covered his sternum and was reddish-brown like the horse tied up outside.

"Mose," Johnny said, "I won't say I'm glad to see you."

"Yah, I wish it was not like this."

"Vernon, do you know what it means to be an accessory to a crime?"

The boy's face was sprinkled with acne. He wore suspenders over an aqua shirt. His voice was a whisper. "I don't think I—"

"Speak up, boy. I'm in a bad, bad mood."

Vernon studied the brim of his straw hat. "I'm not sure what that means, no."

"It means—even if you weren't inside the hardware last night, even if you didn't make a run for it like Mitch and your brother Lloyd, even if you turned yourself in—you still acted as a lookout and might go to jail. Do you understand my meaning now?"

"Yah, I guess so."

"Do you have any idea, Vernon, what a fifteen-year-old boy would face at the prison downstate in Plainfield? Do you have any idea what those men would—"

"He knows he's in a world of trouble, John," Mose Troyer said. "You'll get nowhere scaring the daylights out of him."

Johnny pounded his desk so hard a calendar jumped off the wall. "And you'll get nowhere telling me my goddamn job. Your son and mine are violent criminals now. Their lives will never be the same."

"That may be true for your boy," Mose said calmly. "It ain't true for mine."

Just like the Amish, Johnny thought. Simple as the cows they milked by hand, women dressed like crows on a telephone line, yet they had a smugness to them that begged to be squashed. He looked at Vernon. "I've known your pa since we were boys playing softball. He's always been more sure of himself than he deserves to be."

Vernon made a choking sound. "Are you going to shoot my brother?" he said. He was staring at the revolver strapped to Johnny's side. "When you find him? Are you going to shoot Lloyd?"

"That's up to him, isn't it? Him and Mitch."

"BOYS AND THEIR WILDNESS, HEY?" Chet Newell said later in the alley between the hardware and the bank. He knelt to hold a dustpan as Johnny swept broken glass into it.

Johnny leaned on his broom and looked toward Main Street, where the loafers peered back through the dust. Anybody worth a damn was at work by now. "This ain't stealing watermelons, Chet," he said.

"No. In fairness, it's not. Even so—"

"A good man was hurt."

Chet stood to dump the shards into a bin. "Ah, Toby's okay. He got his bell rung, is all."

They entered the hardware through the side door, and Johnny began scraping dry putty from the window frame, while Chet fetched a handful of glazier points to hold the new glass in place. Johnny tried not to look at the stain on the floorboards near the shotgun display.

"Mitch is a good boy at heart," Chet said. "Not like that Lloyd Troyer. He's a bad one, that Lloyd." He reached to cover Johnny's hand holding the putty knife. "As long as Mitch pays damages, John, I won't be pressing charges."

"It's too late." Johnny freed his hand and resumed his work. "There was a witness. A man was assaulted during a burglary."

"Toby's okay," Chet said again. He laughed weakly. "Might've knocked some smarts into him."

Vernon Troyer had taken the family buggy into town the night before, he'd said earlier in Johnny's office, and was playing pinball at Schott's on Warren Street, when Mitch and Lloyd pulled up in the teal '57 and honked until he came outside. They needed help with a project, they told the younger boy.

"You don't say no to Mitch," Vernon said. "I would have done anything for Lloyd, but I was afraid to say no to Mitch."

"What do you mean you were afraid?" Johnny asked.

Vernon had looked at his feet. "Everybody is."

Johnny thought of those words as he puttied the new glass into the frame. Twice Chet said, "John. That's good enough," but Johnny Baker couldn't leave a job done half-assed. He smoothed the seal until it was a perfect forty-five degrees all the way around.

"I bet this was Lloyd's idea," Chet said as the two men surveyed their work. "These Amish boys and their wildness. I bet it was Lloyd who hit Toby."

Johnny turned in the dimness of the shuttered store. "It wasn't," he said hoarsely. "Vernon saw it from the window. It was Mitch hit your man. Lloyd was jimmying the gun case lock, and Toby came out of nowhere with a ball bat and didn't see Mitch in the shadows, and Mitch grabbed the bat and smacked him across the skull." He brought his hands to his cheeks. "He hit Toby so hard he dropped like a sack of cement."

"Ah, God," Chet said. "Ah, God."

"This was all my son's idea. Vernon said they were going to sell the shotguns for amphetamines."

"Ah, God."

When Johnny let himself out the side door and walked up the alley, the idlers waited there. Men on disability, men who drank all day, men who relied on their wives to take in laundry. The group parted at his approach and most cast their eyes down, though one or two stared at him.

Johnny walked up to the boldest. "I'm guessing you have something to say."

"Some of us are wondering, Marshal," the man said after a moment, "if you have any leads." He glanced at the others. "This sort of thing can't be tolerated in Mount Moriah." His eyes were pink, and broken veins swirled down each side of his nose and joined at the tip. He reeked of whiskey at 11:00 in the morning.

"If I had any leads, do you think I'd be sweeping up glass in an alley?"

"Be that as it may, some of us can't help but wonder—"

"You can't help but wonder if I'm giving this my full attention because my son was involved."

"Well, some of us…"

Johnny was suddenly happy. "Go ahead"—he smiled and drew so near their chests touched—"tell me I'm not doing my job because of Mitch."

The man's mouth opened and closed. Johnny brushed past him to his truck.

TWO HOURS LATER HIS TIRES RUMBLED over the truss bridge east of town, where Little Indian Creek marked the city limits. The sky was a hard blue behind clouds the color of gun metal. Amish farms stretched away on all sides—houses tidy and square, dresses billowing from clothes lines, gardens plowed under until spring. Unhitched buggies stood in the barnyards. Unbridled horses watched from the pastures.

Mose Troyer had told him that no Amish family would knowingly hide the fugitives, though Johnny had answered that there were enough sheds and outbuildings scattered about to conceal a Chevy Bel Air, and enough boys who knew the suspects and might be thrilled to help them.

"You don't know the Amish," Mose had said. "This isn't a time for law breaking." He was referring to *rumspringa*, when Amish teenagers spent a year or two "running around" before settling down to join the church.

"I know them well enough," Johnny answered. Every season he picked up some seventeen-year-old for drinking or pot possession, only to see the same boy a year later, a bonneted girl at his side, a wispy beard on his chin, an infant against his chest.

Now he drove the dirt roads and peered behind corn cribs and silos. He had alerted police as far west as South Bend and as far south as Evansville, though his gut told him Mitch and Lloyd were still nearby. Once he caught a flash of blue through some trees, though it turned out to be a pond behind a milk house, reflecting the sky.

He'd gone earlier to see Chet Newell's man in the hospital. Toby had been awake, his head wrapped in bandages, an amber liquid seeping through them. He'd been kicked by a horse as a boy and was subject to spells, and the pills he took to subdue them caused him to push out a blue-gray tongue and lick his lips constantly. He winced when Johnny opened the blinds.

"Back among the living, I see," Johnny said.

Toby waved a hand. "It ain't nothing. I've had worse headaches." He put a finger to each eyelid and massaged them. "This one's a doozy, though."

Johnny found a glass of ice water on the bedside table and held the straw to Toby's lips. "I guess those morons didn't know you had a cot out back."

Toby laughed and winced again. He laid his head on the pillow and worked his tongue. "I let Mister Newell down, didn't I?" he said.

Johnny felt an unfamiliar itch at the back of his throat. He put a hand on the man's shoulder. "No sir, you didn't. You did exactly the right thing. You didn't let anyone down, Tobe."

Toby looked up at him. "Mister Newell called earlier. We had a talk." He worked his tongue furiously. "Don't you worry, Marshal. I don't remember a thing." He reached to squeeze Johnny's hand. "Mitch is a good boy at heart."

AS HE DROVE THE GRAVEL ROADS EAST of Mount Moriah, Johnny tried to believe him. Mitch had never been an easy one. As a toddler he'd shown rages so fierce he ran blindly into walls. Johnny knew only to hold him in an iron clasp until the fits passed, though Helen's touch sometimes calmed the boy.

"Go ahead, spoil him," Johnny would shout as she hurried away with the child in her arms. Once when Mitch was three and kicked at him in anger, Johnny grabbed his collar and the seat of his pants and threw him like a sack of meal onto the couch. Each time he tried to escape, Johnny muscled him into the cushions again. Over and over it went—twenty, thirty times—until Mitch surrendered, his face scarlet with fury.

Helen had cried that Johnny was only making things worse, but he knew he was teaching the boy about an ordered world, one with limits and penalties, and the sooner Mitch understood its makeup the better.

"That's the way my pops raised me," he'd said. Rather than break him, his father's discipline had only made Johnny stronger, the way fire hardens steel.

The old man had scorned tenderness, despised waste, hated the idea of someone doing a job he could do for himself. And he could do anything. Let a tire on the Studebaker go flat, and he submerged it in a horse trough and followed the bubbles to the leak. Let a birthing heifer go full breech, and he buried his arm to the shoulder and wrestled the calf into the world. By the time Johnny was ten he could hand crank the old Allis-Chalmers tractor to life on a winter morning. By the time he was twelve he could roof a shed with cedar shingles he'd split himself.

That's all I ever wanted for Mitch, Johnny thought as he scoured the countryside. *To teach him to make his own way.*

Say what she might, Helen couldn't accuse him of ignoring the boy. When Mitch had shown an interest in baseball, Johnny volunteered to coach his Little League team. When he'd asked to go fishing, Johnny had taught him to tie his own flies. On his son's sixteenth birthday, Johnny bought him a Winchester 20-gauge and took him to the skeet range, where Mitch blasted clay pigeons from the sky.

Yet in each case the boy's passion had died before it could flower. He'd shown a knack for the Winchester, exhaling before his shot and leading the clay target even after he'd fired, but the few times they'd gone hunting and a living, breathing rabbit broke from wintry scrub, a panic would seize him. He'd throw the gun to his shoulder and let go wildly, gouging the earth with buckshot a yard behind the fleeing animal.

"What the hell was that?" Johnny said once after shooting the rabbit himself, but Mitch was stalking away, leaving Johnny to fetch the dead creature from a red pinwheel in the snow. "Get your head out of your ass," he'd shouted at his son's back.

"Don't fret," Helen said that same spring. "He'll make you proud one day." By then Mitch was seventeen and spending night and day with the older Troyer boy. When summer came, they passed their afternoons at Fish Lake, where they misted their hair with lemon juice so the sun would bleach it. The juice didn't take for Lloyd, but Mitch's curls, already blond, turned snow-white. He wore skintight jeans and sleeveless black t-shirts and a rawhide cord around his throat.

"Just look at him," Johnny said to his wife. "He's a hoodlum, a good for nothing."

She begged him to wait out the phase, even after tales of fights—a meanness to their son that frightened even older boys—began to reach their ears.

When the teal '57 came up for sale and Johnny found that its straight-six engine had bad compression, he'd snapped it up for a song. He saw himself and Mitch changing the engine mounts and dropping in a rebuilt V-8, passing tools back and forth, hands foul with grease, knuckles bloody from when a wrench slipped off a head bolt.

"You won't be sorry," he'd said the day he parked the car in the pole barn. He lifted the hood and leaned in, snuffing like a chef over a pot roast. "Any man who doesn't know the internal combustion engine regrets it sooner or later."

Mitch had lolled beside him, chewing a thumbnail, but he kept the old crankcase filled with oil while they waited for the new block from the machinist, and sometimes Johnny came home to find him soaping down the Chevy in the driveway.

AS JOHNNY CROSSED THE LITTLE INDIAN back into town, the sun glancing off bridge struts blinded him, making him weak and dizzy. He was starving—he hadn't eaten since the night before—and he drove to the house for a sandwich. There Helen met him at the back door to say Chet Newell's man was dead. An autopsy would say for sure, but doctors surmised that the injury Toby had suffered years before had created a swollen place that had never fully subsided, and the blow from the bat had caused it to weaken and burst.

"He went to sleep and never woke up," she said. She stood on the deck—the deck Johnny had built ten years before, while Mitch played among the tools and cords and stacks of weather-treated lumber—and hugged herself against the October chill.

Johnny stared at her, large hands hanging at his sides, then walked to the pickup, hoisted himself onto the driver's seat and drove away.

MOSE TROYER LIVED AT THE END OF A DIRT LANE, with poplar trees lining the sides and a disordered collection of buildings at the end. As Johnny parked, he saw there were two houses on the property—a large one from where Mose and Vernon and a passel of younger children emerged to meet him, and a smaller house beyond, where an old man watched from a doorway. A barn sat on a stone foundation above the houses, and grain bins and sheds lay randomly about. The big sorrel gazed at Johnny from a pasture, motionless but for the flicking of its ears.

Johnny stepped from the truck and walked toward the main house.

"I don't like the looks of this," Mose said as they came together. He was hatless, his sleeves rolled above his forearms. Vernon stood at his elbow, and the other children hung back and stared, their faces innocent as dew melons. "I'm guessing you have something for me, John."

Johnny opened his mouth, but the dizziness from the bridge came over him again. He gripped Mose's shoulder. "We need to talk"— he looked at Vernon—"alone." The two men walked toward the pasture where the sorrel waited, and there Johnny leaned against the rail fence and waited for his head to clear. "Mose," he said at last, "Toby's dead."

"*Ach, Mein Got.*"

"He's dead," Johnny repeated. "Our sons are murderers now."

The Amish man's lungs filled like organ bellows, and he began to mutter words Johnny didn't understand. The horse nickered softly and pressed its nose into Johnny's chest, and he cupped one hand beneath its silky muzzle and lifted the other to grip its mane, and he remembered eight-year-old Mitch in the crook of his arm as the two looked at the Sunday comics—Blondie, Gasoline Alley, Orphan Annie— and Mitch reading the words aloud because he was a good reader and Johnny was not, and Johnny squeezing a fistful of the boy's hair the way he now squeezed the sorrel's mane, and the urge coming on him to squeeze harder and harder until Mitch whimpered and squirmed, and then he, Johnny, letting go and stroking his son's hair smooth and being proud of the boy's toughness and the clever way his voice went high or low depending on the character he was imitating.

Johnny pressed his face to the horse's neck and, for the first time since he was a child, let go a half dozen hard, strangled sobs. The sorrel tried to pull away, but Mose clicked his tongue and the animal stood fast, its giant heart thudding against Johnny's cheek. After a while he straightened to rest both hands on the fence. "Mose," he said, "it was Mitch swung the bat. It likely won't matter to the law, but Lloyd didn't hurt anyone."

"Yah, Vernon told me."

"As for Vernon, he didn't know what was going on. He told the truth the moment he had a chance. There'll be no trouble on that score."

"Yah, *danke*."

Johnny turned. The Amish man was staring away over the empty fields, his arms crossed upon his chest. "Ah, Mose, we've lost our boys," Johnny cried out.

Moses Troyer shook his head. "You don't know the Amish," he said, not unkindly. A tear ran unchecked down his cheek and into his beard. "When Lloyd gets out, however long from now, and if he wants to come home"—he looked toward the smaller of the houses—"I'll be in the *daadiheiser* by then, and Vernon in the big house with a wife and kids of his own." He turned to Johnny. "If Lloyd wants to come home, there'll be a place for him at the table. There'll be cows to milk."

Later as Johnny climbed into the pickup to drive back to town, he heard Mose call his name and saw the man walking toward him. He rested his forehead on the steering wheel until Mose reached the window.

"John," the Amish man said, "there's something else. I don't know what it means, but Vernon"—he spoke with great sadness—"sometimes I think the boy's a mite touched, but he thinks the world of his brother." A tear spilled down his face again, and he wiped it with the back of a fist. "Vernon said something to me three times—not once, but three times—about when Mitch and Lloyd drove away from Newell's last night." He stared at Johnny, his eyes burning with a strange light. "He told me that when the car went east out of town, it was...lifted up. He stood at the corner and watched 'til all he could see was taillights, and then the car was lifted up, he said, like Elijah was lifted up in a whirlwind."

Mose put a hand on Johnny's arm. "John, Vernon thinks God lifted Mitch and Lloyd into heaven, and that's why you won't find them. I don't know what it means, but three times now he's said it."

THE SUN WAS LOW AS JOHNNY CROSSED the bridge into town. The clouds had disappeared, and the sky was a hard, twilight blue. He would go to his office and get on the phone with the law up and down the state. How the Chevy hadn't been spotted yet, he didn't understand, but experience told him nobody ran for long. They always panicked. They always made a mis—

He braked so hard the nose of his truck nearly touched the pavement. He sat in the middle of Warren Street and stared ahead, where the town's only stoplight changed from red to green five blocks away, and the white front of Newell's Hardware gleamed beneath it on the corner.

He pulled onto the shoulder and turned the pickup's nose east toward the bridge, on the path Mitch and Lloyd had taken out of town. He looked in his mirror and watched the stoplight change again behind him. An Amish boy standing at the corner of Main and Warren would have an unbroken view to where he sat.

He remembered Mitch throwing the shotgun to his shoulder, losing all acquaintance with his training when a living target presented itself. Or Mitch casting a fly into the Little Indian and tangling it in a snag and succumbing to a rage so fierce he threw his rod into the water. Or Mitch running the bases like a boy possessed, ignoring the third base coach and tearing for home, where the catcher waited calmly with the ball.

Mitch in a blind panic, driving a teal Chevy away from where he'd just beaten a man to the floor with a baseball bat.

Johnny swore and leaped from the truck and ran to the grassy overhang south of the bridge. The bank sloped steeply to the water's edge, and he saw fresh gouges on the decline, fresh scars in the stands of milkweed and wild carrot and lambs' quarters, where a car might recently have tumbled, its taillights lifting to the sky as its nose plunged toward the dark water.

He shouted and half-scrambled, half-fell down the bank. Boys had forever used the slope as a daredevil place in the winter, tilting over the bluff on saucer sleds and down to the ice, but now the Little Indian was swollen from September rains and flowing fast. He reached the water and waded in but was immediately waist-deep, the current nearly taking him off his feet. He lurched to the bank and struggled back up the slope.

He topped the bluff and ran to the middle of the bridge and stared down. The evening light reflected the sky back to him, but even so he could make out the Chevy's shape beneath surface, its teal color obscured by swirls and eddies and the ghostly fingers of underwater reeds, and because the Bel Air rested on its roof.

WHEN HELEN BAKER HEARD THE SIRENS, she stepped onto the deck and listened, deciding finally they came from town, not the country, where Johnny had said the boys were hiding. There'd been an accident, or maybe a heart attack in one of the stores.

She went inside and sat on a kitchen chair. She held a sodden hanky in her fist, though she was done with crying and had begun to bargain indignantly with God. Surely the fact that Mitch had no criminal record would mean something. Surely the fact that he hadn't meant to kill poor Toby would figure into a judge's decision. Surely the fact that her husband was a town marshal and a respected—no, beloved!—member of the community would impact what came next.

She gestured angrily to the dark room. If a miracle allowed it, if Mitch was ever a member of the household again, things would be different. Johnny was a fine man, but he'd never given the boy his proper due. He'd never seen how gentle Mitch could be, how happy he was to have a real friend at last in Lloyd, how the two of them lazed around the house when just she was home and joked with her and each other.

She rose and tidied the countertop for the third time that day. Then she heard the sound, a tolling that might have come from a distant church, but more uneasy in timbre and less regular in occurrence. She went to the deck again where Johnny's pickup sat outside the pole barn, its headlights pointing into the open door. The sound was coming from within, she realized, and she stepped onto the grass and hurried toward it.

She entered to see her husband in the glare of the headlights, beating the engine block with a sledgehammer. The engine bucked crazily on its chain, its shadow monstrous against the wall, sparks showering from the blows. Johnny was shirtless and he grunted with each swing, and in his nakedness, in the chaos of light and shadow, in the sparks that flew, he looked like an ancient ironsmith shaping the earth's most essential parts.

Johnny's trousers were soaking wet, as was his shirt where it lay at Helen's feet. A terrible truth came upon her, and she began to scream his name. She screamed and screamed, but her voice was lost in the din of hammer on steel, tolling in her heart like a cold, rebuking bell.

Acknowledgments

Gratefully acknowledged are the following publications, where stories appeared in previous versions:

"The Continental Divide": *The Hudson Review*
"Bird Fever": *Philadelphia Stories*
"Please, Mister, Please" (as "The Samaritan"): *Barcelona Review*
"Little Dude": *Bull Lit Magazine*
"Lady Liberty": *The MacGuffin*
"Her Precious Things": *The Common*
"A Vigorous, Mostly Happy Couple": *Vol 1 Brooklyn*
"Tell Me About Bobby Kennedy": *The Common*
"The Half Hour": *The Hudson Review*
"The Devil's Age": *American Fiction* (New Rivers Press)

* * *

After I graduated from the Iowa Writers' Workshop, rent and groceries and a new baby son required that I put down my writing pen and get a 9-5 job. I didn't expect the hiatus to last for decades.

Then at lunch about ten years ago, I sat in a bar with a group of coworkers, including my young friend Josh Taylor.

As I mused on reawakening my dormant writing life, he grabbed a handful of unshelled peanuts from a bucket between us and said, "Write about these nuts."

I went home and wrote a story titled "These Nuts," and I never looked back.

So, I want first to thank Josh for getting me started writing again. This collection wouldn't have happened without his prompt over lunch that day.

I also owe enormous gratitude to Dr. Ross Tangedal, Cornerstone Press Director and Publisher, for accepting my manuscript, and to his editorial, sales, and media teams—including Brett Hill, Sophie McPherson, and Ava Willett.

Many thanks to editor Douglas Silver, who read every story in the collection, and whose advice that I "take off my hat and loosen my tie" helped push my work into unexpected and better realms.

Thank you to mentors from my Breadloaf family, especially Robert Cohen and Amy Holman, who believed in me early and enthusiastically. And to Kenyon workshop friends EJ Levy, Louise Marburg, and Erika Wurth, who taught me the ins and outs of this frustrating business and helped me expand my network of writer associates exponentially.

I must also acknowledge a host of other dear people, who never failed to say Yes! when I asked if they might read a new piece. These include my sister Beth Johnson, Iowa workshop classmate Robert Nelson Jacobs, Biblical scholar Leonard Beechy, poet extraordinaire Scott Stubbs, grade-school friend Gloria Miller Holub, and many more.

Finally, much love to my sons Nick and David Johnson, who forever cheered on my reborn writing career, and to my wife and most important critic Cindy Ward, who always, always, believed, even on the days when she looked up sadly from a new story and said, "I don't get it."

ACKNOWLEDGMENTS • 211

What followed was me huffing and puffing and defending the piece, before ultimately deciding that she was (usually) right.

And of course, I'm delighted to share this collection with you, the reader. Thank you for picking it up and taking a chance on it.

BOB JOHNSON is an award-winning short story writer and graduate of the Iowa Writers Workshop. His work has been published by *The Common, Philadelphia Stories, Vol. 1. Brooklyn, The Barcelona Review,* and elsewhere. His story "The Continental Divide" was named Short Story of the Year in *The Hudson Review.* He lives in South Bend, Indiana.